SECOND CHANCE

A ROMANCE VIDEO GAME NOVEL

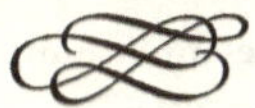

CHRISSY WISSLER

BLUE CEDAR PUBLISHING

ALSO BY CHRISSY WISSLER

Home Run Series

Home Run

Romance Video Game Series

Second Chance: Novel

Anything Possible

Changing Perspective

Enchantment Avenue

Searching for Sanctuary: Novel

Dragons in Preschool: Short Novel

The Blessings Bridge

Pixie Dust Cupcakes

Christmas Weather Witch

Unfreeze a Heart

More than Nurture

Elven Heritage Series

Hidden in Mist

Hidden in Truth

Hidden in Shadow

Hidden in Fire

Hidden in Flight

Hidden in Spirit

Hidden in Desire

Hidden in Memory

Hidden in Time: Novel

Hidden in Lore: Collection #1
Hidden in Myth: Collection #2
Hidden in Legend: Collection #3

Little League Series
Swing Away: A Little League Novel
Prom Dates & Softball Bats
Throw Like a Girl, Catch a Date
Fly Away
No Crying in Softball
More to Life than Softball
A Pitcher's Unexpected Date
A Catcher's Christmas Wish
Stolen Bases, Stolen Kisses
Softball Baby
Off-Balance
Batter-Up Pucker-Up: Collection
Everlasting: Collection
All or Nothing: Collection

ACKNOWLEDGMENTS

Really, the first people I need to thank are my parents. They might have refused to buy me a Nintendo, or a Super Nintendo, or a Game Boy—but they eventually relented and allowed me to buy a Sega Game Gear (with my own money, of course). And while I fondly remember asking for those tiny cartridge games for Christmas (and I only got one because they were $50—a bunch of money back then), my real love of games began when I played my first role-playing game, Final Fantasy 7.

Years later, when growing up meant less time for 100-hour games and less patience for frustrating controls, my enjoyment in games has changed. While the storytelling has improved (marginally), a few games pushed the game industry boundary and introduced romance subplots. It is to those game developers I want to thank, and to my friend Annie, who I called to tell what so-and-so-hero said to me, flirted with me, asked me on a date—the kinds of things only the best of girlfriends (who also played games) could understand.

Thanks also goes to my husband, who backed me up when I pitched my romance game idea to a bunch of his video game buddies —thanks, Dear. Knowing you believe in me, and my dream of seeing this game a reality, means a lot.

To Sean—
Who never laughed at my dream to play a romance video game.

CHAPTER 1

Rachel slipped Nick's house-key into the pocket of her wool coat, carefully balancing the pizza in one hand, homemade chocolate pie in the other, and did her best to not think about the glorious bottom her life had reached.

At least she had chocolate pie. And her brother. In that order, of course.

"Nicky, you there?"

No answer. Not like she'd expected one. Even from the front door she heard the unmistakable crack and pop of machine guns. For fun, an explosion was tossed in there, too.

No way Nick could have heard her. Or even a real bomb going off in his neighbor's white-fenced, always fresh cut lawn.

She nudged the door closed with her sparkly new shoes, complete with the first forming blister on her big toe, and headed straight for the living room.

Eight o'clock on a Friday night? There was only one place Nick would be: Playing video games, by himself (unless she counted the online voice-chat thing, which she didn't).

As if she could talk.

Rachel Clare, bestselling writer of romance fiction, a household name for mothers and young women alike, and how did she celebrate her next sale? "At my brother's," Rachel grumbled. "Drinking beer instead of wine."

Definitely rock bottom. But at least she had someone to celebrate with, even if he was her brother and an unwilling celebration partner.

Nick's house was pitch dark. He'd come home and hadn't bothered flipping on a single light switch. But Rachel knew her way around and could maneuver through the trenches with her eyes closed.

Sort of. As long as he didn't get the bright idea to move furniture—like the table.

Rachel smacked her shin into a chair, bit her tongue, and nearly lost hold of the pie.

"Nick," she growled. "Learn to turn a damn light on!"

He still didn't hear.

Rachel moved through the unkempt, very bachelor-esque house still working on her balancing act, and followed the flickering blue glow coming from the living room.

Wasn't it sad when the smell of pizza put a zip into her step and signing her newest, carefully vetted contract—with a sizable, high six-figure advance—didn't?

Sure enough, Nick lounged on the couch, chest slightly bent over, his fingers working the buttons on his X-Box controller. On the coffee table, a beer waited patiently for him to remember its existence.

Actually, that was the second bottle. The first lay discarded on its side.

"Let me guess, you didn't hear me?"

Nick jumped up, nearly knocking over the beer, but managed to straighten it in time. Unfortunately, the zombies took advantage of his inattention and had a little pizza party of their own on Nick's video game character.

The screen darkened and the words 'Game Over'—complete with congealed, dripping blood—appeared on the large plasma screen.

Video game shooters. Always a class-act. "Good timing?"

"Damn it, Rachel." Nick tossed down his controller, but not hard enough to break it. "Don't you ever knock? And who said you could come over whenever you wanted?"

"You gave me a key didn't you?"

"Yeah, to water my plants when I'm gone."

"It's not my fault you never take a vacation." She held out the pizza box. "Now stop whining. I brought dinner."

He opened his mouth, probably to protest a little bit more, so she held up the pie. "And I brought dessert."

That shut him up. It usually did.

"I'll get the paper-plates."

She mentioned turning on a few lights and got a grumble in reply, but at least he flipped on the living room one, allowing her to set both the pizza and chocolate pie down, then her coat. She finally kicked off her shoes and sighed in relief.

Nick came back out, paper-plates in one hand and a beer for her in another. "I didn't expect to see you so soon."

Soon, meaning her unannounced visits.

"That mean you sell another one?" he asked. "How many books is that, anyway?"

"I have no idea." She served them each two slices, taking the slightly bigger ones for herself. "How many games have you made?"

He frowned. "Four."

"Okay, bad comparison." After all, games took at least a year to make, usually longer. If it took her a year to write a single book she'd be both out of a job and broke.

Nick snorted. "What a rough life you lead. Hey, next time—which will probably be like next week or something—can you bring lobster? Or maybe some out-of-season crab legs?"

"I worked hard to be here." She poked him in the stomach. "And I still do. Every damn day."

Too bad not a single member of their family (excluding Nick) actually thought of what she did as 'work.' Normal people put in eight hours. From writing to actually running her business (and yes, what she did was a business), Rachel put in over ten hours a day, six days a week.

Her 'hard work' just happened to mean quite a few books every year. Her readers loved it and she loved writing the stories.

"Yeah, yeah, I know." Nick waved. "Writing all those steamy sexy scenes is tough."

She smacked him again for good measure, though she really just wanted to smack herself. She was the one who came here after all and what a lousy celebration it was.

"Says the guy who makes video games for a living," Rachel shot back.

Darling, Nick. Her baby brother of a whole three years, had the perfect guy-job. He made video games for a living, got to go to work in jeans and flip-flops, then came home and played more games.

This was somehow acceptable to their parents, while Rachel's work wasn't.

In reality, Nick's life wasn't much different than hers, except hers revolved around romance. And no matter how much she'd liked to have a little romance when she came 'home,' the only romance she usually found was in another book.

But after her very short, very disastrous marriage to Daniel, romance in a book was much safer. And the best part? She'd get a happy-ending. She couldn't say the same about marriage.

"Look. If you're just going to be a jerk I'll take my pie and just go."

Nick's smile faded. "You know I'm just kidding. Come on, I'll put in another game. No zombie killing."

"You sure? Because I brought the perfect book. Romance, beer, and killing hordes of the undead go great together."

"Nah." Nick pulled out the disc and popped in another. "You'll like this one. Its got a story and everything."

She arched her eyebrows as she bit into a glorious slice of pizza. "Story, huh? You mean find the Dagger of Doom and save the princess?"

"Ha, ha. Very funny. You'll get a kick out of this; there's a romance sub-plot too."

Romance? In video games?

"I'll believe it when I see it."

CHAPTER 2

Rachel had every intention of curling up on the couch and losing herself in the newest Nora Roberts romance, but Nick's comments kept pulling her away from the story.

Yes, she had money. A lot of money, actually, and she'd worked her butt off for it. But she didn't write for the money. Heck, she didn't even know what to do with it all.

She cared about writing. And proving herself. Proving to those jerks like Daniel she was a writer and what she did mattered. Even if it was writing romance.

So why did her life still feel so empty?

Nick helped himself to a third helping of pie without taking his eyes off the game. It was a role-playing game, the kind where you played a specific character and were thrust into a 'story' as you played the game.

A story. Right. It also included big-ass spaceships and hot babes in very tight spacesuits.

Rachel had played her fair share of games growing up, at least until she realized what she played for was story and let's face it, stories weren't exactly a video game's strong suit.

She winced as Nick's character 'hit' on the babe in the tight spacesuit. Apparently, in the decade or so since she'd played, the stories hadn't gotten any better.

"You call this romance?" Rachel pointed her fork at the screen. "I mean, you literally went from 'hi, how are you doing' to asking her to take off her clothes."

"I did not." He frowned at her, in the cute way only Nick could. "It was the best of the four options."

Rachel snorted. "If I was that girl and a guy said that to me, trust me, that's how I would have taken his meaning. I'm guessing this was written by a man, who also never read a romance in his life, and who's probably never written a story in his life."

Okay, so she had this slight problem when it came to contrived and obvious plot points. Video games were right up there with those big-blockbuster movies who wouldn't know a plot if it bit them on the ass.

And Rachel, being Rachel and being in such the celebratory mood that she was, couldn't keep her mouth shut.

"You mean, the story is the quest? Like go gather this magic sword —or spaceship or whatever, then get the blue-colored one?" She was dumbing it down, hoping to prove her point. "That's not a story. There's no conflict. No tension."

Nick sat straighter and straighter in his couch, controller clutched tightly in his I'm-going-to-kill-Rachel death grip.

She scooped another helping of pie into her mouth. It really was great pie, unlike this 'story.'

"When's the last time you even saw the bad guy?" she asked. "He probably has some fantastic conflict. If they'd just—"

"You know, Rachel, you don't know the first thing about designing games. Or telling a great story for a video game."

She blinked. "I hadn't realized there's even been one. A great *game* story, I mean."

His shoulders tensed. Okay, maybe she'd gone a bit too far with that last one, especially since this was what he did for a living.

"You didn't work on this game so why are you getting defensive?" she asked.

"It's your snobby attitude," Nick snapped. "You know everything there is to know about stories."

"I don't. Why do you think I write so much?"

That's why she constantly practiced, trying to get better. Every time she sat down to write, she learned something new. She doubted Nick would understand, especially if he thought of her like that.

"Look, I didn't mean to make you mad. I just can't believe you consider this great storytelling..." She clamped her mouth shut. He had a point. She was picking a fight.

"That is exactly what I'm talking about. You look down on me and the games I make."

"I do not—"

"The only kind of stories you write are about people falling in love. Not," he pointed to the screen, "intergalactic warfare or epic fantasy stories."

She could, though.

All she had to do was read several books, get a feel for the storytelling style, and give it a shot. Maybe she should? Maybe dabbling in a different genre would perk her life up a little.

Nick's scowl darkened. "You're not even listening to me. Fine. I'll tell you what. You do better."

"Huh?"

"You heard me. Do it better than them." He nodded to the screen.

"Of course I can do better." Now she was getting riled up. If Nick wanted a fight, she had no problem giving him one. "In fact, I can think of at least a dozen romance novels that would make great games."

"Romance video games." Nick snorted. "That would never sell. One, there's no market, women don't play games in case you noticed."

That's when he continued to list off an every possible reason in existence of why a game made for women, real women, not those little pony riding or doll-dress -up games, would never work.

No market.

No money.

No chance.

He didn't believe in her.

Nick was standing now, hands on his hips and towering over her. "And, you'd have to convince a game developer to be crazy enough to make a game like this."

She might not be wearing her heels, but she wasn't about to let her brother tower over her. Thanks, but she'd gotten enough of that shit from Daniel.

Rachel jumped to her feet. "I can do it."

"Okay," Nick said. "Fine. Then put your money where your mouth is, Rache. Go find yourself a developer and fund this thing yourself."

She blinked. What? Fund a video game?

Nick, as if sensing her hesitation, waggled a finger at her. She hated it when guys waggled their fingers at her.

"See? You don't think you can do it. That's a whole lot of money to put on the line—"

"I'll do it."

The words rushed out of her before her brain translated what the hell she'd just said.

Nick's mouth dropped. "You're not serious. Do you have any idea how much money it takes?"

"It doesn't matter." She had the money.

And like that, the idea took root.

Rachel turned from Nick and paced up and down the narrow living room, stepping over empty beer bottles. It was quite obvious with their conversation that Nick—and the game industry—didn't respect women as a viable market.

She knew it was. Her bank account could attest to that. You just needed to reach them right, just needed to appeal to the kinds of games women wanted to play.

They wanted to read romance. Why wouldn't they also want to play a romance game as well?

Eyes narrowing as determination swept through her, Rachel glared at Nick. "Do you know any developers who need a game project?"

CHAPTER 3

Mark rubbed his forehead and wished it was Friday. Except, of course, it *was* Friday. Friday night, actually. And once again, he'd spent another late night at work.

He leaned back in his chair, shoulder muscles groaning as he stretched. When was the last time he'd even got up? An hour ago, two maybe?

From his window, the best view in his opinion, the world outside seemed to have dimmed. Few cars rolled by on the lit streets. No pedestrians either, even though it wasn't raining.

For once. In Seattle—and the eastside of Lake Washington—it always rained. Even when it wasn't raining, people commented about the rain.

The handful of Bellevue high-rises felt subdued, as if those big companies and their hard working employees had called it a night as well.

This, he thought to himself, this was why he worked so hard. To be here, right here.

And now he might lose everything.

The expansive office, spacing an entire floor in sought-after downtown Bellevue for once was quiet. No chatting employees or the background noises from the QA department. No dramas he was pulled into by HR. For a game company, he had no idea it was possible to have so much drama.

Quiet. And if he didn't come up with a project publishers were interested in, it'd get a whole lot quieter, and fast.

He glanced at his phone, hoping to see a blinking red light magically appear. There was none.

A light switched on in the darkened hallway and Scott, one of Mark's co-owners, wire-rimmed glasses and fully buttoned polo shirt, poked his head in. "You still here?"

Mark didn't bother a reply. Obviously he was still here. His stomach growled. And hungry, too.

"When's the last time you've been home?"

Mark shrugged. "Tuesday? Or maybe it was Wednesday? No. It's not that bad. It just doesn't feel like I've slept in that long."

He probably hadn't.

"You look like hell." Scott let himself in, pulling back the cushioned chair. "I'm guessing there hasn't been any interest."

"Not even a bite. With the market and what's going on," Mark shook his head, "publishers are tight with their money. Too many studios are failing, games aren't selling the way they used too. They want a sure-fire hit."

FastPlay didn't make those kinds of games. They took their games beyond the horizon and into uncharted territories. That's what they were known for. That's what he'd spent the last seven years working for.

No way in hell was he going to give up now.

Of course that's also why Mark, even with pleading and begging, couldn't get a publisher to go for even a single project idea.

Scott slumped in the chair. "You're trying. Me and Ethan know that. Maybe, you know, it's time to try a different tactic."

Mark, who'd been thinking about how he really was hungry and how he should really eat something, some time today, jerked his attention back to Scott. "A different tactic?"

"Nothing big. Just an idea, of course. We've got a lot of talent here.

We could make one of those big, splashy games publishers are looking for."

"We don't make those kind of games." Mark didn't make those kinds of games. He'd been there once, did that. He was through. "That's why we built this company into what it is."

Scott raised his hands in a defensive gesture. "All I'm saying is it'll keep us afloat. Give us time to get something else lined up. Unless you want to lay off half your team?"

He didn't. That's the last thing Mark wanted. He'd hand-picked his team, working from the bottom up until they could afford the talent they had now.

"Something will come along." Even if he had to work all weekend long, he wasn't giving up.

"I know it will, Mark. Like I said, we believe in you. But we do have a fallback option and just in case. I've got a few ideas I've been tossing around. The kind that falls more in line with what publishers are looking for."

Ordinary games, he meant.

Mark forced a smile, even though smiling was the last thing he wanted to do right now. Actually, jumping up from his desk and telling Scott to get the hell out of his office sounded pretty good.

He was just stressed and tired, that's all.

And he knew damn well playing king-of-the-company, especially when you had partners, was always a bad idea.

"Thanks, Scott. I'll keep that in mind. We may have to go in that direction if something doesn't come up."

Something better damn well come up.

Scott beamed at him, relaxing into the chair. In fact, he nearly put his heels onto Mark's desk before he caught Mark's glare and immediately lowered them.

Scott might be good with investors, reviewing contracts, and running the general day-to-day aspects of the company. But an office manager didn't equal a game designer. And someone like Scott wouldn't know 'fun' if it bit him on the ass.

But if it hadn't been for Scott, Mark would never have taken this chance to begin with. He'd never taken a chance with his own company.

Something would come along.

His phone rang.

Mark and Scott stared at the phone and the blinking red light. What the...? Was this video game gods at work or something, or what?

Scott blinked. "You, ah, you're going to get that, right?"

And like that, Mark's fatigue washed away. He straightened and his sore muscles vanished. The soreness would be back later with a vengeance, but for now he was in charge, the CEO and Creative Director of FastPlay.

And that meant he had business to take care of, business that didn't include Scott. He nodded towards the door. "This could be Nintendo getting back to me."

It was a local number after all, even though Nintendo had already given their answer and it wasn't an uplifting one.

Scott scrambled out, waved goodnight, and shut Mark's door. Not that there was anyone else in the office, but at least Scott couldn't overhear.

Mark took a deep breath and answered the phone. "Mark Ashe, how can I help you?"

The person on the line paused briefly, but the second he spoke Mark's hopes crashed back down to earth. It wasn't a publisher calling. It was Nick Clare, a designer he'd worked with when they'd both gotten their start in the business.

A social call, then, one he didn't have time for if he wanted to save his company.

"Look," Nick said, "I know you're busy and from what I heard, running out of time."

"I'm not about to talk about my company's confidential information," Mark growled. "Not when my employees don't even know what the hell's going on."

Which begged the question: how did Nick know?

Sure they were friends, but Mark made it a point to keep silent on business matters. The only ones who knew how dire their situation was becoming were Scott and Ethan. But it couldn't have been one of them. Could it?

"I'm not asking you to," Nick said, pulling Mark away from his thoughts. "But look, this might sound strange, but I might be able to help."

Mark's hand tightened on the phone. He nearly slammed it into the receiver. He didn't.

Why? Because he was desperate—and in a very short while, Scott and Ethan would realize just how desperate their situation was.

"Unless you've got a couple—and I do mean several—million dollars on hand, there's nothing you can do to 'help' my situation."

There. That should make his point quite clear.

Friends or not, Nick should mind his own damn business.

"You're right. I don't have that kind of money... Hang on a sec," Nick paused, said something to another person Mark couldn't hear, then he was back on the phone.

Mark didn't slam the phone down. Instead, it slipped through his fingers at Nick's words.

"I don't have the money, but my sister does."

CHAPTER 4

Mark caught the phone just before it smacked onto his desk. His reflexes were definitely not what they usually were. He blamed it on the lack of sleep and food.

And shock.

"Your sister."

He was really glad Scott had shut the door and there was no chance of him listening in. Within seconds, Scott would be demanding for Mark to step down as CEO. If he caught even a whiff of this ridiculous bullshit the other two owners would turn on him.

"Thanks, Nick."

He managed to keep his voice courteous, but there was no hiding the anger rolling through him. Nick would hear it, and if he had any sanity or ounce of survival, he'd back off and leave Mark and his company the hell alone.

"But unless your sister has about ten million to spare—"

"Hang on." Nick covered the phone again and started talking to the other person, the sister Mark guessed.

This time, it was sheer force of will and remembering that—at one point—he and Nick had been friends, that kept Mark from hanging up.

Nick came back on the phone. "She does."

"What?" Mark blurted. "Who the hell is your sister? Married to a CEO at Microsoft?"

"Shit, Mark, do you really want to know, or would you just rather her tell you in person?"

Wariness crept through him, tingled along his back the way it usually did when he needed to tread softly. He didn't get this far in the business by jumping at the first opportunities that came his way. Diligent thought was needed, right now more than ever.

The company couldn't afford to be picky. They couldn't afford for Mark to hang up the phone if Nick's sister was absolutely serious.

But there was always a catch. The other party always wanted something in return, something he'd learned the hard way from dealing with publishers.

With ten million dollars on the line, there was definitely a catch.

A big one.

When Mark didn't say anything, Nick went on. "Look, she wants to talk to you. In person."

"Okay. I'm interested, but only to talk. No promises." The tingle didn't go away, not completely, but it lessened. He'd talk with Nick's sister, learn what she was after, and then make a decision.

After a long, good night's sleep.

"Thanks, I know how odd this sounds and all, so thanks for meeting with her." The phone was covered again. More muffled voices. "Damn it. All right, fine. Hey, Mark? One more thing. I'm not allowed to be there."

Mark sat forward in his chair. The tingling down his back with a vengeance. "Why not?"

"Because she thinks I'll screw everything up and you won't give her a fair shake." Nick didn't even try to hide his anger. "Just meet with her, okay? What can it hurt? You need a game project and she's got the money. Hell, she's got nothing else to do with it."

Mark heard a slap through the phone and winced. What kind of sister was this?

"Never mind," Nick said. Mark heard the barest wince in his voice.

Apparently Nick's sister hit hard. "She'll tell you and you can decide for yourself."

Mark thought back to his conversation with Scott and his barely concealed threat. Tingling or not, they needed a game, and fast.

What could it hurt? At least he could tell Scott he was meeting with an interested party. And if he asked what publisher?

Well, that answer was fairly simple. An angel investor.

Mark nearly laughed. Scott, who liked everything around him in nice, controlled situations would fall over.

"You there, Mark?"

"Yeah. I'm here." And with that, Mark made a decision; one he hoped wouldn't hurt the company in the long run.

"I'll meet your sister at Daniel's Broiler in Bellevue tomorrow, 12:30. Sound good?"

Nick confirmed this worked, but before Mark hung up he asked Nick what her name was.

"Rachel Clare," Nick mumbled.

Mark shrugged and hung up. It *was* only a meeting right? What could it hurt?

But why did that name sound familiar?

MARK TOSSED his keys to the valet at Bellevue Place, who immediately came forward in his dark, neatly pressed uniform. Sure, Mark wasn't expecting this to be a long lunch (or a very successful one for that matter), but parking was enough of a pain to enjoy the simple pleasures in life.

Like not hunting for parking spots, especially around lunch hour.

Just before he stepped through the glass doors, a flashy red Corvette rumbled behind his much more sensible, and better gas-mileage, Civic. Some people apparently had money to burn. He preferred investing his. Into his company.

He turned, but a pair of mile-long legs grabbed his attention. He blinked, and since he was early, took a moment to lean back and enjoy the view.

It was a pretty good view.

Long legs gave way to a snappy, skirted business suit, killer pink heels—which he had no idea how the woman could even walk in—and loose, flaming hair that matched the car.

If nothing else, he'd have to thank Rachel Clare for the view—something he'd have totally missed if stayed in his office and worked all day. Again.

Mark was pretty darn sure he wasn't the only one taking a long, deep breath before brain activity functioned again. The poor valets had to jump to a lot faster than him, exchanging her keys for a tag, which she neatly slipped into a purse that again matched those killer shoes.

Women, he thought, had this habit of matching things. He was lucky his khaki pants were still clean, only slightly wrinkled, and went with anything.

The woman slipped off her sunglasses, which were totally unnecessary for Washington's usual mixture of rain and clouds, and which she clearly wore as a fashion statement.

And to be honest, they looked good on her.

She glanced at him, a smile tugging at her lips, before he offered that she go ahead of him. She did.

He followed after her.

Not because he enjoyed the view (he did—this woman clearly worked out and had the butt to prove it), but because they were going to the same elevator.

The restaurant was located on one of the upper floors, while the bottom half of the building was reserved for the Hyatt Regency hotel and some high-end, frivolous shops that Long Legs there probably enjoyed shopping at. Seemed up her ally (and her price range).

"Going up?" she asked when he reached the elevator.

"Lunch at Daniel's Broiler. You?"

Her eyes, a deep brown, narrowed the tiniest but then shrugged and hit the elevator button. "Me as well. It's one of my favorite restaurants."

Then whichever gentleman picked the restaurant made a smart move, he thought, because he figured only a lucky guy would meet a woman like her.

Ah, well. At least he still had a chance to enjoy the scenery.

Come to think of it, Nick hadn't told him what his sister looked like. And if Mark had been his usual self and more on top of things (like sleeping and eating), he'd have done a quick internet search.

He hadn't had time this morning, what with running over to the office to tie up some loose ends. He'd forgotten to look at Scott's latest financial report, and if anything good (or not good) happened with this lunch meeting, he'd need some back-up plan to discuss with Scott.

But he'd slept for a few hours and had a nice, refreshing shower. A shower and sleep did wonders to a person, especially when you're stressed and overworked.

Lost in his thoughts, it took a few moments before Mark noticed Long Legs had her back pressed against the elevator, her eyes closed, one hand clutching her purse.

"Are you okay?"

"Thank you. I'm fine." She didn't open her eyes.

Now, any idiot would catch that as a hint for 'leave me alone.' He caught the hint and totally ignored it. And considering this wasn't a short elevator trip, even though they were flying up, he'd rather be a cautious stranger than the polite one.

"Not to be rude, but you don't look okay. Do I need to call someone?"

Someone, meaning 911.

"No." Her eyes snapped open. "I'm sorry, no thank you. I have a thing with heights and elevators aren't my favorite invention."

She made an effort to release her purse. They'd almost reached the restaurant.

Mark held his arm out, offering it to her. "You do look a little unsteady. Let me help. We're going to the same place after all."

She glanced from Mark and back to his arm. She slipped her arm over his. "I usually take the stairs, but in these heels and with this many flights, I'd probably miss my lunch meeting and not walk for a week."

He held her out for a moment, getting a good look at those shoes. The heels had to reach his ankles they were so tall. "They don't look very comfortable."

She groaned. "They're not, trust me."

He smiled at her, suddenly liking a woman who could complain about her expensive, uncomfortable shoes. "They do look great, though."

"That is the point."

They shared another smile, one that transformed her from Long Legs into someone else, an actual person and not some hot babe driving around in an equally hot car.

A name, he suddenly had to know.

"I'm Mark Ashe, by the way. Your escort for these last few floors."

Her smile fell, but only a second before it was back in place. It wasn't quite so radiant and shining this time, but more normal.

Business normal.

Expensive clothing. Expensive car. He didn't need to ask her name.

"And let me guess," he said, his own smile changing from friendly to business, "you're Rachel Clare."

CHAPTER 5

"**A**nd let me guess. You're Rachel Clare."

Rachel's hand on Mark's arm loosened. There wasn't even a hint of surprise on his face whereas she was reeling, and probably not doing a good job of hiding it.

"I am."

Did he know who she was?

A simple internet search would have brought up hundreds of pictures. All saying the same thing: Rachel Clare, bestselling romance writer.

But if he did know, then why come at all?

Nick had been quite clear to keep her mouth shut about the romance writing for as long as possible. Get Mark interested first, then tell him about her game idea.

The elevator stopped and the doors slid open. They stood there for a moment, staring at each other. No, she realized, *she* was the one staring and *he* was the one waiting for her to take the lead in this dance.

After all, she'd invited *him* to lunch.

This was business. Not a date.

She smiled, readjusting her grip on his arm, giving the cue she was

21

ready. Mark obliged and led her to the *maître d'* who asked—Mark, of course—for the reservation name.

Mark glanced at her, a slight uplift of the eyebrows. "I'm guessing it's under Clare?"

"It is," she answered. A business lunch, she reminded herself.

Definitely not a date.

A date, after all, would just remind her about her failure with Daniel—and all the failures since then. Best to keep this as professional as possible, especially since the only resemblance Mark had to Daniel was blond hair. Not the clearly muscular, cut body.

She blushed and immediately looked away.

While they waited, the silence stretched between them, even though there was a gentle of hum of movement, silverware clinking against plates. A calm, quiet atmosphere that in no way reflected her current state of mind.

Mark hadn't let go of her arm, although she was perfectly capable of standing on her own two feet now that she'd exited the death machine. She didn't remove her hand. After all, that'd be rude.

"Nick didn't tell me what to expect," she said. "I was expecting someone more like..." she let her voice trail off. Fat and ugly? "Someone more like his co-workers."

Who were fat and ugly.

She hadn't expected disarming and handsome. And polite. When she saw Nick again, she was going to kill him. Some warning would have been nice.

"I could say the same thing."

Mark didn't even bother to hide his smirk. He was laughing at her! "Oh?"

"I expected you to look like your brother."

"My brother."

Mark held her at arms length for a moment and made a showing of scanning her from the bottom of her heels all the way up.

She tried not to shiver.

The smirk was back on his face. "You're...taller than your brother."

She had a feeling that wasn't what he wanted to say, but she had to admit it was a much safer comment, especially when his eyes darkened as he stared at her.

Definitely safer.

"It's the heels," she said, and was thankfully saved from any other idiotic comments as they were led to their table.

Like always, the view was truly breath-taking. Just past Bellevue, Lake Washington stretched out before them and Seattle's high-rises stood straight, tall and elegant. On a sunny day she could spend all lunch simply staring into the distance, allowing her characters to come alive, to speak to her.

Mark coughed.

Lunches she'd usually spent alone. A habit from her 'Daniel days' and needing to think, and hide.

Rachel tore her attention from the view. "Sorry. Bad habit."

"Hardly. It's one of the reasons they charge so much here. That, and the food is amazing."

Small talk. Safe and easy small talk.

The waiter arrived, just as crisp and polished as the valets, and gave them both a friendly, warm smile. "Welcome to Daniel's Broiler."

He went through his usual spiel, the 'have you been here before' line and the lunch specials. Rachel's gaze wandered back to the view. She tried to remember all of Nick's points, the best tactic for getting Mark to at least hear her out before shutting down her idea.

"Are you two celebrating a special occasion with us today?"

Rachel's attention jerked back to the waiter, who's smile had changed from friendly and warm to sly and leading. He thought they were on a date!

"Ah, no," she said before Mark could. "Just a business lunch."

"My, my apologies. Please, allow me to take your drink order." Which he did, along with their lunch order, and immediately disappeared.

Rachel hoped her face wasn't nearly as red as the waiter's. That really would be embarrassing. This never happened with her because she hardly came here with anyone.

Mark, though, took it all in stride as if the comment didn't phase him in the slightest. Or that he was surprised. He probably wasn't. A man as handsome as him probably ate out a lot, and he was probably never alone.

Not like her.

Oh, don't be silly, she thought, even as her glass of Riesling arrived. She had a big enough challenge ahead of her, convincing this guy to take her—and her game idea—seriously. She didn't need to add unrealistic romantic notions on top of it.

Mark took one sip of his Stella, then set the beer down. She knew that look; it was the look with a purpose, a stop beating-around-the-bush look.

"I'm not a fan of being left in the dark, and Nick told me next to nothing about this deal, why you're interested in my company, or heck why you even want to invest your money into a game."

He leaned back in the cushioned booth. "I'd just like some straight answers so I know I'm not wasting your time."

He left the second part unsaid, the *'you're* not wasting *my* time'* part.

"Fair enough."

She set down her wine even though her gut was telling her this was too soon. He was too hostile, too closed-minded to listen to her. And she was too distracted by the dark and stormy look he gave her.

Way too distracted.

And maybe she *was* wasting both of their time. Maybe Nick was right, that this kind of game would never work.

No. That just wasn't good enough for her.

Women deserved a chance.

"So, why don't you tell me what you do for a living?" Mark asked when she didn't say anything. "I mean, a couple million dollars isn't something most people have laying around, and something most people don't want to throw away into a video game."

Stay cool, Rachel, she thought. "Nick's told me about some of the problems development studios are having with publishers, securing funding and..."

And not getting screwed over. She didn't say that part.

"That's right." Friendly, smiling Mark disappeared into hard-nosed, company owner. "He tell you about us?"

"No. He said you needed a project, I inferred the rest." Meaning Mark hadn't been able to get funding from the usual sources, or at least in some way he was okay with swallowing.

"But you're interested."

"I might be."

His eyes narrowed. "You still haven't told me what you do for a living."

So he didn't know who she was. That might just buy her enough time to play her cards right.

"I'm a writer."

CHAPTER 6

Awriter." Mark said the words a second time, hoping some light bulb would click in his brain and this whole crazy situation would make sense.

It didn't.

Writers, everyone knew, made little money. So little money in fact they had to have a day job just to pay the bills. Then again, she'd driven up in a freakin' Corvette. Nothing said money like owning a sports car in Washington.

When he talked to Nick next, and he would, he had quite a few choice words for him. Thank God Mark hadn't told Scott about this meeting; he'd have been laughed right out of his CEO position.

"What the hell kind of writer are you? Stephen King?"

Rachel's eyes narrowed. He'd thought she was attractive before, now even with all that anger, she was stunning. Too bad that anger was directed at him.

Angry women, he could handle. It's when they cried that he was really screwed. Thankfully Rachel didn't seem like the crying type. More like the gouge-out-your-eyes type.

"No," she said. "I am not Stephen King and thank you very much, but I worked hard for that money. Every damn dollar."

A sore spot, clearly. Mark raised his hands in defense. "No offense was meant, it's just what you said goes against everything I've heard of writers."

"What you've heard," she snapped, "is from the thousands who enjoy the idea of being a writer and never actually sit their butt down and do the damn work."

Ouch. Definitely a sore spot.

She practically snatched up her wine glass, maybe as some kind of lifeline to keep that spitfire temper of hers under control. He hoped so. Stunning or not, he needed to head back to work after this 'business lunch' and didn't have time to change into a clean, and dry, pair of clothes.

"Nick said you're the Creative Director."

He had no idea where this was going, but he'd play along. So long as it kept him dry. "I am."

"Which means you come up with the concept, the kind of game and experience you're offering players."

At his nod, she continued. "And I'll bet you started out as a game designer? Someone who had to learn, and practice, what makes a game 'fun?'"

This Rachel Clare was surprisingly quick and surprisingly understanding. Not even half the people he'd met in the industry, maybe not even a quarter, understood what she so simply, and elegantly, stated.

"That's...that's right."

She nodded, clearly expecting that she was right. "So. Can just anyone be a game designer?"

"No."

How did she know so much? Nick? Everyone and their brother wanted to be a designer. Heck, even most programmers thought they could be a designer without actually understanding the foundation, the way of thinking necessary to see past the 'creative' ideas and look at what actually works.

Look at, and understand, what's 'fun.'

Mark lifted his beer glass in salute. "Point taken, Ms. Clare. Everyone wants to be a writer; everyone wants to be a game designer."

"And the only ones who will succeed are the ones who work their tail off, who put the time in, and practice." She glanced back at the view, a view that kept pulling her attention since they sat down.

Maybe Nick had been right about this whole thing. Maybe this deal might actually be something worthwhile and not a joke. If she meant what she said, if she actually understood how this industry worked; how making a game worked.

"I worked for my money, put in those long hours just like you're doing now. I had something to prove and I still do." Her gaze jerked back to his. "Mr. Ashe—"

"Mark."

"Mark." Her cheeks blushed slightly at that, and he tried not to think about how he liked her saying his name.

Business, he reminded himself. *This is about business.*

And like that, her cool and composed mask was in place. The business mask. He had no idea what he was in for, but he had an idea Nick had left out a lot in their brief conversation in setting up this meeting.

"I have something I'd like to prove in your industry and I think it's about time someone did it."

"I'm just here to talk about getting another project lined up, Rachel. I don't care about secret agendas."

"There's nothing secret about this. Actually, the game itself is the agenda."

Mark set down his beer and leaned across the table. They were sitting, so he couldn't use his larger frame to tower over her, but he would tower and he would make her see he wasn't kidding around.

This was his company. His game.

"Let me get something straight, Ms. Clare."

"Rachel."

"Fine. Rachel. I decide what game's my company makes. That's why I'm called the 'Creative Director.'"

Her eyes narrowed at this, but he plowed on. He would make damn sure she understood exactly what and who she was dealing with.

"I decide the game project," he said, "you supply the money and fund the game. The game's released and hopefully both sides make money."

Okay, so it didn't quite work like that. Especially since half the deal when you signed on with publishers was Mark's idea becoming theirs —they became the owners of the intellectual property in return for funding it.

She didn't need to know that. Unless Nick had already told her, which was possible.

Gone was the attractive woman stepping out of her flaming red Corvette, replaced with a woman practically spitting fire at him. Cold fire. The kind that froze and burned at the same time.

He pitied the guy who had to deal with her temper, probably on a daily basis too.

"Now," she said, "let me set you straight. Mark. If you want my money, my ten million dollars so you don't have to lay-off half your company, then you'll make the game I want you to make."

It took all his control not to slam his fists onto the table or hell, even pour his beer all over her. If a guy had been sitting across from him and just spun that shit to him, a punch would have been thrown.

He had no idea how to tell a woman not only did she step far, far out of line but she was in danger of ruining just more than her suit.

"Your game," Mark purred, low, rumbling, and deadly. "And what kind of game would that be?"

She leaned back, carefully crossing her mile-long legs. He just glimpsed the smooth skin before the legs were thankfully hidden back under the table.

"You never asked about the kinds of books I wrote, Mark."

He hadn't. He'd been barely able to think past the rich and millions part.

"Why should I care? Angel investors supply the money, not the project's concept."

"If you want this game to be a success, if you want it to make your millions—and if we do this right it will—then you better care about the books I write."

He had to sit on his hands to keep from strangling her. At this point, he didn't know if he could stop himself.

Or if he wanted to.

"I write romances, Mark. And I want you to make the first romance video game."

He definitely wanted to strangle her. Too bad their food arrived just as he reached across the table.

CHAPTER 7

$\mathcal{N}$ick had told her. He'd flat out warned her to tread carefully, smoothly and gently. And what did she do? She slammed the elephant right down onto the damn table.

"You want to make a what?" Mark roared as he towered above her.

The poor waiter shrank back, trying to balance their plates and avoid Mark's swinging, angry arm movements.

Oh, yes. Nothing subtle about that, Rachel.

"A romance video game," she said again. "Now. Will you sit down so we can discuss this like adults? Or are you going to knock over our lunch just to prove your point?"

"And what point is that?"

Ah, yes. That was definitely a growl. She'd written about men 'growling' in her stories. She'd never actually heard one though, and that, definitely, was slightly more intimidating than anything she'd ever written.

She swallowed.

Or maybe this just happened to be one of Mark's special talents. At least he wasn't swinging his arms like an ape anymore.

"Your point," she pointed her fork at him, "is that you're mad and highly insulted that I dare suggest such a thing. Now. Will you sit down and eat?"

Mark sat, and the waiter practically dumped both their plates and ran towards the open kitchen. This, she imagined, wasn't the normal way their clients acted. Either they were going to get asked to leave, or the *maître d'* would personally thank them for the entertainment.

She was betting it'd be the former.

"I'm not mad," Mark said. "Furious is more along the lines of what I'm feeling. And you're right. How dare you suggest that my company, a company I've spent years building, make a game so belittling it will destroy everything I've worked for?"

Rachel snapped her fork down. "I didn't realize making a game for women was 'belittling.'"

"A romance video game, as you called it, would be the laughing stock of the industry. It'd destroy our name. Hell, it'd ruin our chances for future projects, and that's only if I could convince my employees not to hand in their resignations the second they learned we were making a 'romance' game."

She scooted to the edge of her seat, her calm and patient mask melting away with every word that left his mouth. How could she have possibly thought Mark would be any different from every guy she'd met?

Different from Nick?

Different from Daniel?

A guy who might actually respect what she did for a living.

She threw her napkin down, right into her untouched steak salad. "You know what? You're right. I'm sorry for absolutely wasting your time, but I was under the impression your prestigious game company was in danger of closing half its doors because you needed a project."

"We need money, not a project. There's a difference. And I'd rather close half the doors than make a game that will ruin years of my hard work."

"Then by all means," her voice rose, "be sure to tell that to your team when you lay them off. That you had a perfectly good deal lined up, a deal you wouldn't even *talk* about because your ego was so damn big you couldn't see around it!"

She stormed to her feet, but Mark was right there with her.

"My ego? You're the one waving millions in my face just to prove a point."

"That's right," she snapped. "A point which you are clearly supporting, that women aren't deserving enough to get a fair shake, that *my* industry, which makes billions, is beneath your notice. Fine. I don't need your business and will find someone who does."

Rachel dug into her purse and threw cash onto the table.

"The hell I'm letting you pay." Mark dug out his own wallet.

She turned on her heels and stomped just as fast as she could to the elevator.

The *maître d'* took one look at her, rushed over and hit the down button for her.

She would have made it to the elevator first, but Mark beat her. Only because she was wearing heels and he could stomp a lot faster in flats.

She glared right back, joining him in the elevator and the doors slid closed.

Rachel crossed her arms and concentrated on stoking her anger. Anything to keep from thinking about the elevator and the feeling of her stomach leaping into her rib-cage.

Or those wonderful visions her creative, and very adventurous, imaginative mind decided to spin up for her about the brakes giving out and her plummeting to the ground floor.

They stood at the opposite ends of the elevator, which unfortunately, wasn't nearly far enough.

Mark snuck a glance at her, at the way her fingers dug into her arms, and swore. "You really are scared of elevators."

"Heights, actually. And it's none of your damn business."

"By all means, freak out on your own."

The elevator dropped another few floors. Not nearly fast enough.

She concentrated on breathing, and when that didn't work, she concentrated on her anger—which also meant concentrating on Mark.

"Why did you even bother showing up? If you weren't even going to listen to what I had to say—"

"I did listen and I'm not interested." He swung that piercing blue gaze back at her, and for a brief moment, she forgot about the elevator, about their downward spiral.

She even forgot she was angry.

"In fact," he said, "you should have just told me over the phone instead of wasting my time. Romance? In a video game?" He snorted. "It'll never happen. It'll never work and it sure as hell would never sell."

Like that, the perfect vision of his blue eyes vanished and she crashed right back into reality, elevator and all.

"I guess not. As long as there are bigoted men running things, men who think the idea of 'women' and games is a pair of gigantic tits and hips larger than a boat."

His gaze darkened and she could practically hear him grinding his teeth, ready to lash back at her. "We got the image of 'bodice-rippers' from someone else after all."

She managed, just barely, not to throw her purse at him. She was so tired, so damn sick and tired of people looking their noses down at romance, looking down at the intelligent, bright women who *read* romance.

Women who just wanted to fall in love and have a happy ending.

The elevators slid open. Cool air brushed her face and she could suddenly breathe again. Not because of Mark and once again being in this confined space with him; it was only because of the confined space.

It had nothing to do with Mark and his arrogant attitude.

They stormed out of the elevator, and then both had to wait while the valet brought up their cars. She refused to step away. If he wanted to be on the other side of the curb, that was fine. He could be the one to walk away from *her.*

He didn't. He stayed right by her side.

"Why the hell would you want to make a romance game?" he asked.

"Why the hell wouldn't you want too?"

"Never mind." He jerked his attention back to the driving up cars.

"Fine."

Thankfully, hers was first.

She would never again put up with someone looking down at her, looking down and demeaning what she did.

What she wrote.

She forced herself to smile.

"Good luck with your game, Mr. Ashe. I'm going home to work on the latest romance novel I just sold, and which will continue to sell, and be reprinted long after your games have disappeared from shelves as they make way for flashier, better and newer titles."

She slid into her Corvette and slammed her door shut.

She caught a single glance of fury from Mark and it made her day that much sweeter.

Of course, writing about two strangers falling completely in love was just about impossible right now. No matter. She was a professional and she'd sit down and write until those two characters fell in love.

Or she killed someone.

When in doubt, or if you're stuck, kill a character. Death always brings out the best conflict.

And apparently, so do handsome, arrogant game company executives who refuse to even listen to a good, legitimate offer.

Rachel gunned the engine and drove off.

She tried not to think about her suddenly tight chest and why the pain there felt so familiar.

CHAPTER 8

$\mathcal{I}$t was pure amazement Mark made it into the office without getting into an accident. Or driving after Rachel Clare and killing her himself.

He ripped off his jacket and tossed it onto his chair. The office was still empty. Even the team working on *Last Man Standing* was out. No overtime yet.

Good. That meant he had some time alone. Time to cool off.

He paced back and forth in his office, running his hands through his hair.

Who the hell did that woman think she was?

Other than damn good-looking.

Women who wore those kind of tight clothes and drove that kind of car knew exactly what they looked like. And how to use it.

Attention-grabbing and attractive. The very last combination he needed in a business partnership.

The perfect combination for his bed and hopefully, the homey smell of scrambled eggs and bacon in the morning, but definitely not in a business relationship.

Mark growled. This wasn't working. He needed to work off this anger, and this unwanted attraction. Maybe then he could think straight, focus, and get some work done.

FastPlay needed him focused right now.

Mark grabbed his gym bag from the closet, always available just for this kind of occasion, and headed down to the building's gym on the first floor. It was empty, and he worked up a hell of a sweat, pushing his body to the limit and then a little beyond, but it didn't help much.

He still couldn't stop thinking about Rachel, from her long-ass legs to her temper as she stood up to him.

Alright. If the work out didn't work, then a cold shower would.

Also, his stomach was rumbling pretty insistently and he knew if he didn't eat something soon he'd drop.

Being exhausted, hungry, and shocked awake from the shower actually did the trick. He didn't have the energy to think about Rachel Clare or her insulting offer.

It was time to focus, get back to work, and maybe grab something to eat.

That had been the plan, at least until Mark got into his office and found Scott there, waiting for him.

Waiting in Mark's chair.

Talking on Mark's phone.

Feet propped up on Mark's desk.

Mark threw his bag into his closet and it banged. Loudly. Scott jumped to his feet, glasses nearly sliding off his nose.

"Ah, thank you Mr. Burslman. Truly. If you want to email me the document? That'd be great."

Scott's eyes flicked back and forth to Mark, who stood there, arms crossed over his chest.

"Yes, of course. I'll speak with him. He's here right now actually and I'm sure he'll be thrilled."

Thrilled? Thrilled didn't even begin to cover how Mark felt about finally ripping a new one into Scott. Being in Mark's office, regardless of how badly he wanted Mark's job, that was going over the line.

Scott hung up, gave Mark his biggest smile, and then immediately dropped it. "Well, I was going to say that I had great news for you, but you look a little angry right now."

Angry? Huh. Not even close.

"Can't you tell? I'm thrilled."

He locked his gaze with Scott's, who stumbled out of Mark's chair. The chair he'd hand-picked when they'd moved into their new, higher quality office building.

"Right, I'm, uh sorry about that. I was just coming by to see you and then realized I forgot to call one of the publishers; you know, I mentioned I'd put out a few feelers. Just in case."

Scott babbled on, even as Mark circled him, arms still crossed over his chest. He circled Scott until Scott had his back to the doorway.

"I know you're mad about me going behind your back because you are the CEO. Ethan and I, of course, respect that."

"So much that you made yourself right at home?"

The only thing Scott respected was being king of the company, which wasn't going to happen. Not unless Mark screwed things up that badly. And he hadn't. He still had time to make this work, to find some solution without resorting to Scott's 'alternatives.'

When Mark didn't say anything, Scott took another step back, then tried to cover by looking menacing in return. It didn't work. He looked like an idiot barely keeping control of his bladder.

"Look. I've given you a chance to set things right, but let's face it, we have no game and no time."

"There's still time." Mark ignored the chill creeping down his spine. He still had time.

"No. You don't. Because I've lined us up another deal and I know you won't approve, but it buys the company time and gives us the money to keep the team going."

Mark may have restrained himself from killing Rachel, but that was only because she was a woman. And smoking-hot.

Scott?

He'd squash Scott like a bug.

Scott might be good with numbers, might be good at office management, but the only reason Mark had agreed to the partnership was because he needed the investment money, money which Scott had in abundance.

Money, just like Rachel Clare had. He was damned if he would be forced into the same situation with her. No thanks.

Mark closed the distance between them and Scott backpedaled out of Mark's office. A good thing no one was here. Seeing the owners fighting was never good for company morale.

Fighting was only allowed in private. Like now.

"You respected me so much you went behind my back, worked to get a game deal, and then even made the call from my office?"

With your damn feet on my desk, he thought.

"It's a game, Mark," Scott snapped. "Which is more than you can say for all your efforts. How long have you been at this? Months? Well, Ethan and I are tired of waiting. The team's getting nervous and talk has started about whether they should look for jobs elsewhere. Is that what you want?"

No. Scott knew that.

"I know you won't be happy, but the game will sell," Scott said.

"How would you know whether or not it sells?"

Publishers played a guessing game, trying to hit a moving target with a BB gun. And unlike Rachel and her books, each game cost a hell of a lot of time and money.

Scott straightened his button-up shirt, realigning until it settled perfectly over him. It was one of his games for control, trying Mark's patience.

Too bad Scott had no idea how frayed Mark's patience was today.

"It's a media tie-in. Perfect and flashy and will draw a lot of attention."

Mark's fists clenched. Media tie-ins were the laughing stock of the industry. Bottom of the barrel, worst games to ever make, worst kind of design gameplay on the planet.

And the damn things did make money.

"Did you accept this deal?" Mark asked, voice low and rumbling.

"Of course not!"

"Good."

Scott pushed his glasses into place and waved towards Mark's office. "I thought we could sit down and look over the contract together, before bringing Ethan in and making a—"

"No."

The single word echoed through the empty, wide-open office. If his teams were here, they'd be poking their heads above their cubicle walls. They also wouldn't dare say a word.

Not when Mark was in this kind of mood.

"Excuse me?" Scott, however, was an idiot and couldn't see a waving red flag if it was an inch from his face.

"I said, 'no.'"

"You have no right. I found us a deal and it's—"

"We're not accepting the deal."

Mark closed his eyes, briefly, and wondered how his life had gotten this screwed up.

No way out. No choices left.

Except for one.

What was worse? A media tie-in game that was bound to be terrible, or taking the heat from the entire video game industry for daring to make a game no one had even thought of?

He knew what Rachel would say.

She'd tell him to grow some balls.

But at least the threat of her game would buy him some time, keep Scott off Mark's back long enough for him to line up another deal. He might find some publisher willing to make the kind of games Mark wanted to make, the kind of respected games his company made.

"We're not accepting the deal," he said again, "because I already found us one. I found us an angel investor."

CHAPTER 9

*R*achel slammed her front door shut and threw off her heels. One landed by her salt-water fish tank, the other vaulted over the vase and lilac bouquet she'd bought the other day.

Not like it mattered if she broke either of them.

"I'd just buy more with my stupid millions."

Just the thought of her 'money' and how Mark threw her offer back in her face just made her want to scream.

He hadn't even listened!

"And I am never ever going to see that man again. Even if he comes back begging."

She didn't need him or his game company.

Normally an hour-long drive with the wind wrecking havoc on her hair would do the trick, but not this time. This time, she still wanted to kill the man.

"Gorgeous. Handsome. Arrogant. Asshole."

Tears pricked her eyes. And she hated, absolutely hated it when she got so upset her hormones decided crying was the best remedy.

She wiped at them, glad they hadn't spilled over during lunch, if you could call the two of them yelling and storming out as an actual lunch.

Her stomach growled, reminding her she hadn't actually eaten anything. The hunger broke through enough of her anger to realize she was standing in her empty foyer. Alone.

Alone in this giant house she didn't need and didn't even like. Just like all the money to 'prove' Daniel wrong.

Her stomach didn't like being ignored and gave her another good kick.

"Alright, alright. Hold on." She headed for the fridge, ready to make do with her own, homemade salad. "Not as good as the restaurant, but it'll do."

The doorbell rang.

She froze. For a second, her heart hammered. There was no way it could be him. It was...well, it was impossible.

The door rang again.

"It's not him," she reminded herself even as she stomped barefoot to the foyer, with her stomach swirling, and yanked open the door.

Not Mark. Just Nick.

Nick smiled up at her, the sweet smile that said 'I'm sorry and please forgive me.' But it wasn't the smile that made her push open the door further allowing him entrance. It was the wondrous smell of pizza.

He'd brought her pizza.

"I thought you'd need cheering up," he said as she let him in, taking a long look at her hair. "Although, I hadn't thought to bring a hair brush. You look like hell."

She didn't even bother to reach up and straighten the mess, a gesture she would have done automatically with anyone else. With Nick, she didn't care how she looked. There were no cameras here, no one snapping away at the famous author.

"What are you doing here?"

Although, she couldn't help but peak at her reflection in the giant hallway mirror. Yep. She looked like hell.

"I thought that was pretty obvious. I'm here to cheer you up."

"Well, you brought food. I'll take that."

She got out some plates and napkins. Much better than eating from the box as Nick preferred.

He grinned. "I thought we'd find a compromise, especially since the lunch went as well as expected."

"Shut up." She didn't need the reminder that he'd been right about the lunch. "And how do you know, anyway? Did you... did you talk to Mark?"

Nick's eyebrows raised at that, but he shook his head. "Wild guess. I know Mark and I know us game developer types."

Rachel didn't know what she thought about that—especially the way her heart beat a tad bit faster when she thought of Mark talking to her brother. About her.

She slammed the cupboard closed.

"Well, you were right. I screwed up as much as he did with me. If Mark really was desperate enough for a game, he'd at least have listened."

"Rache," Nick slid his arm around her shoulder. "I don't think you quite understand just how scary women's stuff is for us men. And romance? Scariest thing in the world, especially those books you women seem to eat up like they were chocolate."

She tossed Nick's arm off her. "They *are* chocolate and that's the reason you 'men' haven't figured out how to actually make a real game for real women. Not those chicks with gigantic tits."

Chicks who didn't exist in normal, everyday life despite Mark's reference to the bodice-ripper romances. Those women at least had been proportionate.

Kind of.

"I'm sorry about Mark," Nick said. "Really, I am. I'd thought he'd at least listen."

It was the way Nick said it, that kind of sly reference that set off her brother-alert sirens. The kind of sirens that warned her Nick was meaning a hell of a lot more than he was saying.

She rounded on him, making him fumble with the pizza and nearly dropped it on the floor instead of his plate. "Why, Nicky? Why did you think he'd listen?"

"Shit, Rache. I'd think that was kind of obvious."

She crossed her arms and glared. "My looks? That's the reason? That's why you picked him out of all your friends?"

"Well, you are hot. For my sister, anyway."

She smacked him hard in the arm. It made her feel a little bit better.

"Oww. Hey! I didn't mean it like that."

He dodged as she smacked him again, somehow keeping his pizza plate out of reach and out of danger.

"There's nothing wrong with looking hot," he said. "In fact, you should use it to your advantage. Why do you think all the game booths at conventions have 'booth babes?' Heck, our PR girl has boobs falling out of anything she wears. Why'd you think they hired her?"

"I hate you so much." She swung at him again. "I hate your industry and I hate...," she hit him again, "hate that I even thought of this romance game for even a second! It's a complete and total waste of my time!"

"It's not a total waste." Nick held out his plate to protect himself. "It's a good idea, but I told you it wouldn't be easy."

"Easy? Easy doesn't even begin to cover what my 'lunch' with Mark had been like."

If all the game developers were as stuck up and arrogant as him—then damn it, Nick was right and she'd *never* make this game.

"I mean," Nick went on, "Mark's pretty attractive himself. I thought that would at least get you through the introduction, long enough to explain—"

"*He* didn't give me a chance to explain anything," she snapped. "The second I said 'romance' he was finished listening to my offer."

And that's part of the reason why this hurt so bad. Because they *had* been getting along, even though he hadn't known who she was, hadn't known she wrote romance for a living.

And the second he found out?

He turned out to be exactly the same as Daniel. Like all of Mark's respect for her vanished the second the word 'romance' came out of her mouth.

The dreaded tears were back and she wiped at her eyes, feeling her mascara smudge.

Nick froze when he saw her tears. "Ah, hell, Rache. I didn't mean it like that."

"Yes, you did. Just like he meant what he said."

She busied her hands with own pizza, hoping it'd distract her sad and pathetic hormones, hormones that again had to point out she lived alone with a tank of fish.

She didn't even have a dog.

Maybe she should get a dog. Their parents always had at least two Labs while they were growing up. Maybe a big, dopey, always-loving-her dog would do the trick and get her out of this funk.

She sniffed. "Just look at me? Successful writer, proving everyone —including her ex-husband—wrong, and I'm so lonely I'm thinking about getting a dog."

"Hey," Nick handed her a tissue. Actually, it was the pizza-labeled napkin, but she took it anyway.

"You're not alone," Nick said. "Though, this place is a little boring. And clean. You could use some dog hairs clumping around the corners."

She smiled as she dabbed at her eyes, just thinking about how it'd mess up the decor and how the stylist she'd originally hired to help 'decorate' the place would freak.

"Maybe. But not white hair. You can see white hair on just about everything."

"Except white?" Nick chuckled. His iPhone rang and he pulled it out, eyebrows shooting up. "Well I might not be able to do much about the dog, but your game might not be totally out of the water yet."

"What do you mean?"

"Mark's calling."

Rachel snorted. "Yeah, probably to tell you how 'great' our lunch went. You can just tell that jerk I don't want to talk to him. Ever again."

Nick ignored her and answered the call.

Rachel tried to ignore how her chest tightened and the way her eyes watered up again. Damn it. She ate a huge bit of pizza, letting the wonderful mix of bread, cheese, and red sauce flood her mouth.

Heaven. At least, it would have been if Nick wasn't on the phone with Mark.

This was simply ridiculous. She was absolutely done with that man and all arrogant men like him.

Finished.

Nick pressed the phone to his chest. "He wants to apologize. He also wants to meet with you again."

"Why should I? I've already been humiliated once this weekend, why shoot for a second time? Besides, I've just decided no more men in my life. I'm done."

Nick shrugged. "Fine with me, I mean the men part that is. You don't have much luck in that field. And you don't have to meet with Mark, but I know this guy, Rache. If you're serious about this game, he's the one that can make it happen."

Rachel sank into her dinning room chair, pizza in one hand, plate in the other and noticed her life, laid out for her on her table. Her life in book publishing, a life she wasn't satisfied with anymore, though she had no idea why.

Strewn across her table, instead of nice place-settings, were her contracts. And previous contracts complete with rulers so she could compare them, line by line, to her newest one.

Did she want to make this game work? Didn't she have enough on her plate as it was?

"Rachel?"

She closed her eyes. What was she thinking. She was crazy! She had deadlines set for the next year or two. But still...her gaze drifted to the contracts, to the same old life she'd been living.

The life that wasn't working anymore.

"Tell him yes. Tell him it's crazy, but yes. I'll meet with him."

And this time, she'd have to be better prepared, and better armed to protect herself against Mark's harsh, soul-piercing words because that's exactly what she'd be facing again.

That's what people like Mark and Daniel thought about her and her work. But she wouldn't run away. She'd at least meet with him and see if this project was worth pursuing.

"You can also tell him my decision has nothing to do with how good he looked either," she threw in before Nick hung up.

Because it had no baring, none whatsoever, on that tiny, slim little excitement about seeing him again.

Nothing at all.

CHAPTER 10

This time when Rachel met Mark at Daniel's Broiler, she'd made sure to get there early just so she didn't have to share the elevator with him. And just in case they had to share the ride down, she'd worn more comfortable heels so she could take the stairs.

At least, as comfortable as heels could be. Regardless, she'd survive the trek down if necessary.

She took the liberty of not waiting, seating herself and ordering their drinks. This time, if it went badly she'd at least stay and enjoy her meal. Since the *maître d'* had actually seated her, rather than tossing her out, she planned on giving them a good tip.

Mark was on time. Nearly on the nose, actually. This time, though, he didn't look quite so prim and proper, what with his hair tossed back and the handful of strands that seemed to go in whatever direction they wanted to go.

It also didn't help that he ran his hand through his hair twice since he sat down. Still, even rumpled and disheveled he looked... way too good. And she hated that Nick had been right about Mark being good-looking. Not like she'd ever admit it.

To either man. Hell no.

She leaned back, crossing her arms as he ran a hand through his hair yet again. Was he...nervous?

That was completely absurd. People like Mark didn't get nervous, and certainly not over meeting someone from lunch. They kept their confidence close to the chest, rarely letting people in or opening up. Sort of like her.

The thought didn't make *her* any more comfortable. But regardless, this was definitely not the man she'd met yesterday.

After another minute of him not saying anything, Rachel decided to take the man's approach and be direct. "Are you nervous?"

He dropped his hand when she pointedly looked at it. "Sorry. I'm not great at apologizing."

"I can believe that."

He scowled and there was that dark, piercing look she'd remembered from yesterday. "I normally don't have people 'above' me that I need to apologize for... unless its a publisher, and they're the ones usually screwing me."

She's had a few book publishers like that, but she wasn't about to let him off the hook. Not yet. "What you mean to say is you're not used to being held accountable for your actions?"

There went the hand again, but this time he caught himself. "You can say that."

She hooked her wine glass and sipped. "It's fine."

It wasn't fine, and deny or suppress all she wanted, his words had hurt. But she couldn't let him know that.

"Fine," he echoed, "as long as I promise not to do it again?"

"A promise would be nice."

He'd break it though, and they both knew it. He was Mr. Big Man in Charge and if they did this project, together, they'd be storming out of a restaurant a couple more times.

At least.

She wasn't about to roll over for him. Regardless of how handsome he looked, even disheveled and slightly off his game. He wasn't about to roll over for her either and that was the only reason she'd agreed to the meeting.

She missed this, missed having someone to... not fight with, but someone who challenged her. Rachel shoved the thought aside. There was nothing she wanted Mark to challenge her about, nothing at all.

Nick had to be crazy to think *this* was the guy who could make her dream a reality.

Mark watched her now, and she squashed a blush before it could take hold.

"Why don't we try this again," she said. "And this time, since you know exactly who I am and exactly what kind of game I'd like to make, why are you even sitting here? You made no secret of what you thought about me and the books I write. So, why are you here Mr. Ashe?"

"It's Mark, remember?"

Mark.

She managed, just barely, not to smile.

Maybe they could at least pick up where they left off—crossing out all the yelling and hurtful things they'd both said to each other. She wasn't exactly blameless on why things went south, herself.

The restaurant noise faded to a dull hum, just the usual clinking of plates and quiet chatter in the background. Lunch crowds were always calmer for these kinds of meetings and she already found herself settling into her element.

Like Mark, she was used to being the one with the power, the one in the driver's seat, and the one who could say no and walk away from a publisher.

Right now, he was the one who could walk away from her. She needed his company. He needed her money.

You'd think it'd be a win-win situation, but it sure as hell didn't feel like it.

Probably because of the way he looked at her, with just enough intensity to make her squirm.

Rachel didn't like squirming so she gave back as good as she got.

"I'll tell you," he said, "but first I need to understand you."

She blinked at this. "Understand me?"

"Why do *you* want to see this game made? Why does it matter so much? You mentioned an agenda. I'm not a fan of agendas."

Rachel swirled her wine, watching the white, yellow-tinted liquid circle her glass. The question looked so simple on the outside, but in truth it was brutally honest because the question wasn't just about video games.

Part of the question asked who she was.

"You say there's no market for a game like this, which means there's no female market. I know you're wrong because I used to be one of those girls."

He gave her an incredulous look and she smirked.

"Yes, I played all the big, hours-long role-playing games. I played for the story and in the end the stories always let me down."

She told him one reason she became a writer was because of the stories, of the characters and the need to see what happened next to them, to be there beside them on that journey.

"The stories in video games were never enough," she said. "So, I spent all my allowance on books and not games. Unlike my brother."

Mark fingered his beer. He hadn't had any yet. Actually, he hadn't taken his eyes off her since he sat. "But why a romance game? Why not something you know will sell, something you know will make money?"

"I don't care about money."

"Everyone cares about money." He finally took a small sip of his beer and she looked away.

She hadn't just been staring at his lips.

"Money isn't a big deal to me and I don't write romances just because I know they'll sell. Look, I don't expect you to understand."

And she didn't. Most people didn't understand what an amazing story was, why readers kept buying her books. Instead, they liked to sneer at her.

The waiter appeared, paling slightly when he saw them, but took their order with an efficiency that made Rachel wonder if the staff was hoping to feed them and shoo them off before they got into it again.

"Alright," he nodded. "But then why romance? Other than the fact that you write it."

"Because I want to make a game for women and there's no better genre to grab its players by the heart and yank them in. If we do this right, you can give players the kind of experience they've never had before, something the best games out now barely scratch the surface of."

How to make him understand?

"Women know the ending of a romance book," Rachel explained. "They pick it up and know how it's going to end. There'll be a 'happy-ever-after,' in some fashion, but readers keep coming back. They keep reading, they keep buying."

Rachel leaned over the table, her blouse dipping lower. Mark's eyes flashed to her shirt, then jumped back to her face.

"Why?" he asked.

A smile pulled at her lips. For the same reason men enjoy and admire a woman's chest.

"They love to fall in love."

She watched as his blue eyes darkened and he studied her with his unreadable expression, even as her own cheeks flushed. She must look like an idiot, letting her passion take control.

But idiot or not, she couldn't back down.

He leaned back and it was like his nervousness from earlier disappeared, leaving behind the man she'd met yesterday. Cool and confident, and in complete control. She had no idea why the change occurred but it had and she couldn't help but feel nervous by it.

This was the kind of man who went after what he wanted, the kind of man who played for keeps.

"You think a romance game can do all that?"

"I do." If they played their cards right; if they made the right kind of game.

"Women are historically not gamers."

"How many games have you actually made and marketed for intelligent, free-thinking women?"

He blinked. "Well there are quite a few Nintendo titles..."

"Real games," she put in. "Not a dance game or a game to help you lose weight. A woman's equivalent game to your shooters, like *Last Man Standing*."

He frowned at this, but she wasn't sure if he understood where she was going. Or if he even believed her. That's when it clicked. He had no idea of the kinds of titles being marketed towards women.

"You don't know, do you?" She kept her voice quiet, as if she didn't want their waiter, who set down their lunch, to hear. "You have no idea how to make a game for women."

Mark picked up his fork, thoughtful. "I don't believe there's a market."

"Have you looked?"

"Have you?"

She smiled at this, the kind of smile that showed *him* the kind of confidence she carried. "Honey, I write for that market. I know there's a market."

"But that market doesn't play video games."

There he went again with the arrogant, condescending tone. She grabbed her napkin and snapped it onto her lap. What she wanted to do was reach across the table and slap him. But she restrained. Barely.

"Are you not listening to a word I've said? No one has ever tried to make a game for women. You slap a pony on the cover and think suddenly it qualifies for a game women will buy."

Her temper rose.

Mark wasn't listening. He wasn't hearing a damn thing she said. He just kept his mind closed off. Just like Daniel had always done with her writing.

"Why are we even here if you have no intention of listening?"

She stood, forgetting her vow to at least eat the food before she stormed out, when Mark touched her hand.

His touch, like last time, sent heat waves through her. Then chills.

This was entirely too much body reaction for a man she didn't like, a man she wanted absolutely nothing to do with.

She yanked her hand back.

"I'm sorry," Mark said. "Really. I'm skeptical... and, no I don't really believe you."

"Oh, well thank you Mr. Smooth. That makes me feel so much better."

His lips curved at that and he gestured to her seat. "I owe you lunch, but you'll have to forgive me for my... disbelief. Because you're right. About women in my industry."

"What about them?"

"We don't have many and I don't have much perspective."

She lifted her eyebrows.

"Or any," he added, "at all."

That statement alone stopped her from leaving. She hesitated, drawn in by his sincerity and wondering, once again, why he'd even called. But if she left now in a huff (again), she'd never find out.

And Nick trusted this man.

Rachel slid back into the booth, picked her napkin off the floor. "I'll stay, but only if you answer me one thing."

"Fair enough. Shoot."

"Why are you here?"

He watched her for a long moment, forgetting about his steak sandwich, even as she stabbed a forkful of salad. She didn't eat, though, but watched him in turn.

A nervous flicker flashed in his dark eyes, so quick she thought she'd imagined it. But she hadn't. She knew she hadn't.

"I'm here," he said finally, "because I need a game. It's either your game or lay off half my company."

"But you don't believe in my game."

"No."

She could see the sincerity in his gaze, and was that a bit of regret? She'd expected as much, though, just as Nick had warned her.

"But that doesn't mean I'm not interested," Mark added.

Rachel chuckled, it was self mocking and though she hated it, couldn't help it. "Mark. If you don't believe in my game, then it'll never work. I'll be wasting your time—"

"And I'll be wasting your money, I get that. I already told you, I don't know the first thing about romances and I have no idea if there's actually a market for one."

Which they'd covered. She felt like they were circling a drain. They hadn't quite emptied out the conversation completely, but they were nearly there.

"I don't know anything about romances," Mark said, voice quiet as if he didn't want the whole restaurant to hear. "But I'm willing to learn."

Rachel straightened. "Learn? About romances?"

"Why did Nick ask you to contact me?" Mark asked, dodging her question.

She frowned, unsure where he was going with this. "He mentioned your company being in trouble, but other than that, just said you were the guy for the job. I trust his judgment."

And that was why she was still here rather than throwing the towel in and finding someone else more interested in her game, in charting new territory, creating a whole new genre in this industry.

Mark nodded. "I am the guy for the job. All our games are innovative, different. We push boundaries. That's what I've built my company on."

She heard something there, something he kept close to his chest, but it was there. He wasn't happy with her game; that much was clear and she didn't know why.

Well, she could take a few guesses, but why was romance so threatening?

Probably because like Daniel, Mark didn't understand it.

Rachel closed her eyes for a moment, letting the memories of Daniel drift away. He hadn't been willing to listen, to learn. She didn't know if Mark could either, but would it be so bad to pursue this a little further?

She still had time to turn him down.

"So you're saying I need to convince you." Rachel picked up her fork, stomach growling. It was time to stop dancing and just enjoy the lunch.

"That's about right. Make me believe in you and your game."

Her shoulders loosened. Mark had no idea, none at all, how big the romance genre was.

He had no idea how big a market women were.

She smiled and stabbed another forkful of her steak salad. This, she thought, was something she was going to enjoy. A lot.

"Alright, Mr. Ashe. I'll bring by some numbers, show you business reasons why this will work, but here's the deal." She held her fork out, few pieces of lettuce pointing at him. "You come with an open mind, willing to learn. If you do that, I might just be interested in making a game with you."

Mark gave her a slow, very sexy smile. She immediately ate the salad so she had something to do, something to distract herself from noticing how good, how predatory he suddenly looked.

"Ms. Clare, you've got yourself a deal."

CHAPTER 11

*N*ow, Rachel was used to standing in front of people, doing speaking engagements, and working with a crowd of hundreds (sometimes thousands). That was no problem.

In fact, she was even comfortable as a speaker, which was an unusual trait in a writer.

But standing in front of three video game owners in a boring, drab little conference room, with their arms crossed, scowls on their faces (okay, maybe not *all* but definitely the mousey, ugly one), she realized she'd met her match.

To think her 'match' would come from men. Not just any man. Mark Ashe.

Mark was even more cool and collected than when she'd first met him, as if this was his serious game face. The problem was she didn't know if that game face was for her, or against her.

Not to mention the fact he might be her only support right now.

Once she reached his building, Mark had escorted her inside, even remembering to be the gentleman and carry her box—a box he had no idea was filled with her romance novels. He'd shown her around, introducing her to the other two owners, Ethan and Scott, before giving her a quick tour of the building.

It was her first look into the kind of game company he ran. And a first look into the man who ran it. Orderly, efficient, and for the most part projecting a pleasant atmosphere.

Relaxed, enjoyable. At least this was the quick vibe she got when he rushed her through, veering away from anyone who wanted to meet her. Which was quite a few people, seeing as how most of the employees were men, and even with her dressing in a snappy business suit, Nick had been right.

She did look good, and therefore quite a few people wanted to be 'introduced.'

Except for Scott, the mousey, ugly owner. He'd taken one look at her and said, "Mark, can I speak with you in my office?"

Mark had said sure, but at least he put it off until after the meeting.

Which left Rachel here, facing three unhappy owners. She finally glimpsed what Nick had warned her about. She might have numbers on her side, incredibly big money-making numbers, but that wouldn't mean a damn if they weren't willing to listen.

She hoped she wasn't wasting her time; hoped Mark hadn't pushed her into this knowing she'd never succeed. She'd hate to hate him all over again.

Not like she stopped hating him after their first lunch. He'd also managed to trample over every temper-pushing button of hers during the few brief times they'd talked on the phone, setting up this meeting.

A meeting she wasn't sure would turn out in her favor, even if they needed her money.

Scott cleared his throat. "Some of us have jobs to get back to." Scott glared at Mark, but his tone was definitely for Rachel.

So much for playing nice. "Well, then, best not waste any more of your time, especially since you're in desperate need of a game. And the money to fund it."

Scott's eyes narrowed, but he kept his mouth shut and she remembered Mark was the one ultimately in charge.

Mark settled into the chair nearest her and she tried not to notice how she could just make out the chest muscles under his shirt. Why did the man have to wear a shirt quite that tight?

This was definitely not the right time to be admiring the view.

Good view or not.

Rachel explained to the owners she'd taken the past week to compile information about her book industry, especially how it compared to other fiction genres. The numbers were damn impressive. But as soon as the words 'romance game' left her mouth, Scott's reaction was damn impressive, too.

The short man shot to his feet and his face got so red she thought he'd burst. "This is your idea of a game?"

Scott rounded on Mark. "You turned down my media tie-in game! And for what? To make a romance game?"

Ethan, the much quieter owner—a programmer, she remembered —just watched. She could see he was worried and if that frown was any indication, he wasn't pleased either.

But at least he wasn't screaming.

"Maybe," Mark rumbled, "you should sit down and listen to what the lady has to say."

Yes, Rachel heard the threat in his voice, but she also felt it settling in her gut. She'd pegged him for a predator at lunch, but she'd had no idea how close she'd been to the mark.

This wasn't a man to mess with. Good to know. She'd watch her step, carefully, and if he was smart he'd watch his around her because she wasn't going to lose this chance.

She'd done some digging on FastPlay Games—Nick had been right. If there was a company who could make her game happen—and not just make the game, but actually make it a good game, then she needed Mark on her side.

She needed him to believe in the idea. She needed him to believe in her.

Easier said than done.

"This presentation is a waste of our time." Scott spit. "Just like you wasted the *company's* time pursuing such a ridiculous, completely unrealistic project. Do you have any idea what would happen if we actually considered this? If we went through with this?"

Mark leaned back in his chair, slowly crossing his arms over his chest. "You mean we might make a shit ton of money?"

Mark didn't look at Rachel, but she could see the anger pulsing through him. "I suggest you listen to her Scott. She knows what she's talking about."

Rachel straightened at the sudden faith he had in her, which was very different than the man she'd seen at the restaurant. Back then, he hadn't been convinced, but maybe now he was willing to listen.

Her fingers itched for her notebook, to write down the details of his jaw, the tension in his entire being as he glared back at Scott. A glare that sent her pulse fluttering.

A woman of her age and her disbelief in men shouldn't have a fluttering heart.

Those were left for her heroines, not for Rachel.

But damn. Mark really was an alpha hero. He'd even be perfect for the game's hero.

No, she thought quickly, pulling her attention away from Mark's narrowed eyes and the way her breath seemed to slow. Best not to think of Mark as any kind of hero, especially not as a hero in her life.

After all, heroes had to prove themselves before the girl could fall in love. And she was no way near to falling in love; been there, done that. She'd stick with being alone. It was safer that way.

While she'd been daydreaming about not falling in love with the sexy game owner, Scott had kept up his sputtering tirade and after a moment, she realized she hadn't missed anything except maybe being even more insulted.

"This will never work." Scott shook his head so hard his glasses nearly slid off his nose. He shoved them back on. "There is no money in romance! We'd never make another game again. No publishers in their right mind would trust us."

If Scott wasn't careful, she had no doubt that the Mr. Mean Mark, the guy who'd put a company together from scratch, was going to come out and rip the little jerk to shreds.

She hoped he would. Because if he didn't, she would.

And right now, she was close, damn close to doing just that.

Stay cool, she thought, *this was what you expected.*

And it was exactly the lead in she needed.

Rachel rose from her chair, immediately drawing the eyes of three owners. "I was told I needed to convince you this game was not only possible, but if we did it right, it'd make this company a lot of money."

Mark was the last one to meet her gaze. After a moment, with her pulsing still fluttering, he nodded for her to continue.

"Considering romance made nearly 1.4 billion dollars in 2009, I think you'd better shut your mouth about there not being 'any money' in romance."

Rachel slapped the industry report she'd brought onto the conference room table. And every number on that report, going back the previous ten years, proved her point in big, black decimal points.

Scott blinked at her. "Yes, but surely in comparison—"

"Nothing else comes close. Religion and inspirational fiction comes in next at a mere $770 million. Like I said, there's a market out there, if you're willing to take the chance."

If they were willing to give women their fair shake.

Even standing here in this room of men she was reminded of the David and Goliath fable. And this wasn't even the real Goliath, this was just her trying to convince three men to give her a chance. To give women a chance.

Maybe Nick was right and she was crazy, but for the first time in years, she was excited.

This was her chance to show this male-dominated industry that women mattered, and not only did they matter, but they should be respected.

They deserved to be respected.

In the back of her mind, she pictured Daniel with his trademark frown when she brought home another armful (okay, two armfuls) of books. He'd always said she couldn't do this, couldn't make a living as a romance writer.

Now these men were saying the same thing, but about women and video games.

Well, screw them. She *would* prove them wrong.

Scott, despite his dislike, was the first one to start drooling as he gazed at the reports, mumbling to himself. Apparently he was the geeky, numbers guy.

She knew, deep down, he wasn't the one she needed to convince. It was Mark and even though he watched her with those dark, unreadable eyes, she knew she hadn't convinced him of anything yet.

That's why she had to bring out the big guns.

She took a deep breath. She didn't like talking money, or in particular, talking about her money and her sell-through numbers, but she needed Mark to understand the kind of market her name alone brought to the table, to this crazy, completely nuts venture of theirs.

"Over lunch," she said, "Mark asked me how to market to these women."

When she said his name, Mark glanced up. He studied her, waiting to see what she had up her sleeve.

For the first time, Ethan stirred in his seat. Good to know he was actually alive and paying attention. "It's a good question and Mark is right. People who read books don't play games."

"But they could." *Here goes.* This time, her fluttering heart had nothing to do with Mark. "They could if you have the right marketing tool. If you have the right brand."

She slid out her report. Three copies, one for each owner.

She forced her hand to stay steady, to not reveal a nervous twitch. It was worse than seeing readers pick up one of her books, shrug, and then put it back down. Somehow, this was much worse. She was giving them her career, what she'd worked so hard for and built for years, to be judged.

Judged by men.

The last man she had allowed to judge her work ended up in a divorce.

"Gentleman, these are my numbers. This is how many books I've sold and how many for each title. I think the numbers speak for themselves."

Silence lingered in the room as they each reached for their copy. Silence as the blood drained from Scott's face. Silence as Mark looked at her, eyebrows raised. Pure and utter disbelief, but was that possible...did she see a small amount of admiration?

No. Impossible.

Except, her twisting stomach and her fluttering heart had other ideas—that he might believe in her, that he might... *absolutely not.* Rachel shut the thought down. Those ideas truly didn't belong in this room, let alone coming from her.

Still, she waited for the judgment she knew was coming. The judgment that'd rip her right open again, even as she prayed it'd be otherwise.

The report slid from Mark's fingers and he frowned at her. And just like that, she knew she'd lost. He didn't want to make this game. He didn't want to make her game.

And yet, her damn heart had to go and twist like he'd just broken it. Which was impossible since she definitely hadn't given it to him.

Nor would she. Ever.

CHAPTER 12

Mark stared at the report—at Rachel's numbers—in complete shock. Holy shit. Not even their bestselling game came close to even her lowest numbers.

Who the hell was this woman?

For that matter, who the hell were all these women buying her books?

Mark set the report down and tried not to think of how much money every book of hers made. If he did his head would spin out of control.

And she just had all this cash laying around?

Rachel looked different now, not nearly as confident as when she first walked into the building. Because of showing them how many books she'd sold?

But that was ridiculous, she had nothing to be nervous about. Heck, if they sold half that amount in games he'd be boasting about it every chance he got.

Still she stood there, face slightly pale, fists clenched at her sides. It was a look he didn't like to see on her. He liked the confident, angry woman instead, which was silly since *that* woman tended to drive him crazy.

"You weren't kidding were you?" he asked as the report slid from his fingers. "This is a huge market. You're a huge market."

She blinked and her fear slowly replaced with shock.

What had she expected? That he get mad because her numbers weren't better?

He wasn't sure they could be.

Mark slowly stood from his chair, noticing that neither Ethan or Scott had recovered yet. Not a good sign.

Good for Rachel, not good for him—or his company. His other two owners were impressed. Impressed enough to give this hair-brained game a chance?

He'd started FastPlay to make the kinds of games he liked to play, the kind of games that pushed the limits; and while Rachel's game would 'fit' with that innovation, it was the last game Mark wanted to be caught dead making.

But shit. These numbers *were* impressive.

"Rachel. Why didn't you—"

A knock at the door cut him off and Meredith, their receptionist poked her head in. "Sorry to bother you, Mark, but you've got a call from Forged Legends Interactive on line three."

A call he'd expected months ago. A call that would most likely be a denial.

"Should I ask them to call back?" she asked.

Mark glanced once at Rachel and she shook her head. "No, please. I can wait. I know how publishers can be."

How did she know Forged Legends was even a publisher? He didn't have a chance to ask because Scott jumped up from his seat.

"Yes, of course Mark can take the call. Ethan will wait here with Ms. Clare, get her some coffee if she likes."

Then Scott darted out the door, taking Rachel's two reports with him. He wouldn't answer the phone right away, but if Mark took too long, he wouldn't hesitate.

"It's all right." Rachel touched his shoulder, a touch he felt shiver through him.

"Thanks, but, uh. Don't drink the coffee. I can take you out for some real stuff when we're done."

Why did he say that? Wasn't he already considering brushing her and her game off? Good-looking for not, leading her on about the game wasn't fair, but the words sort of jumped out of him.

He was tired and stressed. That was all.

"Not sludge coffee?" Rachel smirked.

"Yeah. Not sludge. There's a place around the corner." He wanted to say more, but truthfully, he had no idea what to say. Or what to think.

He'd seen that look on Scott's face when he saw Rachel's numbers, knew Scott was already sold.

But Mark wasn't. His chest tightened at the thought of making her game, making a romance game.

He didn't say any of that. Couldn't.

"I'll be right back."

He kept the door open a crack, then walked at a brisk pace across half the length of the office. More than a couple employees watched him pass, brows raised, but Mark ignored them.

Right now he needed his head on straight. This could be the opportunity he'd waited for. A call that could save him from making a game that would destroy his company's reputation, destroy everything Mark had slaved for.

Even if she might actually be right.

As Mark expected, Scott hovered over Mark's phone. Another minute and the ass would have answered it. Mark glared at him, which made Scott shuffle away—though not far enough.

He settled in the chair to wait. Scott didn't move, just stared at him.

Mark swallowed his temper, put his game face back on and answered the phone. He'd expected another denial, another 'this game looks great but not right now.'

Instead, Forged Legends Interactive made him an offer.

Mark sank into his chair, limbs suddenly weak. He'd done it. He'd stayed in there long enough and he'd—

Then the rest of what Mr. Lawrence said caught up to Mark's brain. Lawrence liked the game, but he wanted a bigger scope—wanted the game on multiple platforms otherwise it was no deal.

Multiple platforms—consoles, hand-held systems, computers—was always a pain in the ass. It'd been something he'd decided against just this past year on *Last Man.*

But Mark kept all that in the back of his mind. He nodded at the right places, watched how Scott's eyes narrowed. But Scott was actually more interested in the numbers—Rachel's numbers—than with Mark's relayed conversation with Forged Legends.

Mark didn't know what to think and he definitely didn't know what to feel. This was the call he'd been waiting for, but the more he listened the more he realized this wasn't quite the game he'd pitched to them.

It was worth it, right? Worth it at least to pursue the matter, see if he and Forged Legends could come to a compromise on some of those points?

Anything was better than a romance game.

Right?

The second Mark hung up, Scott slapped Rachel's reports onto his desk. "You need to call them back."

"I do?"

"You need to tell them no."

It took all of Mark's control not to reach across the desk and slam Scott's face into those numbers he loved so much. No one told him what to do, not in that kind of tone, not when they tried to run his company and steal it out from under him.

"And why in the hell should I do that?"

"Because we're going to make Rachel's game—because we're still small time, we don't have the staff or funds to make two—but with her game we're going to make a shit ton of money."

"Is that right?"

"We'd be idiots to turn her down. If we even got half of these women, our numbers would be off the charts. And we could make the game right, with you at the helm, and with Rachel's help... we've never had such an amazing opportunity before!"

Mark didn't give a rat's ass about opportunity. "I'm not about to see this company's name get smeared all over the industry for making a romance game."

Scott, finally noticing Mark wasn't on board with this plan and wasn't happy at this moment, frowned. "If you didn't like the game why'd you even bring it to us?"

To buy me some time asshole, Mark thought.

"You needed to hear her offer. I heard and I'm not interested, especially when we have a chance to make a real game." Mark nodded at the phone.

Rachel had unknowingly done her part. She'd given him time, time to get Scott off his back.

His stomach twisted at the thought of telling her they weren't going to make her game, but she would be prepared for disappointment. Nick would have prepared her.

Scott carefully gathered up the two reports, neatly lining them up and stood. "That's your vote, then. And you know mine. I guess it's up to Ethan to be the tie breaker."

"Fine by me." Mark shot to his feet.

Ethan would see reason. He always did, and he always sided with Mark when it came to games, when it came to making business decisions.

Mark followed after Scott, fury growing with each step and he realized Scott was practically glowing with smugness. Why the hell would he...?

Mark entered the conference room and froze. Ethan was sitting beside Rachel, in Mark's abandoned chair. She'd crossed her mile-long legs and her skirt had ridden up just enough to tease, just enough to hint at what lay underneath.

Scott stopped, too, and Mark was more than sure he was seeing the same thing. And enjoying it—a little too much.

He grabbed Scott's shoulder and pushed him to his chair. Ethan, however, wasn't noticing her legs at all. Instead, he leaned in, holding something in his hands—a book—as he laughed.

Laughed.

And talked.

Ethan did neither. He was the shy, quiet owner. The techie guy, the guy who kept to himself and did all the crazy, hard programming for Mark.

And was Rachel seriously flirting with him?

Mark yanked out a chair, hard and fast, which caused them both to glance up. And for Ethan to lower the book onto the table.

A book with a perfect, chiseled male chest on the cover. Complete with a half-undone bowtie circling the man's neck. No face was needed. Neither were the sparkling letters or pink background.

There was a God damn romance novel on his conference room table.

First Scott. Now this.

Mark's hand tightened on the chair, but he didn't have a chance to tell her off, to tell her to take her trashy novels and get out of his building.

Ethan smiled. "Rachel's told me more about her idea, about these novels in general, and I think we could really make it work. I think we should do it."

Mark's entire world came crashing down around him and Rachel sat there with her sleek, long legs and the most beautiful damn smile he'd ever seen.

Two votes against one. They were going to make her damn game and there was nothing he could do about it.

Beautiful or not, he wanted to kill her.

CHAPTER 13

*R*achel was an expert on body language, on the subtle hints a person gave off revealing their mood, their hidden, inner thoughts. She needed to be observant in her line of work.

Right now, there was absolutely nothing hidden about Mark and how pissed off he was. Nope. Nothing hidden at all.

A smile pulled at her lips as he lost his serious, calm mask. She smiled because she knew she'd won. She may not have convinced him yet, but she would.

Given enough time, she'd get through to him just like she got through to Ethan.

"You think we should make the game," Mark bit out. Even she could see the words pained him. "I think we should talk about this more, at least before we decide."

Scott waved him off. "There's plenty of time. We still have to work out a contract, negotiate. Lots of time."

Scott's gaze slid to her crossed legs. "You know, Ms. Clare, if you don't mind I'd love to take you out for that coffee. Maybe give me a chance to better understand your... uh..., your numbers."

Her numbers? Bullshit. She had a hunch what he wanted to discuss and she wasn't interested.

Rachel slowly, and making sure she didn't reveal anything Scott was interested in seeing, uncrossed her legs. "We'll definitely need to discuss the business end. Marketing will be tricky to get right. I imagine it'll be much different than what game companies are used to doing."

"Yes, yes," Scott nodded. "And I'm sure today is just the day to—"

"Might as well start today," Mark cut him off. "And I promised you coffee. Good coffee."

Mark slammed his chair back under the table, making Scott jump while Ethan merely watched him, his eyebrows quirked up. Rachel had no idea what was going on.

Sure he was upset about making a romance game, but there were a hell of a lot more vibes in this room and she didn't like not knowing what to expect.

Mark grabbed her purse from the chair and tossed it into her arms, which she fumbled to catch. Then he caught possession of her arm.

Yes, possession was exactly the right term.

"What are you—?"

"Coffee. Now. We'll talk."

And like that—rough, brutish—Mark was again shuffling her through the building. Actually, this time he was practically carrying her out the way his strides covered the distance from the conference room to the door.

"What is this about?" She kept her voice lowered, so none of his employees would overhear, but his gaze still darkened.

"Nothing."

Nothing? Like Mark turning into a sudden caveman over Scott wasn't nothing. And it wasn't like she couldn't take care of herself.

"Are you going to drag me all the way to the coffee shop or are you going to let me walk like a big girl?"

He jerked his hand back as if she'd burnt him. She hoped she had because her arm was on fire from where he'd touched her. "Sure. Yeah. It's right down the block."

She hoped it was. Sensible heels or not, there was also no such thing called 'sensible' heels. "I can walk a block."

He glanced at her shoes, gave her a look of pure disbelief, and mumbled something that could have been "this way."

That, of course, was the point where he stormed ahead of her, as if he was in a race and needed to reach his coffee in the shortest time possible. Rachel scowled at him, hiked her purse strap higher, and followed after him at a normal pace.

There was no way in hell *she* was going to stomp around in her heels. If he wanted to talk with her then *he* could slow down and wait for her.

It took a few minutes, but then Mark froze and checked over his shoulder. He didn't apologize when she caught up to him, just stuffed his hands in his pockets and kept going.

At least this time he kept pace with her instead of leaving her in his dust. But with the angry waves streaking off him, she almost wished she had.

Still, Rachel kept her mouth shut and waited until she ordered one of the most expensive, extravagant, girly, espressos from the menu—and then made him pay for it.

Now, with coffee goodness in hand, she was ready to deal with this man. Or as close to ready as was womanly possible.

The coffee shop had been just down the block as promised, but it was nestled in between two apartment buildings. If you weren't a local, you'd have never seen it was there.

The smells of roasting coffee hung in the air, soaking into her clothes. As mad and frustrated as she was at Mark, the fragrance slowly relaxed her. It was late enough that they'd missed the morning rush, but still too early for the afternoon crowd.

Which meant they had the place to themselves.

The cashier nodded at Mark, asked him how the game was going, to which Mark gave a vague and curt reply, before they settled down into their seats—at the furthest corner from everyone.

Considering how their business lunches tended to go, this was probably a good thing.

Rachel savored her caramel double shot vanilla latte, leaned back in her chair and wished she was here with someone else, someone whose company she actually enjoyed rather than someone she was about to yell at. Again.

Savoring done, she put the cup down and gave him a level stare. "Are you going to tell me why you're so pissed off now?"

"Who said I'm pissed?"

"The entire world knows you're pissed. You hide everything else well, but not your temper." Not to mention she'd seen enough of his temper to know what it looked like—and the signs.

"Fine." He put his black coffee down beside hers. "I'm not happy how this turned out."

"Even though you have a game? A game that will keep your doors open?"

For a moment, she wondered if he was going to give her the honest truth, if he was going to tell her why he was so mad. Or if he'd shy away and make excuses. That's what Daniel had done, both in their marriage and even now when he accidentally 'ran' into her.

Rachel crossed her arms and waited. She wasn't good at waiting, but she'd wait for this man. She'd wait until she got a straight answer. She deserved that much.

"If you weren't interested in my game, then why did you meet me for lunch? Why did you ask me to come to your company and try to 'convince' you? Obviously you had no intention of being convinced."

"You're right. I didn't."

Okay. She'd wanted honesty and that was exactly what he gave her. The jerk.

"Except," she went on, "I've just convinced Ethan and Scott. They want to make this game, don't they?"

His eyes darkened and she watched as the blue became an almost midnight color. A very good color on him.

Her face heated, but she didn't look away. What was it with this man and why did he get to her so easily?

Shit, all she wanted was to dump that scalding hot coffee all over him and let him scream—because that's what he made her feel like. Like she was getting burned all over again by Daniel.

Mark nodded. Once. "They like your game. I don't, but it looks like I can run my mouth all I want. You convinced them."

Ahh, so that's why he was pissed at her, but it didn't answer the other part of her question. The important part.

"You have a game. You'll keep your teams in tact. But you're still mad and I need to know why."

Mark grabbed his coffee again and cursed because he'd burnt his tongue. "Jeez, can't one thing just go right for me today? All right. You want to know the truth. Fine. I've worked too hard to make this company into what it is and if I come out with a romance game..."

He waved his hand. "I'll lose all the respect I've spent years earning. Respect is the problem. I don't respect your game. I respect what you're trying to do, but I'm not the guy for this project."

Rachel's arms snaked around her waist and for a moment, she felt so helpless, like she'd been transported back to a time in her life where she wasn't the confident, successful, best-selling writer.

Instead, she was the woman being told over and over she wouldn't succeed, she'd never make something of herself.

Something she'd finally started to believe.

A failure.

The thought of being a failure, straightened her spine. Rachel reached across the table, grabbed Mark's shirt—feeling the tight chest muscles underneath—and pulled.

He hadn't expected that and nearly lost his coffee over them both. But she leaned in, nose touching his.

"I am not and never will be a failure," she growled. "And I will not allow this game to be a failure because your dick is so big you can't see around it. Either give me a god-damn chance to prove you wrong or tell your buddies the deal's off."

She released him, snatched up her purse, espresso, and stomped out as quickly as her heels would allow.

She didn't get far.

Mark burst through the door, slamming it behind him. He'd forgotten his coffee. "Fine! I'll give you a damn chance."

"Why should I?" She shot over her shoulder.

He caught up with her in two strides, then slid in front so she had to stop, had to face him. She still had her coffee. She still had the opportunity to dump it all over his arrogant chest.

Stupid, good-looking chest.

"Because I'm all you've got," he said.

Rain opened up from the dark, gray skies and came down in fast, steady drops. Great. Now she was going to be soaked and mad.

"From where I'm standing, there are quite a few game companies in the area."

"Yeah, but I'm the only one who can make this work." He stepped closer and even though they were on a wide, empty sidewalk, it suddenly felt like she was trapped in the elevator with him. Again.

Trapped, and barely able to breathe.

This time, she wasn't trapped by the closed in space. She was trapped by Mark, by his angry, furious eyes. Trapped by his body and the way her heart just went into overdrive.

Trapped because his eyes flicked to her lips and she suddenly, very much, wanted him to kiss her.

CHAPTER 14

The second Mark jumped up from the table and ran after Rachel, he'd stopped thinking. He'd moved without thinking, yelled at her without thinking.

And now, with her mere inches from him, inches where he felt every part of her as if she was radiating heat in this pouring, cold rain, he threw 'thinking' out the window.

He was pissed. He was beyond rational. He was losing everything and somehow, it was all her fault.

She tilted her head up, just enough to glare at him. That was enough. Because the second she tilted her head, he suddenly had a wonderful view of those lips, lips which the rain lightly touched, droplets trailing from her lips and down her neck.

He growled, low and deep. And like she'd done in the coffee shop, he grabbed her arm and pulled her to him.

Her eyes widened, but then she was falling into his chest. Her heels not enough to dig in, to prevent gravity from taking control.

Like the way he was taking control. At least in this.

His lips met hers and he kissed her, kissed her until she stopped thinking as well, until he felt a moan roll up her throat.

The rain continued to pour around them. He buried his hands in her hair, distantly thought the strands were just as silky as he'd imag-ined. Then wondered if the rest of her was just as smooth, as silky.

A car drove by. Honked. Someone shouted out the window, "Good job, Boss!"

Like a bucket of cold water dumped on him, in a way the rain wasn't doing, Mark immediately let go. Stepped back.

Rachel wavered on her feet, not quite steady in those heels, hair disheveled from where his hands had been. She still held onto her purse. And her coffee.

She stared at him, mouth open, probably ready to deny what had just happened.

He wasn't going to let her, not with his body still humming from her closeness, from her heat. Not when he just wanted to grab her and kiss her all over again.

"I'm the only one who can make this work." He stalked back towards his building.

This game was a terrible idea on so many levels it wasn't even funny. But he had time, time enough to set up the deal with Forged Legends. As long as the contract with Rachel wasn't signed, he still had time.

He'd convince Ethan. He had to because there was no way he could work on a game with Rachel.

No freakin way could he work on a romance game, not with a woman who probably kissed exactly like the characters in her books.

ETHAN REFUSED TO BUDGE. Even when Mark mentioned Forged Legends' interest, Ethan merely shook his head. "They've had months to consider your proposal and they're just getting back to you? Not to mention that we decided no more multi-platform titles."

They sat in the conference room, with Rachel's box of romance novels on the table. He'd looked, briefly, and barely managed to hold in a shudder. The damn woman was serious about this.

Ten million dollars serious.

So, apparently, was Ethan—and that hadn't been something Mark expected. He was sure he'd sway Ethan to his line of thinking, but whatever Rachel had said, she'd done her job well.

Ethan sipped his coffee—company sludge coffee—while Mark dripped on the carpet. The rain had come down fast and hard after he'd left Rachel. But he felt a little better knowing she'd gotten just as drowned as him.

Her designer clothes would be ruined, or would need some serious dry cleaning. He'd just toss his into the wash when he got home.

Whenever he left work, that was.

"Working with her will be a heck of a lot different than working with publishers," Ethan said. "No more political bullshit, no more publishers holding back royalty payments because some ass in corporate doesn't like signing such a big check to us little developers."

Mark didn't care that Ethan was making a good point—hell, all of his points were great points. Ethan was right, but that didn't change anything.

FastPlay *couldn't* make a romance game.

Ethan listened to Mark's complaints, to his very good reasons why they shouldn't make this game. He left out the kiss, but that was also a good reason not to make the game. Conflict of interest and all that.

When Mark finished, Ethan merely shrugged off everything he'd just said. Everything.

"Her game would be doing exactly what our company's mission statement says, but in this case... damn, we'll be blowing everyone out of the water for sure. *Innovative* is one thing, but starting a whole new genre?"

Ethan whistled to prove his point. Another good point; damn him.

Mark slumped in his chair, not caring he was getting it all wet. "I know you're right, but that doesn't change anything. This company's reputation—"

"Might be on the line."

"*Will* be on the line," Mark corrected. "Yeah, we might get some points if the game sells, *if* it sells. But what about our future? What if we can't get another publishing deal?"

"That's the gamble. It's always been a gamble, Mark. You know, it's no different in Rachel's case. She's making a gamble on us."

"I'd rather her gamble on someone else."

Ethan tapped his fingers on the table, watching Mark. He might be quiet but there wasn't much that slipped by him. "I know why you brought her in. You're getting worried about Scott."

Mark shrugged, hoping it'd show he wasn't concerned. Ethan didn't buy it.

"Look. You're doing a good job and I'd rather have you sitting in the hot seat. Definitely rather have you there then me." Ethan smiled. "It's nice blaming everything that goes wrong on you. Really, though. If you're this worried about making a romance game..."

"I am."

"Okay, I can respect that." Ethan tapped the table again. "I think you're wrong, though. Wrong about the game and wrong about her. She's in this for the long haul and she'll treat us right; better than any of our publishers ever did."

And that was ultimately what Mark wanted, to be completely free from publisher control, to not need their money and yet still make the kinds of games which got him into this business.

The kind of games he remembered and enjoyed as a kid, games that lost their place on the shelves for bigger and flashier titles.

He remembered Rachel as she'd grabbed him in the coffee shop and told him exactly what she thought.

"I do believe in her," he said quietly, "I just don't believe in her game."

"So. What do we do now, boss?"

That was the question, but even if Mark was CEO, this company was a partnership and two of three partners had spoken their mind.

"We haven't signed a contract with Rachel yet, and heck, I don't even know if this game's possible."

Ethan nodded. "True on both points."

Mark didn't want to give in, not even this much, but he'd relied on Ethan in the past and everything Ethan had said was spot on. "I'll talk with her more, work out the details. Do you have a problem if I still pursue the Forged Legends deal? Just talk, no signing. Then maybe when we get a better idea of both projects the three of us can sit down and decide."

Ethan fiddled with his coffee, forehead furrowed. Finally, he sighed. "I'm fine with it, but you know Scott's not going to be. He wants the money Rachel will bring to the table."

"The money isn't a for sure thing." But being embarrassed and publicly humiliated? That was for sure.

"And I'm gonna say this right now. When Rachel finds out about Legends—and I'm bettin' she will—she's going to be a whole lot more pissed than Scott."

Ethan grabbed his coffee and stood. "And you're gonna take the heat for that. All of it."

"Fair enough." Mark stood as well. He'd thought he'd feel relief, that he'd succeeded in extending his deadline, gotten the time to work out a deal for *his* game.

He didn't feel relief. Instead, he felt a settling in his stomach. Not disgust, but definitely not comfortable.

Not when he couldn't stop thinking of Rachel glaring at him in the rain and then with her lips pressed firmly against his.

"I'll take the heat for this," he told Ethan. "Believe me, I'll deserve it."

CHAPTER 15

Rachel waited in her car, dripping, soaking wet onto her recently cleaned upholstery and thought of all the wonderful, fabulous ways she was going to kill Mark.

Her hands, still wrinkled from the water, tightened on the steering wheel. She didn't need the heater to warm her up; she was producing enough heat to warm up the whole car.

Nick knocked once on her window and slid into the seat. "Whoa, didn't expect it to come down quite so hard."

Then he turned and got a full look at her, hair frizzing in all directions, water-stained blouse, and her tight, furious face.

"Umm, something wrong?"

"You and your recommendation," she growled. "How could you think even for a second that *he's* the one to make my game?"

Nick's confusion fled and he nodded, as if a wise sage. She'd wise sage his ass. Right onto the curb.

"Well... Mark can be a bit... difficult sometimes."

"Difficult?" She dropped her voice. "Difficult?"

"Okay, maybe that was too nice a word. Hey! Where are we going anyway? You said this was an emergency?" He smiled, all nerves but determined to steer the conversation away from her impending temper explosion.

"I'm getting a dog."

"Oh, good that's an excellent—" Nick clicked his mouth closed. Blinked once. Then his explosion came. "A dog? You called me out of a meeting because you need to get a dog. Right now?"

"Yes."

She shifted gears and tore into the street. She needed a damn dog because apparently she was lonely enough to let a jerk like Mark kiss her.

Apparently, she was lonely enough to kiss him right back!

Yes, a dog was just what she needed to save her sanity.

"It's going to be female dog. A big one. No damn males in my house."

"Uh, right, Rache." Nick fumbled with his seat belt. "I guess your meeting with FastPlay didn't go so hot?"

"Oh, it went great. Two owners want the game."

Nick's eyes widened at that, impressed. From the corner of her eye, she watched as realization sank in. "But not the third one."

"That's right."

Not the one who mattered, the one who had to understand everything about romance to pull off a game like that. The owner who she'd need to spend time with, lots of time, to make sure he understood.

"And that's why you're getting a dog?" Nick asked, voice tentative.

"That's right."

No more lonely Rachel Clare. Now, she was going to be lonely, but she'd have a dog who'd love her unconditionally, shed fur all over her house, and refuse to stay off the couch.

A dog was exactly what she needed.

ONE LOOK at the giant Alaskan Malamute and she knew this was the dog she needed. All one hundred pounds of her, fluffy tail and all. The dog was friendly, absolutely in love with people—all people, especially her—and best of all, the dog was a girl.

The clerk at the Seattle Humane Society smiled, bright and cheerful, but her gaze kept straying to Rachel's ruined clothes. Nick, thankfully, distracted her. Not that it was a huge problem since the girl was cute.

Still, it got them out of Rachel's hair long enough for her to bond one-on-one with the dog. Rachel threw the tennis ball in the enclosed exercise area and the dog wasted no time running after it.

Giving the ball back was a different experience, but when offered a treat, the ball was discarded in a second.

Rachel laughed despite her pissed off mood, despite her wet and now sticking clothes.

"Wow." Nick came up behind her, tucking his hands into his jean pockets. "Didn't think I'd hear you laugh again for another week at least."

She smiled, but only because the dog nudged her hands with her giant head. "See? I need a dog."

"You're also a little emotional right now. You sure about this?"

He was right. She *was* emotional and decisions like this should never be made without careful thinking things through. "Yes, you're right. But look at her?"

Rachel knelt and gave the dog a good ear rub. "How can I leave this sweet thing here?"

"Okay, it's your house. You sure you don't want something else? Like a little bird or something that's not going to eat your furniture?"

"This sweet thing," she told Nick, "would absolutely eat the bird."

He shrugged. "Your choice. Haven't a clue how you're going to get that beast in your car though."

Right. Her Corvette. "Back seat for now?"

Well, Nick had been right about her spontaneous decision to get a dog, especially a dog that was only twenty pounds lighter than *her.* She'd survive.

Her house, on the other hand, might not.

One step into her house, and the dog—now called Allie, claimed her spot on the couch. Well, at least Rachel had the loveseat to herself, which was fine since it was only her who lived here.

And to be fair, Allie didn't start eating the furniture until Rachel left to pick up some much needed dog supplies—like a kennel, dog leash, and bowl. When she saw the very much nibbled on coffee table, she shrugged, decided she needed a new one anyway and got to work with the training.

Dealing with Allie was the perfect distraction. She was exactly what Rachel needed after the meeting today. Okay, not so much the meeting but Mark.

Mark and his stupid kiss.

She glanced at her dinning table and the contracts littering its surface. Not to mention she still had a book to write.

"Okay. I've played around long enough. Time to get back to work."

She stood, brushing her hands on her very comfortable and very dry jeans. She'd put together the wire kennel and Allie jumped down from her couch to inspect it.

Rachel ran her hand through Allie's fur, finally relaxing after the rain-soaked kiss. She'd figure this out and if the game didn't happen? Well, Mark was wrong. There were plenty of other people who could make this game. Plenty of people who'd be dying to make her game.

"I don't need you," she said aloud. It made her feel better.

At least up until her cell rang and caller ID informed her two minutes of relaxing were up.

Mark was on the phone.

CHAPTER 16

Rachel crossed her arms and glared at Mark, who sat at the other end of the conference room table. Poor Scott and Ethan were on either side of them, fidgeting and sneaking not-so-covert glances between the two.

Scott cleared his throat. "Is there, uh, is there something you two would like to discuss before we get started? Ethan and I can step out."

"Nothing to discuss," Mark growled.

He looked the same, except his shirt was slightly rumpled, as if he'd pulled it from the top of a clean laundry pile. She simply hated that he could still look rumpled and good at the same time.

Hated it.

"Nothing at all," Rachel snapped back. "You called me, so why don't you tell me why I'm here."

Scott cleared his throat again. "I, uh, I thought Mark told you we'd like to move forward with the game? We're interested, Ms. Clare, if you still are."

Mark had told her, but that didn't mean she believed him. She still didn't. Oh, she believed Ethan and Scott thought this was a great idea. Okay, maybe not great but not at the piss-bottom of the barrel like Mark seemed to think.

"It depends," she said finally. "On Mark, really. Are you going to give this game a chance or should I go spend my millions on another company?"

"I will. No point in *wasting* your millions on a company that'll make a shitty game."

His eyes narrowed to tiny little blue slits. Good. She'd gotten to him. Because even with her new found dog for company, she still couldn't stop thinking about him.

And that damn kiss.

Scott pushed up his glasses, then shuffled some papers either to keep his hands busy or to make some noise in the dead silence lingering in the conference room. "We, of course, have details to work out, a contract to negotiate."

"As well as explaining your *'vision'* for this game," Mark said. "Can't start on the core design and game play without that."

Okay, the way he said 'vision' was about as condescending as he could get. She watched as Ethan, who was sitting next to Mark, kicked him under the table.

Mark only grunted, then finally dropped the 'I hate you' look for an 'I'll tolerate you' look. Fantastic. What a team they were going to make.

So why didn't she just say 'no thank you' and walk out the door? She could. And she could find another company, but damn, Mark. He was right about him being the best.

And after talking with Nick she realized not just any company *could* make this game. Some companies didn't have the culture that could change their mindset in order to make a game, well, make a game for women.

Mark could. Not only could he, but based on all their game reviews, he knew how to make a game fun.

Rachel huffed and finally dropped her arms into her lap. "Fine. I'm interested. I'd like FastPlay to make this game—if we can work out the details and *if* we both decide we can make this work."

She said this last to the three owners as much as she did to Mark. If they couldn't work together there was no way this would work.

After a moment, with Scott and Ethan watching him closely, Mark nodded. "Agreed."

For some reason, that one word was like magic because before Rachel could blink, Scott and Ethan had jumped up from their chairs, shaken her hand and then scooted right out of the conference room.

She heard a small click and swiveled in her chair to stare at the door. "They didn't... they didn't just lock it did they?"

"Sure they did. For their own protection."

Rachel turned back and dialed up her glare full throttle. "Their protection, huh? So who's going to protect *you*?"

"Who said I need it?"

She raised her eyebrows at that. Clearly, he was also an idiot if he didn't think he needed protection.

"But they are half right. We are going to spend a lot of time together." He leaned back in his chair, crossing his legs as he studied her. "At least I'll enjoy the view."

"If I remember right, you enjoyed more than that."

Stalemate. Their eyes met. Held.

It was the first time either of them had referred to the kiss-that-shall-always-be-forgotten. But now that she'd breached the no-talk zone, Mark smirked, a slight and very sexy pull of his lips upward.

"You're right. I did."

Rachel fists clenched in her lap. Oh, how she wanted to slap that smirk off his face, show him exactly what he should be afraid of.

Business partnership, she reminded herself, *business.*

Nothing he said was personal; couldn't be personal.

Riiight. Just like they could actually get along.

"The only reason I'm still here is because I think you're right," she said.

At that statement, his smirk turned into a full on ego smile.

Rachel grabbed her folder and slapped it onto the table. "You can make my game, so long as you can get your head out of your ass long enough to learn what women want."

"Rachel, I know what women want."

She smiled back, except it was more like a lip-curling sneer and literally slam-dunked the ball into his court. "Clearly, you don't. Now. Are we going to play nice or what?"

It was *his* turn to be the professional and at least try to meet her halfway.

Mark's eyes never left her face. "Okay. Let's give this a go—and by 'go,' I mean *working*, not you kissing me. Probably not very professional for the work environment."

Why that asshole! He'd been the one who kissed *her*.

She didn't have a snarky reply because Mark pulled out her box of romance novels (which they'd hidden in the corner) and he dumped the books onto the table. And the books did make quite an impressive pile.

"You mind telling me why you brought all these?" He held up a book, a Scottish Highlander on the cover. The first of her Highlander romance series.

"Research."

Now it was her turn to smile, especially when his face paled. Rachel stood, plucked the book from his hand. She leaned in close, so close her blouse sleeve brushed him.

For a brief moment she had a flash of that rainy kiss and she shoved it aside. Business. Professional.

Of course, how could she deny herself the pleasure of making him feel uncomfortable?

"How do you expect to make a romance game if you don't know what women want? Or more specifically, the kind of *romance* experience women want?"

Mark scowled back, then leaned in toward her—much, much too close—to get the book back. He flipped through it, pausing every couple pages. Which wouldn't normally be a problem.

Except he didn't move away, back to his side of the table. Or heck, at least back into his seat. Meanwhile, with her butt pressed against the table there wasn't anywhere she could go, unless she went through him, which was looking more and more enticing by the second.

"You're kidding." He turned the book to the side and tilted his head. "Is that position even possible? I mean, I can't put it in the game if I don't know how it works."

"Give me that." She snatched the book and tossed it onto the pile. "Trust me, it's possible."

"Is that right?"

"Yes."

"You know from experience?" His arms slipped on either side of her, resting on the table with her trapped in the middle.

Perhaps she shouldn't have taken the book away from him.

"I do, thanks very much. I was married."

Even if that marriage had ended long before Highlander was written, let alone published. Mark, however, didn't need to know that.

Mark gave her a long, slow smile. "Was, uh?"

"Yes. Not that it's any of your business."

Nor was him being in her space any of his business. She shoved at his chest, pushing him off her.

After a moment, a moment where he showed her he was only choosing to back off, he did back off.

He began picking through the books, tossing some to the side and keeping others. "Okay, Rachel. I get why you need me to read these. I'd have asked for them myself, actually, so you saved me the trouble."

"Really?"

"Hard to believe, huh? I may not be pleased about it—and don't think I'm going to be caught dead with these outside of a locked, secured area—but yes, I do need to learn your genre."

"Oh." That went, surprisingly better than she'd expected. She'd thought she'd have a full fight on her hands.

"In that case," she picked up her purse, thinking they'd finish up later—like when her breathing returned to a normal, steady pace. "I guess I'll be—"

Mark's hand shot out, stalling her. "Not so fast Miss Romance Princess. I need more than just reading books. I'll need to pick your brain."

Which meant lots more Mark time. Great. "Okay."

"You're one of the Queens of Romance, so you clearly understand your audience." He shook the Highlander book in her face. "So I need to know what you know."

"I can try. A lot is instinctive and—"

"That's not all I need," he cut her off again. "I need you to do research, too."

"Me?" What kind of research would she possibly have to do.

"There are a few games I'd like you to play, one or two have little romance subplots." Mark gave her the smile/sneer she'd given him earlier.

Payback, then.

"You want me to play video games?"

"You bet, Princess. I'm gonna need your help pin-pointing exactly how we can convert this," he held up her book, "to this."

This time he held up a game with a handsome space guy on the cover, and with a sexy brunette in a skin-tight outfit posing next to him Video games. Nick would be laughing his ass off if he heard this.

Rachel immediately thought of her writing deadlines, some looming closer than others. Why hadn't she thought of this?

"I'd say that's a pretty fair assessment. I don't, however, have any consoles and Nick won't let me borrow his."

Mark snorted. "You couldn't buy any with your millions?"

"Why? Just so they can gather dust as soon as I'm done with this 'research?' I don't play games for a reason."

He backed off slightly, eyes drawn in a frown. "Curious. I'll tell you what. You come by my place, bring your favorite books you want me to check out. You can play the games and I'll read romances. That sounds like a fair trade to me."

Rachel didn't think so. She'd be dealing with frustrating game controls, a story that a six year-old could write, and long, endless hours only to 'accidentally' die because some game developer thought to make level 9 a tad bit harder.

Meanwhile, Mark got to read steamy sex scenes.

Definitely, not a fair trade.

"Fine." She snatched the game from him. "When do you want me to come over."

A slow smile spread across his face and her stomach curled at the promise there. It was a promise she didn't want anything to do with, and yet, there was her stomach curling on its own.

"How about tonight?"

She hated the stomach curling and she hated that smile of his. Hated them both enough to take drastic, evil measures. Evil as in pure terror—the rampaging, giant-tail wagging kind.

"Alright, but how do you feel about dogs?"

*M*ark glared at the two steaks, patiently waiting for the grill, and asked himself for the hundredth time: what the hell was he doing?

He should have insisted she just buy a game system. She had the money, she sure as hell could afford it. *But nooo, he had to go and let his ego get in front of his head.*

Not to mention she was bringing some dog of hers. A dog she'd just gotten from the Humane Society and didn't want to leave by herself. Which didn't explain what the dog was doing while Rachel had been at the meeting, but no, the Queen of Romance wouldn't explain that!

"You got yourself into this, Ashe," he said. "Now you've got to deal with it."

Deal with it in a way that involved not strangling the millionaire, and no kissing either.

What he should be doing was working on Project Hades, the online co-op game he'd pitched to Forged Legends. He and Ethan had tossed around a few tweaks that afternoon, but now Mark had to hammer out the details before he called them back.

But instead of working on the project he wanted to make, he was stuck reading romance novels and picking Rachel Clare's brain on all things romance.

And why?

"Because you couldn't keep yourself from egging her on."

He'd definitely lost his mind the second he'd seen her mile-long legs. And the infection only seemed to worsen after the kiss.

A kiss she'd mentioned. All on her own. A kiss that wasn't going to happen again.

Mark shook his head. He needed to knock it off, to think straight and do what he needed; do what was best for his company.

Which wasn't Rachel's game, no matter what Scott and Ethan thought.

The doorbell rang. Mark threw the steaks onto the grill, making her wait in the rain a few extra seconds, before he answered it. She didn't smile when she saw him. In fact, she looked about as thrilled as he did.

This should make for an extra fun evening.

That was as far as his thoughts got because he was suddenly knocked backward by a train, a train which then jumped up to his face—a flash of white and blackish-gray fur. It then proceeded to roll out a gigantic tongue and lick the entire side of his face.

"What the hell is that?" Mark shoved the dog back down. "You call that a dog?"

Rachel leaned in his doorway, not even trying to call off her beast, as she smirked at him. "You said you liked dogs."

"I said dogs. Not *beasts*."

The dog jumped up again, but this time Mark was ready and kneed the dog back down, but the second his hands were in licking range— well, that part was pretty obvious.

A giant dog, but at least a super-friendly one. Okay. Maybe a little *too* friendly.

He wanted to stay mad at Rachel, mad that she'd purposefully tricked him into saying 'yes' without mentioning that her dog was a 100 pound walking, licking, wardrobe accessory.

But he was a sucker for dogs.

"This dog equals like four people. You lonely or something?" He looked up in time to see her smile fall and her eyes cloud over.

She looked away. "Why would you say that? Allie, okay, down now. That's enough."

And with a control he never thought possible, she expertly got her crazy beast-dog under control.

"How long have you had this dog?" He didn't try to hide the admiration in his voice. Course, that meant she'd let it—Allie—jump on him on purpose.

"Since the day it rained."

"Ah."

He knew which 'rainy day' she meant, even though it rained seven days a week most of the time in Bellevue.

"Anyway, why don't you come inside, seeing as how Allie's already made herself at home."

The dog bounded about his place, running up the condo's stairs, nose into everything she could reach. He was a gentleman enough to take Rachel's coat (a coat that cost more than his entire wardrobe) and hang it, then gave her a very brief tour of his place.

As in, *there's the bathroom.*

At least she didn't comment on his very obvious bachelor home. And very obvious nerd home.

He had straightened up a little, washed the dirty dishes, thrown away the half-eaten Tupperware surprises. He hadn't done it for her. He'd only done it because with him being so busy trying to find a game console the place had gotten a little rumbled.

He'd cleaned because it suited him.

Not like it mattered as he watched Allie fling her tail across the coffee table and knock over the empty beer bottle from earlier. Rachel had the kindness to at least wince.

"I hope that was empty."

"Me too." He led her to the living room and she paused in front of the 60" plasma-screen TV.

"Nice TV. Big enough for you?"

"I'm betting yours is even bigger."

"You're right." She tossed the bag of books and her purse onto the couch. "It would be—if I had a TV."

"What? You mean you don't?" His mind reeled at the thought. "What the hell do you all day?"

"Let's see, I umm, write? Oh, and I like to read."

Mark only shook his head. "You're crazy."

"Oh, believe me, I have no doubt about that." She held up her leash. "We can throw her outside if she gets too crazy."

Mark shook his head. He could handle crazy, had to be a little crazy himself for having this gorgeous, attractive woman in his home —a woman who kissed like she was on fire—and a woman he'd sworn off kissing ever again.

Christ, it was going to be a long evening. And he'd sure asked for it.

Mark asked if she wanted something to drink, holding out a Stella of his own. Rachel pulled out a wine bottle instead. Who was he to rain on her parade?

He poured them both a glass, 2005 Cabernet Franc, and wasn't surprised she had great taste in wine. It seemed like something right up her ally.

While the steaks cooked, they drank their wine, steering clear of small talk—or any kind of talk for that matter. Allie nudged their hands when petting time came around, but for the most part entertained herself.

Which left Mark to entertain Rachel.

They sat on bar-stools at his counter, which was what he used for a table, and the silenced stretched between them. Rachel crossed her legs, and even in the long, trim fitting jeans, they looked fantastic.

Which was very distracting. For him.

Thank God steaks didn't take long to cook, and a good thing she didn't mind meat since he'd forgotten to ask if she was a vegetarian or not. Allie was definitely not a vegetarian and patiently sat beside them, looking all pretty with her tongue rolling out, waiting for her steak.

"She wants to lick our plates," Rachel interpreted.

"You sure about that? I think she's staring at this slab of red meat."

"Well, that, too." Rachel shrugged and for the first time that night, smiled at him.

Okay, she was smiling at the dog and not him, but that was the first time she'd given a real smile in his presence. He watched as she fluffed Allie's head and decided she was right to get the dog.

Anything that made her smile like that.

That's the point where he remembered his talk with Legends and his plan to turn her project down. It was something that definitely wouldn't make her smile. Not in the least.

And he'd be the jerk for stringing her along and ruining that smile.

"So, uh," he said, "what are you expecting, from our game?"

"Expecting? You mean what my 'vision' is?"

She used the same tone of voice he'd given to her earlier. Right. He deserved that.

"Yeah, that. Mind telling me what you're thinking so I know what to look for in those bodice-rippers?" He nodded to the books on the couch.

"Bodice-rippers were a thing of the 80s," she clarified. "My books are *not* bodice-rippers."

"Could have fooled me with that kilt guy."

She stabbed a slice of steak with her fork. Perhaps antagonizing the woman while she had a knife was a bad idea. "My 'vision' is simple, but not so simple to execute I'm sure."

And for the first time since he met her, well, since he realized she wrote romance for a living and wanted to make a romance game, Mark kept his mouth shut.

He leaned back, stroking Allie's head with one hand, eating a steak with the other, and listened to her.

The more he heard, the more brilliant her 'vision' sounded. It wouldn't be an easy game to pull off, but he was already thinking of design solutions to some of those problems.

She wanted this to be a game where the players—the female players—had a chance to fall in love.

"I've seen Nick play games for years," she said, "and I did get a kick out of the ones where he could chose which dialogue to pick from."

Mark nodded, not at all surprised. "That was a hit with our female audience, especially the romance subplot."

"I haven't played it yet, but it sounded weak."

"Well, it was." He stuffed another bite of steak into his mouth.

How to create a game experience that mirrored the experience of reading a book? Wasn't that the million dollar question?

Still, the only way he knew this was going to work was biting the bullet and reading one of those books. And once he did that, he could at least say for sure a game like this would never work.

Even if now, the more he listened to her, the more he doubted his own reasoning. Maybe a game like that *could* work.

CHAPTER 18

While Rachel had hoped Allie's presence and the destructive nature of her size would infuriate Mark, she was pleasantly surprised otherwise.

He didn't mind the big dog at all. In fact, he seemed to be enjoying her presence about as much as Rachel was. Of course, that sort of detracted from the reason she'd brought Allie in the first place—which was to infuriate Mark Still, this seemed like a better alternative.

It was like having a beast-size, tail-wagging chaperon. And with Allie's presence, Rachel had an easier time relaxing as she sat on Mark's leather couch playing games. He sat on the opposite end reading a romance novel.

Who would have thought after their disastrous first lunch, they'd be here? Not her, not in the slightest.

She also hadn't imagined she'd be playing a game set in space that was half role-playing game, half adventure-shooter. Definitely not the kind of game a contemporary romance writer would find herself playing.

Mark glanced up from the book, a romance with a fluffy white wedding dress on the cover. That was *her* payback for the science fiction game he'd shoved at her.

"Are you still creating a character?"

"Yes. She has to be perfect. And sexy. I can't play a non-good-looking character."

Mark rolled his eyes. "And wasn't it you who said something about stereotypical game chicks with big tits?"

"She doesn't need to have big tits. She just can't look ugly. There's a huge difference."

Mark watched her for another few minutes as she moved the character's cheekbones back from one extreme to the other. "Just, just give me that. I'll make you not look like an alien, okay?"

He didn't exactly wait for her to agree, just snatched the controller from her and like magic, zipped through the cheekbones, the chin size, forehead size. Rachel's head spun at all the 'options.'

Did anyone really ever pick the ugly features? How much time—and money—had been spent into something that could have been sooo much simpler?

Mark finished with the facial structure and moved onto the next step. Hair.

"I get to pick the hair," Rachel said.

"Right."

He toggled through the options and Rachel tried not to grimace. Who'd thought of *that* hairstyle? Ugh. After another five minutes, which then meant another five minutes for her to actually pick the hair color, Mark's shoulders were settling in what she considered his 'tense' posture.

This was probably a good lesson for him in what women wanted—meaning, too many choices was usually a bad thing. Because Rachel couldn't possibly play a character who wasn't perfect; a character she'd spend the next couple of hours/days looking at.

Perfect was important.

"There," he said. "You want to pick the make-up too?"

"Oh?" She straightened from her seat. "There's make-up?"

"Make-up, too." Which resulted in another ten minutes. He tossed her the control. "Now. You can actually *play* the game. Weren't you the one who said something about real games for real women?"

"That," she pointed the control at him, "is half my point. Do you think my books would sell if there was an ugly person on the cover? Man or woman, they need to look like someone you can fall in love with."

He scooped up his book and sank into the couch—right up against her. Their thighs brushed and she squirmed out of the way. Mark focused on her as if he knew exactly what he was doing.

The jerk probably did, too.

Still, he didn't move away and to make matters worse, the comfortable couch seemed to take his extra weight as an invitation to get even more comfortable, and she simply slid back down towards him.

Note to self: make sure Mark sits, and remains sitting, on the other side of the couch.

She didn't move away because that would only further draw his attention to their proximity and her being uncomfortable, which simply wouldn't do.

"Okay, Princess, what does that person look like?" he asked. "I mean, everyone's got their own ideas of who they can fall in love with. So shoot. What does that person look like?"

"Not you." She had no idea, none at all, where those words came from and how they possibly left her mouth. Her mouth. "I mean..."

His eyebrows lifted. "Go on."

"I mean, never mind. Look." She flipped over the book in his hand. "Most books won't have an actual full-bodied person. Some do, some just have the good parts."

"Female legs?" He asked, since that was about the only thing on the cover, along with a giant, foofy wedding dress.

"That is a perfect example. You like my legs. You haven't stopped staring at them since we met."

Mark laughed and swung an arm on the couch, which also happened to fall right in the area of where she was sitting. Rachel sat a little bit straighter.

"Okay, you got me there. But you've got a great pair of legs." To make his point, his gaze slowly traveled down to her feet and then back up again. "Very great legs."

Except this was the part where he should throw in a snarky comment.

He didn't.

He didn't take his eyes off her.

Rachel's breath slowed and she felt his fingers brush against her neck. She shivered at his touch. It didn't matter if she didn't want to, didn't want to give this man any sign he was getting to her, that she was having a reaction to *him*.

This was probably too close. But wouldn't it be nice just to get a little bit closer? Not much closer, just a little.

Rachel leaned closer to him, both of their eyes still locked. Her shoulder brushed against his hard, muscular chest. Another shiver swept through her.

What in the heavens did this man look like without his shirt on?

Allie, a true blessing in disguise, nudged their legs, ready for her please-pet-me attention. Rachel jerked her attention back to the dog as she tried to collect her thoughts.

What was she doing? Heck, what was she thinking? And why wasn't she breathing properly?

Mark didn't remove his hand from where it rested against her neck. And if anything, that smug smile was back. The jerk *knew* what he was doing to her.

Time to move away from how they were each attracted to the other and onto safer ground. Like how she didn't like this man and how she was so mad at him she went and got a dog.

"You should, uh, read this." Rachel held out the book. "And I've got a game to play. Research and all."

Because the sooner she got to playing this game, the sooner she could be done and out of his house. If only life were that easy, and if only the game's storyline wasn't so generic, wasn't so completely predictable.

She'd lost track of how many times she'd cursed out loud, and how many times Mark managed to look up at the right time, which was usually when her character died a horrible death by being gun-downed by walking, space-alien corpse things.

"You're really bad at this."

"Shut up. I write. I don't play games for a living."

"Could have fooled me. I mean, I can't believe women actually read this."

He held out a page to her.

She squinted and recognized it as one of the earlier scenes when the heroine, Kate, realized she was attracted the hero. "What's wrong with it?"

"The heat spread outward from his hand...?" Mark read. "Really? I mean, you're kidding right?"

He looped his hand behind her again, those fingers brushing her neck, her arm. And with that touch was the spark, the heat that *did* spread from his touch. A heat she could feel all the way to her toes.

Oh, yes, Rachel thought. *Really.*

"How about now?" He leaned in, his thumb slowly running down her neck as if a causal movement, but there was absolutely nothing causal about this.

He was playing with her.

Rachel shoved his arm away. "Yes, really. But not your touch, I'm sorry to say. You must not be my type."

"Really?" He sounded curious. He also sounded like he didn't believe her at all.

Rachel scanned the room for the dog, hoping for another rescue, but Allie had crashed on the rug and hadn't moved since. Great. Looked like she was in this all by herself.

But she was used to that, used to standing up for herself. Used to being alone.

It was all the reminder she needed.

"You know, Mark. I think we're done for the night." She tossed the controller in his lap. "You think this is funny, you think this is all a game. Well, fine, but don't waste my time. I have work I could be doing."

He watched as she stood, not protesting or apologizing. Of course not. That would be too much to ask for.

"Work like this kind of work?" He waved her back at her. "This heat spreading and falling in love stuff."

"That's right." She snatched the book from him. "The stuff that's going to pay for your project."

She could tell he didn't like being reminded of that, didn't like that his game would be funded by romance. Good. His ego needed a hit, a giant one.

He still didn't move as she collected her things, including Allie's leash and dog bowl. Allie lifted one sleepy eye to stare at her but didn't seem like she wanted to move any time soon.

"Why do your books sell?" he asked, right about when she was going to give up on him and assume he'd also fallen asleep.

She blinked. Where did that come from?

"What do you mean?"

"Your books. People obviously read them, enjoy them since they keep coming back for more. So, why? What do you do that other romance writers don't?"

She thought about that for a second as she slid her purse on her shoulder. "I guess I'm good at connecting with the characters. Romance is all about emotion. Emotions drive everything, especially the conflict. But there's also got to be a reason—a good reason—why the guy and girl can't get together on page one."

"Emotions, huh?" He stood, his rumpled shirt revealing just a hint of his hard stomach before Rachel jerked her attention back to his face. "So if you're so good at writing emotions..."

He stepped closer to her. One moment he was by the couch and the next he was beside her, hand sliding up her purse strap just as it started to fall back down.

And was there heat with his touch?

Oh, yes. There was heat.

"If you're good with writing emotions, why aren't you so good with the real ones?"

"Real ones?" She was finding it hard to think all of a sudden.

"Yours. The real ones. The ones that matter."

She swallowed. "Who said I'm not good with my emotions?"

"Me."

Then, within a blink, his lips brushed against hers, soft and yet confident. Completely in control.

The kiss was a feather touch, lighter than anything she felt before and yet she felt it. Felt every inch of him as if he was pressed against her again, as if he'd kissed her with the same fire as the rainy day.

"Because," his breath tickled her lips, "if you were good at connecting with your emotions we'd have been doing this all night instead of working."

Oh, yes, she was definitely having a harder time breathing.

"Who said I want to kiss you?"

A slight pull of his lips. His fingers brushed her cheek and she lifted her head, just enough to open her mouth to him. Both his hands and his lips vanished.

He stepped back.

"I think that's pretty obvious, Ms. Clare. And, I think it's pretty obvious I *do* know what women want."

His words hit her hard and fast. She sucked in a deep breath. And with that breath she realized exactly what he was doing. Playing with her. Proving his point.

Rachel's hand tightened on her purse strap. Did she know her emotions? Yes, she knew them. Just like now she fought a battle between beating him over the head with her very heavy, very full purse and crying.

The beating was preferable.

"Well, then Mr. Ashe." She was pleased to see how steady, and emotionless her voice was. "If you think you know women so well I guess that means you don't need my help anymore. I'll expect a full presentation of your 'vision' at next week's meeting."

His eyes widened, a look of horror she'd replay in her mind whenever she needed a little smile.

Or a big smile.

Fine. If he wanted to be Mr. Know-It-All then she'd let him do his own swimming in the romance world. She'd let him do this solo and she'd enjoy it as she watched him drown.

Yes, she was quite well connected with her emotions.

$\mathcal{M}$ark waved to Nick as his former designer pal opened the door to the Rock Bottom Restaurant. Nick waved back and headed to the bar where Mark had a beer waiting for him.

Nick took one look at Mark, one look at the beer, then sat down. "Okay. Beer at 2:00 in the afternoon. What's the emergency?"

Always straight to the point, that was Nick for you. Mark took another chug of his beer—his second beer, actually, because he really did have an emergency.

A romance emergency. Or more specifically, a Rachel Clare emergency.

"I'm honestly considering killing your sister. I hoped you wouldn't mind."

Nick smirked. "Gotten to you already has she? She can be a bit hard-headed."

Hard-headed? That didn't even begin to cover what Rachel was. More like arrogant, stubborn, a pain in his ass, and attractive as all hell. Damn it.

Nick shrugged out of his coat and settled into the bar-stool. "This is starting to be a regular occurrence with you two calling me out of work. Good thing I'm one of the guys in charge."

"She called you out, too, huh?" Mark hoped it was recently, hoped he wasn't the only one being driven mad by their 'association.'

"Who do you think went with her to pick up the dog?"

Okay. That wasn't too recent.

Nick ordered himself a sandwich, and then one for Mark after Mark said he wasn't hungry. "I'm guessing we're gonna be here for awhile. So tell me, what'd she do this time? Because last time I checked, *she* was mad at *you*."

"You're checking up on me?"

"Hell no! She just tells me. *Everything.* Comes with the territory of being a big brother to a girl who, other than her new dog, is alone. So I hear the bitching and the crying, which I try to get out of as much as possible. Not that it works."

Mark lowered his glass. In one moment, Nick had told him more about Rachel's life than the two weeks he'd known her, including the Google searches he'd done on her.

He knew she'd been married, but there was only the briefest mention of it since she divorced several years before she made it big as a romance writer. But alone? Crying to Nick?

"She cries? I mean, I thought she was like a stone Greek goddess or something. Hmph. I was thinking of code naming this project after one of them, like Hera. All I've seen is that fiery temper of hers."

And her fiery passion, but best not to mention that to her brother.

Nick glared at him. "That's because you have a gift at pissing her off, just like me. And I'm getting tired of hearing it, so knock it off."

Mark lifted his hands. "I will if she will. And I haven't seen her recently anyway."

Which was part of the problem. And his emergency.

In as few details as possible, Mark told Nick his dilemma. He needed a presentation on the game's concept, an idea for the core game play, as well the scope of the project for the other two owners and Rachel. By tomorrow.

The problem? He wasn't getting the romance thing.

"I've read her books, more of them than I ever want to admit, so don't ask," Mark said. "And I'm not seeing it. I'm not seeing the draw or why she sells so freakin' well."

Nick snorted and fingered the fries that came with the sandwiches. Mark scooped up a few for himself. French fries and beer. The only way two men could discuss romance novels.

Mark also didn't add he'd focused most of his time on project Hades, the one for Forged Legends. A presentation which was due tomorrow as well. And while that one was done and ready to go, Rachel's well... to put it lightly, hadn't gone far at all.

"I think she's right, you know," Nick finally said. "You don't understand romance. Not that I'm saying you don't understand *romance*, but romance readers? I've been to a few of her signings and man, it's an eye-opening experience."

Intrigued, Mark snagged another handful of fries and gestured for Nick to continue.

"They're normal women. The kind you see in grocery stores, I guess. Women who've got happy lives, have kids, but man, there's something they just love about falling in love."

Normal women, Mark thought. "Women who are happy in their marriages?"

Nick shrugged. "I'm sure you've got tons of unhappy ones in there too. Maybe what you should do is talk to your audience. Ask them yourself—because all this right here," he gestured to him and Mark, "is just speculation."

Maybe that was what Mark needed. Not that he needed to look into it very much. He hoped that after the Forged Legends presentation tomorrow he never had to look at a romance novel again.

Still... he didn't like going into anything unprepared, and he had promised Rachel he'd try.

And keep an open mind.

It looked like he finally needed to keep his word instead of just trying to get under her feathers—something that was increasingly hard to do when she ignored his phone calls and refused to talk to him when she did stop by the office.

Mark sipped his beer. "How is your sister, anyway?"

"Busy, as usual. She always says she never worked harder until the day she decided to be a writer. So, yeah, busy. And still mad at you."

That was fine with Mark since he was mad at her too; mad that she'd stormed out of his condo and left him to juggle this romance thing by himself. He'd had actual *questions* for her and she'd ignored his calls, his emails.

Okay, he had deserved it for pushing her the way he had, but he couldn't help it. He wanted to see her eyes narrow, to get her temper all up and snapping at him.

He'd like to see her so he could do it again. Maybe even kiss her again.

Of course, as soon as he turned her project down the kissing thing would be out the window since he was fairly sure she'd be trying to kill him. As he rightly deserved.

Nick probably would want to also. Better keep himself in line if he wanted out of this alive.

Mark pulled some cash from his wallet and slapped it on the bar. "Thanks for coming down here. I appreciate it."

"Where are you going?"

Mark slipped on his leather jacket and headed to the doors. "I've got to do some romance research."

Research that included the local Barnes and Noble right across from the restaurant, but since this happened to be a weekday, as well as in the middle of the afternoon, to say the store was 'dead' would be putting things nicely.

Mark kept his hands in jacket, hoping to appear as causal as possible as he peeked down the romance aisle. Completely empty of women. Great.

This research wouldn't go well if he didn't meet some women.

After few minutes of continued emptiness, Mark squared his shoulders, decided to be a man and entered the romance section.

It was an experience.

One he hoped to never, ever repeat again.

Apparently, you could write romance in just about any time, space, closet, whatever—there was a book about two people falling in love.

Cowboys (always pictured with the cowboy, never the girl, complete with muscular chest and cowboy hat), women in tight, black, leather outfits, some with a sweet looking sword (he read the back blurbs on these), as well as the fluffy wedding dresses, hot pink heels (amazingly like the ones Rachel liked to wear).

So, first research assessment?

Women had quite the varied taste. And the one thing in common? Two people falling in love.

Mark remembered one of the golden rules Rachel told him: there was always a happy-ending.

He wasn't so sure how a hot, kick-ass looking chick would end up with her happily-ever-after, but he was willing to bet she did. Even if that meant killing somebody.

He kept ignoring the 'C' section, but curiosity finally got the better of him. He knelt, following the author names until he came across 'Clare' and nearly fell on his butt.

Rachel didn't just have a space. She had three God-damn shelves devoted to her books.

"I guess that's why she sells so many," he muttered to himself.

"Who sells so many?" A woman asked behind him, and Mark found himself looking up at a very nice, very long pair of legs.

He immediately checked the shoes. Not Rachel.

Then he scrambled to his feet. "The author. Rachel Clare."

The woman smiled at him, which only made her look even more stunning. "Do you read romance?"

He hesitated and she laughed. A laugh just as stunning as her smile.

"No, I don't," he said. "Not normally, anyway. It's for research."

"Research? Like checking up on what your wife's been reading?"

He held up his hand and smiled back, unable to help himself. "Not married."

"Oh, well. Good."

Right. *Good* because he wasn't attached to someone, wasn't sleeping with anyone, and two brief kisses with Rachel didn't count as anything.

Other than kisses.

When he didn't say anything, she glanced over his shoulder. "What are you researching romance for, anyway?"

Saying 'confidential' was on the tip of his tongue. That was what game developers said most of the time to prevent leaks to the press. Except he had come here for research and how could he research anything without talking to attractive women about why they read romances?

And why they would play a romance game?

"You know, you just might be able to help me out. Can I buy you a cup of coffee?"

She didn't need to answer.

Her smile said everything he needed to hear.

CHAPTER 20

Mark watched as Stacy leaned over the small coffee table in the bookstore's Starbucks café, shirt lowered enough to show him two very nice curves. And Stacy's smile curved up when she saw where his gaze had strayed.

Right. He was working.

Convenient of Starbucks and Barnes and Noble to provide the perfect place for him to work—and to admire his research.

"A romance game? That's a fabulous idea." Stacy crossed her legs, hiking up her skirt another couple of inches. "How will it work?"

"I'm not sure about that yet. That's why I wanted to talk to you. I mean, you obviously read romance and therefore, obviously, are my target audience."

"Obviously." There was that sultry smile again.

Mark really needed to thank Rachel the next time he saw her; doing his own research was a fantastic idea. He'd show her; he knew damn well what women wanted.

"Ask away," Stacy said, "and we'll see how much research I can provide."

Now, in normal cases he'd ask for her number.... okay, not normal cases.

And while still holding quite a few moves (thanks to his constantly working out), Mark was a workaholic. He didn't ask women for numbers and, in fact, it wouldn't have even crossed his mind if he hadn't met Rachel.

Rachel. The woman who by simply thinking about her, got his blood pumping. Pumping for a fight.

Behind him, even over the chopping of coffee beans in the background, Mark heard the unmistakable *click, click* of heels.

And one glance at the floor right behind him was another gorgeous pair of mile-long legs and pink heels he instantly recognized.

Mark gazed up at Rachel Clare, who had a Barnes and Noble employee at her side, clipboard clutched to his chest. Rachel looked like a storm about to burst.

The employee looked from Mark back to Rachel. "Ah, Ms. Clare. Is there something wrong?"

Wrong? Mark doubted the only thing *wrong* was her seeing him.

That was the point where Stacy jumped to her feet and exclaimed, "Oh, my God! You're Rachel Clare."

Ahhh, Mark leaned back, the pieces clicking into place. That smoldering gaze wasn't because she'd seen him (that would just rate for a frustrated gaze). But smoldering?

That was because she'd seen Mark with another woman.

Interesting.

In the meantime, Stacy was thrusting her hand at Rachel and asking her to sign a book.

Rachel slid from smoldering gaze to charming smile in about a half second flat. "Yes, I'm Rachel. Pleased to meet you." And then she continued with the pleasantries.

Stacy, however, was clearly not an idiot and recognized that Mark and Rachel knew each other. She immediately filled Rachel in on the, 'oh this isn't how it looks' line about seeing her with Mark. She told Rachel Mark was doing research for his project.

Rachel's eyes narrowed at him. "Research, huh? Imagine that. I hope you have the presentation ready for tomorrow?"

Time to stop taking a beating by that woman's glare. "That's right. Thanks to Stacy here, I think I've got a much better understanding of what romance readers are looking for."

Another narrowing of eyes.

"What are you doing here?" He asked before Stacy or the employee could steer Rachel away. "I thought you were busy."

Employee with the clipboard and glasses answered for her. "Ms. Clare's doing a book signing here in a few days."

He didn't get much further, not with Stacy squealing in delight. She also hadn't released Rachel's hand, and though Rachel kept up that charming smile, he could tell she was losing it.

Mark easily slid between Stacy and captured Rachel's hand for his own. Oh, if looks could kill. Definitely not what she had in mind, but she couldn't exactly chose her heroes now could she?

"Thanks so much for your help, Stacy, but I need to ask Rachel a couple more questions about our project. That is if she's done here?" He asked the employee.

"Oh, well I suppose, but—"

"Excellent." And with that, Mark steered Rachel away from her fan and the nervous, but shadow-like employee. Two steps and he shook his head. "I have no idea how you stand that."

"It's much easier than standing you." Rachel yanked her hand free.

He was surprised at how his chest tightened. He'd thought she'd liked him a little. At least, until she realized he had no intention of making her game.

He'd have to explain it to her, explain why he couldn't do it, couldn't put his company on the line like that. After she'd cooled her temper and no longer wanted to kill him.

Could be awhile though.

"I've called you," he pointed out. "You know it's rude not to return messages."

"Yes. I know."

Guess Nick was right about her being mad. Best to make a speedy exit and finish up on this presentation. "Well, then, I guess I'll let you get back to your busy writing life—"

Rachel rounded on him. Hands on her hips, showing off pink nail polish that matched her shoes. And her purse. The woman really knew how to match.

"Are you really going to be ready for tomorrow?"

"I said I would be."

"That's not the same thing as being ready."

She couldn't actually be worried. Could she? "You seem a little uptight. Something on your mind?"

"No. Absolutely not." Her gaze strayed to Stacy, before she caught herself and glared at Mark. "Everything's fine, just that your presentation is important."

"So important you left me high and dry to figure out a woman's world?"

Oh, there was that glare he'd missed seeing this past week. Made him smile just seeing it.

"If you remember correctly, you were the one arrogant enough to assume you knew—" she clamped her mouth shut. "You know what? Never mind. I have a deadline. I have to focus on people falling in love, something that is absolutely impossible to do while you're around."

"Really? I think I'd be rather helpful with that." If those kisses had been any indication, he was sure he had been.

"Oh, trust me. You're not. Just be ready for tomorrow. It's important."

"Hey," he touched her arm before she stomped away. His touch seemed to freeze them both. It took a moment before he realized he hadn't followed up with any words after the 'hey.'

"Umm, when is your book signing?"

Rachel took in a slow, deep breath, as if hesitating, and then smiled at him—the I-hate-you smile. "None of your damn business, Mark. I'll see you tomorrow. Please take me, and my game, seriously for once. Okay?"

She didn't give him a chance to respond, just clicked on out of the store in her killer high heels, drawing the attention of the few people there. Though, she didn't reach the safety of the doors without Stacy stopping her for those book signings.

Women, Mark thought as he shook his head.

The Barnes and Noble employee passed him, and Mark half-turned, then stopped. Rachel was signing here, huh?

Even from this distance he could see her straight back, tense shoulders. Maybe he did get under her skin, maybe even in a good way.

And maybe he should stop by her signing, support what she was doing and all that. He might not be a woman and he might not get romance, but he did understand her slight hesitation when he'd asked about the signing.

Enough of hesitation that he knew, she actually wanted him there.

Which was strange in and of itself.

Mark scratched the back of his head. "Maybe I don't get women after all."

CHAPTER 21

achel stifled a yawn as she waited for Mark to set up his presentation. Both Scott and Ethan were there and they'd both already offered her the company's sludge coffee.

She'd smiled and said no thanks, silently cursing herself for not bringing any outside coffee with her. She'd been up until nearly 3:00 in the morning, finishing her latest book. Meanwhile, she'd found a nice email from another editor when she'd booted up her computer that morning.

Rachel had just been pleased to find her characters' voices again, and the steamy attraction that went with it. After seeing Mark and the beautiful blonde at Barnes and Noble, it was very tempting to let the black moment—the point of no return in her novel—actually stay black.

Happy ending?

Why should her characters get all the luck when *she* only had an arrogant game designer who apparently flirted with any long-legged woman he came across.

Ethan lifted his eyes at her, and she realized she'd been frowning. Again. She smiled and hoped he saw that yes, she was actually fine and happy to be here.

She wasn't, though, but only because of Mark. Only because she didn't trust him to take her game seriously.

Although, he had read all those books... Rachel tucked a strand of hair behind her ear. She'd withhold judgment, right up until the very end. All she could do was hope Mark hadn't wasted her time, hadn't been leading her on.

She'd believe it when she saw it.

And as much as she disliked Mark, disliked that smile he gave her, the one that caused her toes to curl, he proved it to her.

During his presentation, somehow, he proved he believed in her game. That he believed in her.

Rachel sank further into her chair, her mouth lowering another few inches as she listened.

Word for word, it was nearly the exact same vision she'd had. Not that she knew much about game design, but this...? This was exactly what the game needed.

A game for women. A game that gave women the control to decide how a conversation would play out. The flirting, the falling in love. The player would control those choices.

She'd played more of the space game—and yes, she'd coughed up the money for a small TV and game system. And she'd been infuriated when she realized the wrong choices, or the wrong actual game play choices, would instantly make that romance disappear.

Poor Nick had gotten quite an earful over *that*.

Mark seemed to be one step ahead of her in that area. He thought it was important to allow the game to keep going, to let characters correct their mistakes without actually starting the whole game over.

Rachel found herself nodding, then taking notes as ideas popped into her head. By the time Mark was done, when all three of the owners' attentions turned to her, Rachel couldn't help the smile on her face.

Couldn't help the way her heart beat even faster as she met Mark's gaze. Held his gaze.

He'd done the one thing Daniel had never done. He'd given her work, her career, respect. And he'd come up with the perfect game concept.

"It looks like you were right. I can't make this game without you."

Mark hesitated for a second, as if surprised, and then he was all cool and collected Mark. Until he opened his mouth. "I told you needed me."

Scott and Ethan managed to step in before she ruined the moment by telling Mark to take his arrogant attitude and shove it up a very un-gentleman like place.

There were details to work out, a contract to negotiate, one her attorney and theirs had already started on. There was also a spring in Rachel's step, one that hadn't been there in days.

Her game was actually going to work. And not only that, they would succeed. *She* would succeed.

She'd show this whole industry that women were a powerful force; one to be reckoned with.

The meeting lasted another hour or so, with Mark having to excuse himself earlier, which was fine. Rachel had already texted Nick and he agreed they needed to celebrate after work.

She didn't bother going home and changing. She already looked snappy enough for Daniel's Broiler. She hardly even noticed the Fast-Play employees looking up as she passed, the rumor-mill swirling in full force behind her as everyone speculated on who she was—and if they had another project.

Rachel smiled. She smiled all the way up to Nick's office, picked him up, and then parked in valet. It was fitting, she thought, to come here. This was the place where it had started—and nearly ended—but now it was the place to celebrate.

She turned towards the valet walking over and her smile grew when she recognized a familiar, straight and tall posture heading toward the glass doors. Mark? Mark was here?

She couldn't help the way her stomach fluttered, the way her heart beat at seeing him again.

"Something up, Rache?"

She jerked her attention away from Mark, even as he opened the doors for three men. But Nick had seen where she'd been looking and squinted, his eyes narrowing.

"Is that...?"

"Oh, um, yes. Looks like that's Mark."

Nick glanced from her to Mark's disappearing back. Nick's mouth tightened. "You know, Rache, I think we should try another restaurant. This one's a bit too stuffy for celebrating. I mean, we need to celebrate since you won my bet and all."

"Stuffy? Nick, what are you talking about? You love eating here."

The valet came over, holding out a ticket, but Nick pulled her back towards the car. "Mark's in there. We should go some place else."

Rachel knew her brother and his evasive habits, ones he continually used on her. She put her hands on her hips and ignored the cars piling up behind them, waiting to be parked.

"Nick. Why should I care if Mark's in there? I just saw him. And heck, he just gave one hell of presentation on my game."

The thought brought the smile back. Which only made Nick's frown deepen.

"He also has a habit of pissing you off, and tonight's a night where we should celebrate. Come on."

This time, he succeeded in getting her to the car, then apologized to the valet assistant, handing him some cash for making him wait.

And yes, while the Crab Pot was a bit more 'let loose and celebrate,' and while Rachel did have a good time, Nick didn't. Oh, he pretended he did, but she knew her brother.

She also knew the signs of when someone was lying. But she bit her tongue, decided to simply celebrate and enjoy herself (that was why they were here after all), and didn't complain when Nick asked to end the night early.

Whatever was wrong, whatever was bothering him, had to do with Mark. Had he noticed her smile when she saw him?

Surely she hadn't smiled like, well like she *liked* Mark. Had she?

And that was silly. Because she didn't. Like him that was. She was only excited that he'd given her a fair shake, that he respected her.

Regardless of whatever was on Nick's mind, that thought alone brought the smile back.

Mark respected her, respected her romance writing.

She couldn't wait to get started on the game project. Project Cupid.

This romance game idea was turning out better than she'd ever expected.

CHAPTER 22

Mark asked Mr. Taylor and the two other executives from Forged Legends to hold on, he'd be right back with drinks. Celebration drinks.

He'd done it.

They loved his idea, were interested in the changes he'd made, and wanted to move forward. Somehow, Mark Ashe, CEO and Creative Director of FastPlay, had done it again. Even with the time crunch, even with Scott threatening to unseat him, Mark had done it.

He was going to make the kind of games his company made, the games their reputation was founded on.

He ordered his drinks at the bar, not even trying to hide his smile. Or his excitement.

There were some issues Forged Legends hadn't budged on, like the multi-platform one, but he figured Ethan would come around. So long as they could minimize Forged Legends' 'requests' on how many platforms to port his game to.

It was doable, very doable. Even Scott would have to back down; he'd wanted Mark to provide the company with a game and that was exactly what he'd done.

Twice.

He'd given them two games and now, as his right, he got to choose. After all, they simply didn't have the staff to handle more than one. As if was, their team would be hard-pressed to make the game's deadline.

And this game, this online strategic space shooter, was a much better fit for his company than a romance game.

As he stepped up to the bar and ordered the four drinks. Mark's smile slipped

Rachel.

He'd talk with her, too, explain why it wouldn't work out. She was a romance star, she understood the importance of branding and reputation.

After some yelling.

Okay, after a lot of yelling, she'd understand.

He couldn't help but remember her smile from earlier, her excitement after he'd finished presenting his idea. That smile had hit him, hard. Harder than he'd expected and he couldn't help but feel... happy? Glad?

No. He was just happy he'd nailed it on one try, that he, the man who knew nothing about romance, managed to capture her vision.

Except, he was squashing her vision. Wasn't he?

There were quite a few people in the bar, some enjoying drinks, others enjoying another's company. The music beat at a dull hum and Mark noticed the Mariner's were up in a game. All in all, it looked like a good evening for just about everyone here, so why did his good mood suddenly tank?

It couldn't be because of Rachel's game. He'd done his part, presented a good concept, and he just happened to land an even better deal. Well, a better game idea. Rachel's deal would be better in one way; it would give his company more independence than any publisher ever would.

"I see you've ordered a few drinks there. Looks like you're celebrating." Nick slid up beside Mark, like he came out of thin air.

"Oh, hey. Nick." Mark did not look behind him, at the small group of executives waiting for him.

What the hell was Nick doing here?

The bartender turned, a question in his eyes.

"Go ahead and get this man whatever he likes," Mark nodded back. "We're celebrating tonight."

"Yeah. I suppose you are, aren't you? Nothing for me, thanks."

Mark knew that tone. Nick didn't get mad often, it was one reason he could work so well as a lead designer, dealing with programmers, his design team, the art guys, and the rest of the developer mess.

But Mark had worked with Nick for too many years before he started FastPlay, and he knew better. Mark knew enough of Nick to know he was in trouble.

And that Nick had recognized the Forged Legends guys.

"So what are we celebrating?" Nick asked.

Not one to beat around the bush, that was Nick.

"A game deal." There, that was nice and non-committal.

"Right. You know, Rachel and I just finished celebrating too. She's pretty psyched about all this. Looks like you really came out of left field with your presentation. She couldn't stop talking about you all night."

Mark accepted his beer from the bartender and sipped, giving himself time, giving himself a distraction. She'd talked about him?

"Is that right?" Mark said. "I'll bet that's the first time she hasn't bitched about me."

"Yeah, for the most part." Nick leaned closer, made the very obvious gesture of looking at the three executives. "Thing is, we'd planned on coming here first, except she saw you. And I saw *them*."

Mark lowered his beer. "Nick. This isn't what you think."

Nick just looked at him.

"Okay, it *is* what you think, but you of all people should understand."

"Is that right? Understand that you've led my sister on, just got her hopes up for this game she's putting in a ton of time and money on? And you've what? Made another deal behind her back?"

That was exactly what he'd done. And Nick's anger was exactly what Mark deserved.

"What was I supposed to do?" Mark shot. "I needed time. I've got

Scott breathing down my neck, ready to shove the company out from under me. You think I want to spend the next three years working on a romance game? Do you know what that'd do to my company? To our reputation?"

Either it was his own shame, or just the alcohol, but Mark found himself telling Nick exactly what he felt. Not about Rachel, but the project. Nick had to understand.

"Your reputation," Nick spit, "isn't worth what I thought it was. And yeah, making a romance game ain't exactly my dream either, but it's her dream. And if you had no intention of following through you shouldn't have asked in the first place."

They were getting a few looks now, the bartender hurrying to finish those drinks. But Mark didn't care. Let them stare. He hadn't done anything wrong; they hadn't signed a contract with Rachel yet.

It was his right to find a better deal.

"You're the one who pushed her into this in the first place," Mark snapped. "You're the one who told her it couldn't be done and now you're getting mad at me for finding a better offer?"

Nick got to his feet. "It's not a better offer and you sure as hell know it."

Mark stood as well, forgetting the drinks. "Where the hell are you going?"

"To tell my sister the truth, since you're too much of an ass to do that much."

Mark found himself frozen, rooted to the floor as Nick stormed off. Behind him the bartender coughed, trying to draw his attention, but Mark couldn't move.

And he didn't know why.

He hadn't done anything wrong, not contractually anyway. But he had lied to Rachel. He'd gotten her hopes up even though he had no intention of following through.

"Damn it," he swore to himself, running a hand through his hair. His life had been a whole lot less complicated before she'd stepped out of that red sports car of hers.

He grabbed his drinks, plastered a smile on his face, and went to seal the deal—as much as he could without his partners' approval—with the Forged Legends executives.

But smile all he wanted, he still couldn't stop thinking about Nick and his on-the-nose accusation. Even more than that, he couldn't stop thinking about Rachel and her smile.

A smile he'd just completely, and totally, taken away from her.

When the evening's event came to an end, and Mark shook Mr. Taylor's hand, promising to talk with Scott and Ethan in the morning. He couldn't help but wonder, had he done the right thing?

Of course, he had.

This game was the best one for his company.

And yet, he thought about the challenge, thought about his excitement from last night when the final pieces of Rachel's game clicked into place. When he'd figured out how to give her readers—her players—an interactive, romance story experience.

Excitement he'd felt right up to the moment when he remembered he was going to turn her down. Which he still had to do, if Nick hadn't done it for him.

Mark was betting he had. After all, that was what protective brothers were for, keeping their sisters safe from assholes like Mark.

CHAPTER 23

$\mathcal{M}$ark didn't get far when he came into work the next day. Ethan stood outside his office, arms crossed, hair that hadn't been brushed. He'd taken one look at Mark, glared, and said they had an owners meeting.

Right now.

Oh, yes. Nick hadn't waited to tell Rachel, and knowing Rachel, she'd called Ethan. Or Scott. Or both.

Depends on how pissed off she was.

Mark threw his coat down, grabbed the coffee he'd picked up on the way in, and found both Ethan and Scott waiting in the conference room, wearing matching scowls.

Well, she'd called them both. So she was well and truly pissed.

Scott barely gave Mark enough time to close the door so their nosy employees didn't overhear the shouting before he said, "What the hell were you thinking?"

Mark closed the door the whole way. "Which part? The part about finding us a game? Giving us options?"

"We had a game." Scott snapped down a folder with all his financial notes and charts onto the table. "A game that could have made us millions and what did you go and do?"

"I found us a better game." Mark didn't bother taking a seat. This wouldn't take long.

Scott sputtered, spraying spit onto the table. He didn't stop spraying until Ethan patted his shoulder.

"We're not happy about this, Mark," Ethan said. "You brought us a deal and we planned on moving forward with it."

"No, you two planned on moving forward." Mark pointed at both of them. "You knew I wasn't happy about this, regardless of what the numbers say. I made no secret I was pursuing other avenues and I did. I also happened to like what I heard from Forged Legends better."

Scott got all red in the face, but Ethan beat him to the punch. "That's crap and you know it."

Mark blinked, surprised. Ethan, quiet, programmer Ethan, hardly ever spoke this much about the company's business. He preferred to let Mark and Scott handle the details and just gave high-level support.

Ethan stood and his chair scraped against the floor. "The only part about Forged Legends you like better is the game. Well, too bad. They faxed over the contract this morning. We looked at it and neither Scott nor I are signing it."

"What? Do you have any idea how long I've worked on that?" He'd spent months trying to land a publishing deal and now they wanted to throw it out? "You can't be serious."

Scott pushed his glasses up. "We're dead serious. We're not agreeing to this deal, not when *you* provided us a better alternative."

"That is," Ethan added, "if you can convince Rachel you're not a complete asshole and she still wants to do her project. I told you, I told you she'd be pissed. She had no idea."

Scott nodded. "That's right. It wasn't fair to her, not to mention you went behind our backs about this."

Mark had heard enough. "Don't you guys care at all? Don't you care what her game will do to this company? Do you have any idea how many employees will hand in their resignations when they find out their next game, their three-year project, is going to be *a romance game?*"

Mark already had a good idea. Already knew at least half the team, if not all, would decide against listing a romance game on their resume. No developer in their right mind wanted that.

Ethan sighed. "I'm sorry you feel that way, Mark. I really am. After your presentation I was hoping you'd see the kind of opportunity this was. You said you wanted to make games on the cutting edge, games no one else in their right mind would make. Here's your chance—and what are you doing? Throwing it in her face."

Mark wasn't, at least not intentionally, but Ethan and Scott were done listening. The vote still stood: two against one.

The second they left, leaving him alone in the conference room, Mark slumped into the chair and resigned himself to his fate. There was nothing else he could do.

He was stuck making a romance game, and working with a romance writer—a writer who was pretty darned pissed at him. He had no idea if the company would survive. He had no idea if his partnership with Ethan and Scott would survive.

Everything would go under. And worst of all, now he had to convince Rachel to sign the contract, a contract she probably wanted nothing to do with.

That was his guess after his sixteen unreturned phone calls.

"Shit." Mark hung up the phone again, barely not slamming it back into the receiver. He had to convince Rachel. He'd already said no to Forged Legends, so now FastPlay really needed her game.

Except she was pissed.

"And she has a right to be," Mark grumbled.

There was no other choice. If she wouldn't return his calls he'd just have to go see her in person. Even if that meant going to a romance book signing.

MARK'S one foray into the romance section at Barnes and Noble didn't come close to the mayhem he was facing. The store was packed wall-to-wall with women, many of them clutching at least a half-dozen novels to their chest, all waiting in line to meet Rachel Clare.

He'd hoped to slip up to the front, but the little old lady with her pink-floral shawl gave him the nastiest glare and he immediately stepped back into line. Shit. These women were crazy.

And numerous. He was in an ant line of women—women of all ages from teenage girls with glasses and braces, to the sexy types (he turned his head when he spotted Stacy), and then there were the normal women. The older women like mean grandma in front of him.

Rachel's audience, it was...well, it was huge. He didn't even think Ethan or Scott realized just how big and diverse it was.

Mark also happened to be the only male in line. A very disconcerting thought, especially when the women started giving him that look and giggling.

Shit.

Nick would be pleased as pie if he saw Mark now. And would probably say it was exactly like what Mark deserved.

He'd be right, too.

He hoped Rachel thought the same because he still had to convince her that yes, he was an ass, but he was an ass who needed to make her game. He'd say 'want' but figured she'd see through that lie in a heartbeat.

Best to play it honest. For once.

That was his plan until he shuffled up after grandma, finally reaching Rachel's signing table and the mountain of books surrounding her. She looked up, saw him, and her smile faltered.

Even with the make-up, he could see the bags under her eyes, and yes, those were a pair of stormy, pissed off eyes that narrowed at him. But he also saw the instant of hurt.

Hurt he'd caused.

His chest tightened. He almost wished Nick was standing there and not the Barnes and Noble employee with his clipboard. Nick would have punched him and that would be so much better than the hurt she tried to mask.

And he had no way to make it up to her, no way at all. And now he was coming to her and asking her for a favor.

"Mark," she said, voice sizzling with barely controlled fury.

Grandma with the shawl was still close enough to hear, and zipped her head back around. "Ohh, I thought it was strange seeing a man at the signing. Do you two know each other?"

"Yes," Mark said.

"No," Rachel said at the same time. "But if you're looking for a book, might I recommend this one."

She held out her newest title, *Hot Target*, the one he'd seen most of the women carrying.

"I think it's right up your ally. Lots of action, explosion. Betrayals."

Yep, sounded like just the book for him.

He accepted the book with smile and flipped to the back cover. "Not so sure I need to read about it, since I can hit most of those high-points all on my own."

Mark tossed the book back onto her signing table. Grandma and the women nearest to him leaned closer, like they smelled blood or something.

Or maybe they all just lived for gossip. He wouldn't put anything passed these women.

"Got anything with some straight-up romance? Forgiveness? A chance of redemption? I could use some pointers in that area."

CHAPTER 24

ointers?" Rachel did her very best to keep her voice cool. Unattached. Her fans were here, after all.

Watching.

But it was hard. Hard because this one man got under her skin so much. And couldn't seem to control what she said to him.

Or how she felt.

Which was usually just pissed off.

She smiled up at him. "I think you need a whole lot more than pointers. "Now, if you'll excuse me. I'm a little busy—"

"Okay. I'll give you that. I need more than pointers."

Her heart raced. Not because of all her fans eagerly listening in—and definitely not because of Mark, who had absolutely no business being here. Actually, there was simply no good reason at all why her heart raced.

She was done with Mark. Completely. Out of her life.

Except he was standing there, waiting for her recommendation. With his height he towered above her, making her feel small, helpless. The same way she'd felt when Nick told her the truth, told her why Mark had been at Daniel's Broiler. Told her who he'd been meeting with.

145

Even now, the hurt swelled to the surface. She couldn't help it, couldn't help the way her eyes teared up of their own will.

And that just made her mad all over again.

She'd thought she could trust him. She thought he'd respect her. Boy had she been wrong.

He watched her with his quiet intensity, eyes narrowing when he noticed her watering eyes. Damn it. She would not cry in front of this man; she would definitely not cry because of him.

He didn't deserve it.

"Actually, I don't have a book good enough for that. I suggest you start with the basics. Like apologizing or jumping off a cliff." That last bit had slipped out. Couldn't control it.

She needed to go. Needed space.

Rachel got up. Slow. Graceful. But her hands shook and she tucked them behind her back. "Excuse me, I need a moment."

She didn't wait for the employee, Jason, to tell her yes or no. But he knew his job and told her waiting fans Rachel Clare needed to use the restroom and she'd be right back.

Restroom. And excellent idea. A place for privacy.

Rachel strode around the bookshelves, not hurried like she was running from someone—which she wasn't—but purposeful. She didn't look behind her. She didn't need to.

She knew Mark was on her heels. Literally.

"Rachel—"

"I don't want to talk to you."

"Rachel."

"No." She spotted the restroom sign, pushed open the woman's door, and slammed it shut behind her.

The slamming motion was all it took; for some strange, annoyingly female hormone reason, it was the last button that pushed her tears over. Couldn't even be sure she was alone before she simply... broke down and lost it.

"Damn it."

She wiped at her eyes, dabbing at them so her mascara wouldn't run. Why did he have to show up? Why did he have to be an ass? And not only that, but the same kind of ass Daniel had always been.

No, Mark was a bigger ass than Daniel. When Daniel would have let Rachel go storming off, more than happy to let her cry in privacy, Mark did the opposite. He came in after her.

She rounded on him, swinging her purse at his arm. "What the hell are you doing? Do I need to spell it out for you? I. Don't. Want. To. See. You."

She smacked him again, he didn't block her purse.

"Or talk to you," she yelled. "Or have anything to do with you or your stupid game."

"Rachel."

"Don't 'Rachel' me!"

Another smack.

Someone flushed the toilet and Rachel froze, purse hanging limp in her hand. The beautiful blonde woman she'd seen talking to Mark (nearly a lifetime ago, it seemed) peeked out of the stall, blushed, and washed her hands.

Stacy. Right. Her name was Stacy. And Stacy had just witnessed Rachel's complete breakdown.

"Sorry about that," Stacy muttered as she dried her hands. "Carry on. I'll let the manager know you'll be out in a moment."

Meanwhile, Rachel and Mark simply remained frozen, mid-fight.

Stacy gave Rachel an apologetic smile. "Men can be such asses. Trust me, I know. Hit him again if you need to. We'll be waiting when you're ready."

The door closed behind her.

Rachel sank against the sink and now there was no stopping her tears.

"Shit. Rachel. I'm sorry."

"Sorry? You're sorry? Well, I guess that just makes everything better. I'd actually thought you'd changed your mind. That you were excited about this game, that you actually respected m—"

She slammed her mouth shut. No. There was no way, no way in

hell she was going there. She would *not* let Mark know how much he hurt her.

"Rachel, I've always respected you." He ran a hand through his hair. Hair that was rumpled and still managed to look good.

Not like her messed-up face. God, she hated him! The thought sent a new stream of tears. "You respected me so much you went behind my back and signed another deal?"

Mark paled at the tears. "I didn't, Rachel. I didn't take the deal."

"Well, you should have because there's no way in hell I'm going to work you. I will not be in another relationship like this, another relationship where I'm looked down on, not respected, and not—"

He didn't give her a chance to finish.

Mark growled, swept her up in his arms, and kissed her.

Both her tears and crying stopped. Instantly.

The kiss exploded through her, mixing both joy and hurt. Joy because she was attracted to this man, as much as she hated it, as much as she didn't want him in her life—she still wanted him there.

And hurt because he'd kicked her so hard in the one place that could hurt her, the one place that would send her crying into a bookstore bathroom.

"Why?" She said against his lips. "Why are you doing this?"

Mark broke the kiss and rested his forehead against hers. "Because I was wrong. I've always respected you, even if I didn't always respect the kind of stories you wrote."

She pushed against his chest. This wasn't what she needed to hear. She'd heard it all before, heard it a hundred times from the man who was supposed to support her, supposed to cheer her on, especially in the hard times, the times she needed it most.

Mark didn't let go. "Rachel, please, I was wrong. Hell, I was more than wrong and I see that now. I took a good look at the women lining up outside to see you. *You.* Not me, not to buy any of my games. They want to buy your stories."

She stopped trying to free herself, though she angled herself in the right position that if she needed to, she'd knee Mark between the legs until he let go.

There was no need.

He sighed against her forehead and then stepped back, his arms slipping from her. "That's what I wanted to tell you."

"You don't want to make my game."

Even now, she could see it. He wanted nothing to do with her romance game idea.

"I'm not happy about it, no. But that's because I swore to only make the games I wanted to make and romance, well, it didn't fit into that criteria when I started this company."

He looked away from her, frowning, and she watched him struggle for the right words. But there were no right words.

He was being honest, yes, but that still didn't change anything. Didn't change the fact he didn't believe in the game.

"No, Mark. I can't—"

"You write the stories you want to tell, right?" he asked. "You don't let the publishers decide, don't let your readers decide, do you? It's all you. That's what I'm faced with. It's not easy and I'm not happy."

Rachel stepped back, surprised. She'd never thought of it that way. Even when her editors told her a type of story would never work she said the hell with them and wrote it anyway. Someone would buy it, and if they didn't? Well, she'd put it in a drawer until the right time, the right person came along.

She'd never thought to apply the same reasoning to games, and more specifically to Mark. Was that why he worked so hard? Why he'd started FastPlay to begin with?

"But," he said, interrupting her thoughts, "I also promised I'd make innovative, industry-changing games. I can't think of anything more industry-shattering than what you've dropped in my lap."

He didn't reach for her again, but he might as well have. His gaze held her there. She couldn't have moved even if she wanted to.

"I'm not sure I believe in the game, I'm not sure it'll work. I'm not sure all those women out there will flock to buy a game you helped create. I don't know, but it doesn't really matter."

Mark's hand reached up, and he gently pushed a strand of her red hair away from her face. "But I believe in *you*. If you let me, if you let me be part of what you're trying to do, I'd like to try. It's your call, Rachel. Your decision."

CHAPTER 25

*H*er call? Her decision? If only it were that easy.

She'd somehow survived her book signing with Mark lingering in the background, giving her space but watching. Waiting for some sign she'd forgiven him, that they'd try again.

Except there had been no 'lingering' about it. She felt him, as if he were standing right beside her. Could practically feel his warmth, the same way she'd felt when he'd held her in the bathroom.

By the time the last of her fans had left, she was ready to pull her hair out. Did she honestly think she could work with this man? That she could spend three years together and somehow survive the project? Survive him and his infuriating presence?

And the way he kissed her?

Absolutely not. No way. Except when the 'yes' slipped from her lips it had shocked both of them. But she knew it was right. This man, and his ideas, were right for her project.

If she put aside the need to pull out her hair, her need to slap him again with her purse, or heck, her need to kiss him, she was left with one answer. This man, this company, needed her game.

And her game needed them.

Saying yes had been the easy part.

Making it actually work? Not so easy.

Try infuriatingly difficult, especially with another book deadline coming up hard and fast. And what was she doing with her time?

Playing video games and spending the evening with Mark.

Rachel glanced up from her spot on the loveseat to glare at Mark who had his feet sprawled out in front of him. To make matters worse, he was completely pressed against her because Allie had the couch, and she sprawled about as much as he did.

Actually, to really make matters worse the fantasy game he'd given her, complete with character-specific origin stories, was really pissing her off.

"This is terrible," Rachel snapped for about the hundredth time. "Why do I have to keep playing this?"

If the game had at least been enjoyable, the situation wouldn't nearly be so bad. But considering there was no way she could get a happy ending (without letting her love interest sleep with her best friend—one of the absolute biggest taboos in romance!), it made for a very frustrating, and waste of time, experience.

"Because you need to know what not to do." Mark turned the page of her recent book, *Hot Target*.

"Why? If you know this already, why do I have to play?"

"Your game, too, remember? I need your insight into how to make this not happen."

"Simple." She threw down the controller. "Don't be an ass writer and come up with an ending that screws you in every way possible."

"Not the game." Mark glanced up and smiled. He pointed at her face. "That."

"Me? What about me?"

"You're pissed, and I know for a fact, because I have insider knowledge, that those writer-designers you hate so much thought this was simply 'game story brilliance.' Force the players to make 'hard' choices and all."

Rachel's eyes narrowed. "Hard choices? You've got to be kidding me! Some brainless idiot thought it'd be great to force women to either A. lose the guy they're in love with, or B. make him sleep with her best friend so they can be together in the end?"

Mark's smile grew. "Scout's honor."

"This is crap. I'm done. No more wasting my time on video game bullshit. There's no way *my* game is going to be like this."

Mark had already turned his attention back to her book. "You haven't even gotten to the part where you have to choose whether to let the guy die or you. To save the world and all that."

"Video games suck at storytelling. I just spent how many hours playing and now I have to *die?*"

Mark laughed, actually laughed. He tossed his book aside, pulled out his notebook—continued to laugh, and make notes. "This is why I want you to play these games."

She leaned over his shoulder, which wasn't too difficult since she was nearly on his lap. Ah, yes, a little too close.

Rachel blushed and immediately scooted over to her 'side' of the loveseat. She was still mad at him for pursuing another publisher deal behind her back, and she still didn't quite trust him.

Except it was hard to stay mad.

Regardless of Mark believing in her game, he was trying. And he was taking the game, and the design, seriously.

Sort of.

Other than the constant arguments she overhead between him and Scott, and sometimes Ethan, too. While Scott and Ethan had managed to set aside their creative differences to make this game, Mark still wasn't able to let go.

Not to mention the rest of the company and the slow trickle of information passed down to certain employees. If she didn't have Mark on her side, how could she possibly expect the rest of the company to listen?

She'd finally given up trying to understand Mark and why he dug his heels in with this game; there was some culture in his industry, something that made him so resistant to this game.

If she was honest with herself, she didn't know what to think of that. Part of her hoped he'd change the more they worked on this together. But then, people don't change just because you want them to. She'd learned *that* from her marriage.

It'd be foolish hoping otherwise, except... except Mark kept coming over. He kept spending time with her.

A lot. Though, he said it was because he liked the dog.

Maybe she shouldn't have gotten the dog. Then she might have gotten some more writing done. Not that Mark's presence was preventing her from writing, it was more her *thinking* about Mark that got in the way. Especially when her hero characters developed tiny quirks that hadn't been there before, quirks she knew came from her observing Mark.

Allie poked an eye open to stare at her, thumped her tail in the half-hearted hope of it being walk time. Or dinner time. Or both.

Rachel stretched her hands over her head and groaned, Mark glanced up from his notebook and his gaze dropped to her stomach—a stomach now a tiny bit bare.

His eyes darkened from blue to midnight and she dropped her hands. Her stomach was covered again, removing the need-to-stare temptation, but he didn't stop watching her.

"Mark?"

He blinked and jerked his attention back to the notebook. "Sorry about that. Nearly done here."

She didn't want him to be sorry. She was an attractive woman; there was nothing wrong with him admiring her. Okay, maybe the way her insides turned to jelly was a bit of a problem.

How could his one look do that to her?

He was no one, totally unimportant. Right?

And there was that kiss, three kisses actually... Rachel shook her head. No, thinking about them kissing was certainly not a good idea, not when she could feel every hard inch of him pressed against her.

Crap. Maybe she should play that game some more. Her frustration would definitely distract her from the man sitting beside her, the man she wanted to do more than just sit with.

Rachel jumped to her feet. "Do you, uh, need something to drink? Water? Beer?"

"No. I'm good."

"I'm not good," she muttered to herself and headed to the kitchen.

She needed something to distract her. At the very least to have something for her hands to play with, something to do so she didn't have to keep looking at him, feeling him so close.

Rachel opened a bottle of '08 Cabernet and poured herself a healthy glass. Wine and men were fine. She knew her limit with both and when 'too much' of either became 'too much' of something else. There was a reason she hadn't touched the hard stuff whenever Mark was around.

The vodka was staying safely tucked away in her cabinet.

She swirled the red wine, taking a deep breath, letting the smoky scents sooth her. She was fine. She was in control and when he left for the evening she'd sit down and work out all this sexual tension in her writing.

"See?" She whispered. "Good for something."

"What is?"

Rachel spun and there was Mark, setting down his notebook on her bar counter. One hand rested on his hip, hips quite nicely defined in those jeans.

Jeans which left very little to the imagination.

Holy shit.

Rachel sipped again and nearly choked as Mark moved closer. His hand slipped underneath hers and without hesitation, she relinquished the wine to him. Her body seemed to be completely incapable of moving at the moment.

Her gaze fixated on the glass and the lavender lipstick smudge she'd left on the rim. Seeing it there, seeing him smell the wine just as she'd done, made everything different. More intimate.

He also didn't step away as sipped and savored the taste.

"I, I didn't realize you were a wine drinker."

"On occasion. We're so close to the wineries, it's hard not to at least be familiar with wine." He set the glass down on the counter. "And you do have good taste."

"A hobby of mine. Wine tasting that is."

"Really." He made as if to reach for the glass again, but instead he reached for her. His arm slipped around her waist.

Rachel didn't move, didn't pull away. She let him guide her towards him, let his hands run up and down her back. His touch sizzled through her silk blouse.

Her whole body warmed, quivered.

She knew, logically, this was a bad idea. They were business partners now and getting into a relationship, the kind of relationship his look promised, was definitely a bad idea.

It'd start fun and end badly.

Still, when he lowered his lips, she didn't pull away. She met him halfway. Met his kisses, kiss for kiss. Matched his groans with her own moans while her body ignited.

Bad or not, this felt so good. So right.

She slid one shoe off, then the other. Her heels clacked on the tile floor. Mark's hands tightened around her, held her closer. Pressed her body, her breasts against him as if he couldn't get enough.

As if he needed more.

Some small part of her brain heard Allie jump off the couch, heard the door open. None of it registered until the footsteps. But even then it wasn't until Nick whistled that everything clicked into place.

Nick. Was here.

In her home.

With her ready to yank off her clothes and push Mark onto the counter. Not something she wanted her brother to see—ever!

She turned slightly, looking past Mark. Nick stood there, his head cocked to one side. "So, umm, I'm guessing this is a bad time?"

CHAPTER 26

*N*ick." Mark released Rachel, and she suddenly realized that her shirt had been unbuttoned enough to show her very curvy breasts.

To say her blush traveled all the way from her cheeks to her breasts would be an understatement.

"Nick! What are you doing here?" She wasted no time buttoning up and glared at Nick from over Mark's shoulders. "You're supposed to knock, you know."

Nick was busy giving Allie all the attention she wanted (meanwhile politely giving Rachel privacy), but that grin—oh, she knew that grin. There was no way he was going to let her live this down.

"Well, umm, now that you have more to your life than writing and books, I might have to pick up the habit. Just in case. Isn't that right, Allie?"

"Might be a good idea." Mark swiped up his notebook and she realized his shirt was also untucked.

Unlike Nick, who was casual and untucked as usual, Mark always looked professional... which probably meant she'd been the one doing the untucking.

Or *yanking* in this case.

"Hey," Nick said, "if she starts knocking on my door, I'll do the same."

Mark nodded, clearly thinking this was a reasonable trade-off. "Well, we got a bunch of work accomplished tonight. I should be going. Gotta sleep some time."

She looked away from Nick—and saw her discarded heels on her kitchen floor. Shit.

"I'll see you soon?" Mark asked her.

"Right. Soon." Rachel nudged her shoes behind the trashcan, where she hoped Nick wouldn't notice.

Mark's gaze darkened as he noticed what she was doing. Was he thinking about what had almost happened?

Rachel scrambled to make sense of her thoughts, or the image of what had almost happened in her kitchen. "I didn't realize you were still working late."

Nick straightened and Allie sat like a good girl, still expecting to be petted. "Of course he is, Rachel. Signing the contract with you was only one step in this giant hurdle."

Step?

She looked at them both, confused. "What 'giant hurdle'?"

Mark shook his head. "It's nothing, Rachel. Just starting to let employees know what's going on."

Nick snorted. "More like putting out fires and getting people to follow that non-disclosure statement they signed, but there's always a leak."

Now Rachel really was confused. "I don't think I'm following. What's the big deal?"

Sure non-disclosure statements were part of the business, but with writing it was never that big of a deal. She *wanted* to let readers know what she was working on, what project would be coming out next. Of course, they never got the details, but there was nothing like this paranoia she was sensing from Mark.

"It's nothing, Rachel. Trade secrets. Just the usual in the video game world. You'll come by the office soon?"

Nick had stopped petting Allie completely and he watched Mark with the kind of intensity she wasn't used to seeing on her carefree brother. Mark was still waiting for her reply.

"When I can," she said. "I have a manuscript to finish, but I think you're right. About playing the games. I never realized how much they got wrong about all that stuff."

She waved her hand in the direction of her TV. Right, *stuff*. A perfect explanation from a fantastic wordsmith. What was this man doing to her?

Mark shook Nick's hand. She did, however, notice Nick held Mark's hand a little too long. Probably a guy moment, or a brother-threatening-the-other-man moment.

Rachel distracted herself with the wine, then froze when she realized she'd sipped from the same place Mark had. She stifled a groan and without thinking, dumped the glass out.

She poured herself another and then a glass for Nick. He closed the front door and they stood there, staring at each other for several long moments. She had no idea what to do, didn't even know why Nick was suddenly upset.

Was it something that Mark had said?

Rachel held the glass towards him. He mumbled a thanks, took it, and plopped down on her couch. The actual couch, not the loveseat she and Mark had shared.

Allie jumped up beside him, pleased to have company on her special couch. Nick had to do some quick maneuvering to prevent the glass from being knocked out of his hand.

Rachel covered a smile. His mood seemed to fade, as if he couldn't help but smile around that dog, even when she was being incredibly annoying.

"So," Nick finally said, "you and Mark?"

She shrugged. "I'm not sure, honestly."

"Not sure? Sis, from where I was standing you both looked pretty damn sure."

Thankful for the glass in her hands, and the distraction it presented, she fiddled with the stem. It was an excuse not to look

Nick in the eye. She didn't want to see what he thought, didn't want to see just how much trouble she was in.

Not from Nick, but for herself. It had been a long time since she'd been with anyone; a long time since she'd wanted to be with anyone.

"In the moment, yes, I'd say we were. But when the moment passes?"

Her fingers shook slightly. Rachel stared at them for a moment, then immediately set the glass down onto her coffee table. "You know it's been awhile since, well since anyone really."

"You mean since Daniel."

She recognized the hard edge in Nick's voice. The kind of edge he reserved for their infrequent talks about Daniel.

"That asshole broke your heart and then walked out on you." Nick snorted. "Then had the audacity to stay in your life and try to squeeze some extra money off you."

"He doesn't, Nick."

"Used to."

Rachel frowned. "That was only because he'd lost his job and I was still—"

She cut herself off. She'd somehow, in some tiny place unknown to her, had been in love with him. Still. Even after all the emotional torture he'd put her through.

"It was only one time," she whispered. It had taken only once for her to get her head on straight. One night of dinner, some true romance right out of one of her novels, and then he never called her back.

At least she hadn't called him. She'd restrained herself, though barely.

"One time is all it takes," Nick said.

"Yes. And I'm living with that decision and will continue to live with it for the rest of my life." She crossed her arms, felt her anger sparking. That meant her old self was returning. Conversations about Daniel tended to do that.

She'd grown up since she married him. Grew up even more when she divorced him and realized just where she fit in his life.

She didn't need Nick protecting her.

"Now. Did you come over here for a reason or just to warn me about getting into a relationship with Mark?"

Nick slouched back in her couch and Allie curled up even more on his lap. "I just don't want to see you hurt again. I'm your brother. I love you."

"I know, Nick. But I'm a big girl. I don't need you protecting me."

He watched her, one hand stroking Allie's head. "Are you sure about that?"

CHAPTER 27

Mark unlocked the front doors, trying to ignore the early morning chill and the way his breath puffed out. Damn, it was cold.

He balanced his coffee as he gave the keys a turn, while at the same time trying not to think about how early it was.

First one to the office.

First one in, last one to leave. Again.

Unless, of course, he had evening plans with Rachel—and after last night and what nearly happened on her kitchen counter, he should probably hold off on any more evenings alone with her.

Indefinitely.

He didn't even want to think about what Scott would say. Sleeping with their investor? With the person who'd be writing them checks for the next three years (not counting royalties when the game took off)?

Sleeping with her was a bad idea on so many levels.

Problem was he couldn't stop thinking about her. Or thinking about sleeping with her.

Mark checked his voice messages, not surprised the big executives at Forged Legends had put a few more calls in, hoping to change his

163

mind. Part of him wished he could, that he had the power to call them back, to say the hell with Rachel's game.

He tossed his jacket on the guest chair and sank into his own. The problem was he didn't want her to walk out of his life, and if he made the deal with Forged Legends, that was exactly what she'd do.

And with good reason.

But was it a good reason to want to think about her, several times a day? Hell, he had to start skimming past those sexy bedrooms scenes in her novels because it was getting damn hard not to think about her. And him.

Not to mention reading at work was tricky at best. He figured whenever he got to the bedroom part, he'd just skip to the next chapter.

Problem was Rachel didn't limit her 'love-making' scenes to the bedroom.

Like last night.

Shit.

Mark dropped his face in his hands. This was at least one problem he'd never had working with a publisher. He'd never wanted to sleep with any high powered executives.

Someone knocked at his door. Mark swallowed a groan, wondered who the hell could be up as early as him. Office hours might officially start around 9:00, but most employees didn't show up until 10:00.

Or after 10:00.

Video game developers were not morning people. So someone else being here this early? Not a good sign, especially when it was barely 8:00.

Ryan poked his head it. "You got a minute, Mark?"

This was the other half of the problem, the part he'd kept from Rachel last night. He might have evaded Rachel's questions, but not Nick. Nick knew too damn well what Mark was going up against.

"Yeah, have a seat."

Mark scooped his jacket up off the couch and hung it up, then took a calming sip of his coffee—or it would have been calming if it hadn't gone cold. He steeled himself for what was to come. Still, knowing what was coming didn't make it any easier to deal with.

"You thought over what I said? About Cupid?"

"I did." Ryan didn't look at him. Definitely not a good sign.

Ryan had been one of the first employees Mark had hired once they'd been able to afford 'good' employees. Not just the bodies he needed to finish a project, but the kind of employees necessary to make his company grow, to move away from the phone and hand-held games and break into the big league games.

Ryan was his right-hand man, the lead designer Mark had assigned to Project Cupid. And Ryan was probably one of the few employees Mark would never be able to replace.

"Might as well get this over with." Mark always thought being direct was the best way to go. No need to dance around a thorny issue, just step right in and deal with the pain. "You handing in your resignation?"

Ryan's lips thinned, but after a very long, nervous moment, Ryan shook his head.

No.

Mark let out a breath. Surprised, he unclenched his hands from his armrests. "You, you're not?"

"No. It's not the game I want to make, but I get it. I get why we're doing it." Ryan sighed, but the sigh quickly turned into a yawn. "Sorry, I just wanted to talk with you before everyone else got here and waking up early..."

"Yeah, not my thing either." Mark glanced at his now cold coffee and tossed it into the trashcan. "Tell you what. Let's go for a walk, get some damn good caffeine in us and we'll talk about the project. I'm sure you've got questions."

"You can say that."

Ryan stood and Mark was pleased to see he didn't look quite as nervous. Not happy, but then Mark wasn't happy about the project either.

But it was money on the table and it kept employees like Ryan with a job. It was also a chance to do something daring—something you had to be insane to try.

At least Mark wasn't the only insane one who worked here.

"You know," Ryan said as he waited for Mark to put on his coat, "I'm not going to be the only one thinking about leaving."

"I know." Mark may not want to think about it, but it didn't make it any less of a reality. "I'm sure a few *will* leave."

If not 'quite' a few.

"I've already got HR contacting some people. Interviews will start soon."

"You're uh, planning on bringing in some more women, I hope?"

Mark closed his door and studied Ryan. "I'm guessing that's not just a professional question?"

"Hey, just thinking more women will give us a better chance of pulling this thing off right." Ryan smiled. "Of course, more women is always a good thing."

Mark thought about Rachel, thought about the way she'd look at him on the couch, her hair tousled. A look that said she wanted him, wanted everything about him.

Mark shook of the picture. "I wouldn't say that, Ryan. Women are dangerous."

"Never said they weren't, boss."

That was something he'd have to keep in mind, both when dealing with Rachel and the women he was sure they'd soon be hiring. But first things first, he had to convince as many of his employees to stay and take a chance on this game, and do his best to make sure information about the game didn't leak to the press.

That, he knew, would kill Project Cupid before it started.

CHAPTER 28

Rachel ignored the still silent phone and concentrated on her manuscript, a manuscript that was due tonight.

"A manuscript that's obviously not going to write itself," she muttered. "Rachel, focus."

Oh, she focused all right. Focused on glancing at the damn phone again and wondering for the hundredth time, why Mark hadn't called her.

Nearly a whole month had passed since the evening Nick had walked in on them in her kitchen. A whole month of Rachel wondering what to do about that kiss—and Nick's warning.

She'd decided the best course of action was to do nothing. Pretend like it had never happened.

So, apparently, had Mark.

She saw him often at the office, but their conversations were short and brief at best. He claimed he was doing more research on his own, reading the romance novels (with his door securely closed) to get a better 'feel' for them and how to translate that 'feel' into a game.

Which was fine with her. Perfectly fine.

"Because you have a deadline, Rachel," she'd reminded herself.

Right.

And because what had nearly happened in her kitchen shouldn't happen again.

Of course, that still didn't mean she wasn't irked Mark hadn't called her even once. Okay, so maybe he called her a few times, but she didn't count anything under three minutes, and with her answering strictly business questions, as an actual 'call.'

So, when her phone *did* rang and she snatched it up before she realized what she was doing, she'd been expecting—and hoping—it was Mark.

It wasn't.

"Hi," a very female, non-Mark voice spoke. "Are you Rachel Clare?"

That was a question that never went well.

"Depends. Who's this?"

"Oh, my gosh. I'm so sorry."

If Rachel had a video set up, she was sure she'd see the woman blushing about three shades of red.

"I'm Karen. You don't know me, but I'm the new producer at FastPlay."

At the word 'FastPlay,' Rachel relaxed. Not some crazy fan then, and at least it wasn't Scott calling her. She swore that man called at least three times a day and the only reason she continued to answer the phone was the possibility of it being Mark.

Who it never was.

"Ms. Clare?"

Rachel shook herself. "Right, sorry, Karen. I'm just distracted. I've got a deadline and I—"

At which point Karen then continued to profess her apologies. This was clearly not getting Rachel anywhere in the conversation. "Look, Karen, why don't you tell me why you called?"

And how she got Rachel's number.

Her number wasn't something she wanted anyone to have. She kept it unlisted for a reason. After all, she did have work to do.

"Rachel, it's just, well. I need your help. I love reading romances, especially yours, but... I'm the only employee on Cupid who's even opened up a romance book. The guys don't get it and they're not listening. We just had a terrible design meeting..."

Rachel's back hit her chair with a thud. All thoughts of her deadline forgotten.

She somehow found the words to tell Karen to go on, she was listening. She was doing more than listening. She was developing one hell of a righteous fury.

A terrible design meeting? Ha! That didn't cover a near mutiny with half the designers either bad-mouthing her books or threatening to leave. Every word out of Karen's mouth made her stomach plummet.

Why hadn't Mark told her?

Rachel squeezed her eyes closed, trying to focus on Karen and shove aside her hurt. He should have told her. She could have helped, helped to explain, to ease them into the idea.

But he'd shut her out.

"Karen."

At Rachel's sudden voice, Karen immediately quieted. "Yes?"

Rachel hadn't just invested all this time, all this energy, and yes, already quite a bit of money into the project only to let it fail before it got off the ground.

"What do you need me to do?"

RACHEL YANKED OPEN the door and strode into FastPlay's office. She hadn't even bothered to put on her good business suit. She'd simply thrown on the one closest to her and buttoned her jacket on the drive over.

She'd nearly gone out in her bunny slippers, but since Karen's call had been about professionalism and the viability of the game, she'd cool her temper just enough so she didn't rip her skirt as she tugged it on.

Rachel had been in the office enough times to know her way without Scott playing tour guide. And more importantly, she knew the way to Mark's office.

She narrowed her gaze, taking in the heads popping up from cubicles, the faces staring at her with open mouths. She ignored them and stomped towards Mark.

Some guy in a T-shirt stained with ketchup tried to offer her assistance. She glared at him and he backed off. Actually, she was fairly sure he went running for the door.

Good. Because right now she meant business.

Mark's door was closed. She didn't give a damn about his privacy and thrust it open.

"What the hell is going on?" She slammed the door shut.

Mark turned, phone at his mouth, and looked at her like she was crazy.

Well, screw it. She was crazy. Crazy for thinking she could make a game with him; crazy to think she could trust him!

The thought of 'trust' sent another sizzle of anger through her. She reached over, snatched the phone from him. "I'm sorry, Mr. Ashe has a big problem he needs to take care of. He'll call you back."

She slammed the phone into the receiver.

"Rachel!" He jumped up from his chair. "What the hell do you think you're doing? You can't just come in here and—"

She thrust her finger at his chest, hard. "I *can* and I *will*!" she said, her manicured nail punctuating each word with a jab. "Especially when you can't be honest with me, that you don't trust me enough to tell me what the hell's going on."

"Trust you? Christ, I thought we've been over this."

"Over it, yes, and clearly you're missing the point."

This time, she shoved him for reference. Not like her shove did a damn thing. He didn't even take a single step back, which only made her madder.

"I just got a call from one of your employees," Rachel said. "She was very concerned, very worried about convincing a bunch of boneheaded jerks why we should make this game!"

Mark's eyes narrowed at her words. "I'm handling this."

"Bullshit! When were you going to tell me? And why didn't you give your lead designer my analysis?"

Rachel pulled the reports from her purse and shoved it at his chest. "Do you want him to face everyone down without the right information? Are you *trying* to sabotage this project?"

"Like hell I am." Mark grabbed the reports and threw them onto his desk. "This is my company, my employees, my problem—and I'll handle it like I damn well want to."

"Then do it right! Stop trying to kill my project."

The words escaped before she thought them through. The implication of what she'd said hitting them both like a bucket of cold water.

Rachel's mouth clicked closed. She hadn't meant to go that far, hadn't meant to, but that didn't change the truth. Didn't change the fact she believed it.

Believed in the possibility of it.

Mark stared at her, mouth set in a firm line. "Is that what you think?"

"What am I supposed to think? You don't call me, you don't ask for my help, you're evasive. Even Nick knows you're lying about the problems here. And then I get this call. Tell me, Mark, what am I supposed to think?"

"You're supposed to trust me."

"Trust?" Rachel gave a half-laugh, half-sigh. Mostly at herself. "Trust, yeah well, trust goes both ways." She picked up her purse. "I thought I could trust you to handle this right. I guess I was wrong."

She turned to go, but Mark's hand darted out and grabbed her arm. The very contact, the very touch of his skin against her made her shiver. A touch she hadn't forgotten in the month it'd been since he'd held her in his arms, since he kissed her as she tugged at his shirt.

Rachel jerked her gaze away from his hand. She couldn't think of that. There was nothing between them but heat. She'd written enough romances, enough happily-ever-afters to know that wasn't the kind of ending she wanted.

She didn't want the kind of ending this attraction between them would lead to.

She'd had enough heartache and pain to last her a lifetime. She didn't need Mark and she certainly didn't need his trust to survive.

CHAPTER 29

Rachel." Mark's hold on his temper slipped. He tried to push it away, tried to be rational and professional. But she'd been the one who barged into his office, hung up his phone call.

The phone rang again.

Rachel faced him and sent a questioning look at the phone. An 'are you going to get that' look.

No, not a look. A challenge.

Mark let her go, pulled out his chair and pointed. "Sit."

She thrust her chin out. Another challenge.

The hell with being professional. He grabbed her by the shoulders and shoved her into the chair.

"Hey!"

"You gonna act like a two year-old, then I'll treat you like one." Mark yanked the cord out and the phone silenced. "Now. We're going to talk about this like two adults and you're going to tell me what the hell you're mad about this time."

"I thought I already did that."

She had. He'd give her that, but that didn't mean he wasn't pissed at how she'd acted.

Mark dropped into the chair opposite her, his legs brushing hers.

She tugged her knees away. Good. She was uncomfortable and that was right along the lines of what he felt right now.

That and pissed.

"You can't just come into my office, into my company, and act like you're in charge. Nor can you go about slamming my door and hanging up my calls."

Her eyes narrowed. "Are you going to keep giving me reasons to act that way?"

"Damn it, Rachel." Mark ran a hand through his hair. "Okay, fine. You're right. I'm having a difficult time with this. People aren't adjusting, but that's what I expected."

She leaned forward, but still kept every inch of her body away from him. He tried not to think why that bothered him so much.

"Then why didn't you ask? Why aren't I helping? And why aren't you showing them the data?"

She had a point, but it was a card he hadn't wanted to play yet. He wanted to let people get used to the idea, let them give her romance books a try first, but maybe he had made a mistake. After all, it had taken numbers to get him to even open one of her damn books.

"I gave them the books."

"The books," she repeated. "The books aren't enough and you know it."

"No, I guess not."

He could see that now, but that was only because he had wanted to distance himself from her, from the game. It was the only way he could think straight.

Rachel slumped in her chair and rubbed her forehead. That was when he noticed the dark circles under her eyes. Something in his chest gave a slight twinge at that. She hadn't... she hadn't gotten those circles from him, had she?

"Haven't been sleeping well?" he asked.

She blinked. "What, oh, I've been working late. Pushing myself to meet a deadline. When I signed the contract I hadn't factored in my video game playing time into my writing time."

Now it was Mark's turn to blink. She was still playing the games? Even after he'd told her she didn't need to?

"It's fine, really," she said. "You were right. If you need to understand my books, then I need to understand your games. They are two very different mediums."

She smiled, a half-mocking smile. "At least, our game can't be any worse than the crap I've been playing."

Our game.

A jolt shocked through him. She'd never called the game that before. Heck, he hadn't even called it 'his game' yet.

"Yeah, well, you've got that right." Mark had no idea where his own answering smile came from, no idea how he could go from being pissed off and ready to kill to her to this... whatever *this* was.

They stared at each other. The silence grew, along with something else, the tension between them as if it sizzled in the air, in the small, closed room.

Without wanting to, Mark thought about the night at her place and the last kiss they'd shared. A kiss that had been a mistake, a kiss he couldn't get out of his head.

"Rachel—"

"Mark." She said at the same time.

Neither had a chance to say what they wanted. A soft knock on the door, followed by Ryan and then Karen, poking their heads in, interrupted the moment. Karen was practically cowering behind Ryan, but she stood her ground and gave Mark a somewhat even stare.

"Mr. Ashe this is my fault. I'm the one who called Rachel."

Ahh, that explained it. From what Ryan had explained in their earlier debriefing, Karen had been the only one on board with the romance game idea. Mark had expected her to do the research to convince her team the owners weren't making a colossal mistake, but he hadn't expected Karen to have the balls to call Rachel.

Another oversight. He'd been having a lot of those lately.

"Karen, call me Mark. And it's no one's fault but mine."

He noticed Rachel lifting her eyebrows at that.

Well, it was true. He'd handled the situation badly, but he was man enough to own up to it.

"Tell you what, why don't you schedule a meeting with the design team later this afternoon? We'll bring Rachel's information with us, hopefully ease some fears."

Or at the least, make the choices very clear.

Either work on this game or take a hike.

"Uh," Karen glanced between him and Rachel. "If Ms. Clare has time, wouldn't it be helpful if she joined us? I mean, who better to answer their questions than a famous romance writer?"

Rachel straightened, but he couldn't tell if it was because of the question or because she thought Mark should have asked earlier. Hell, she was probably pissed about both reasons.

"Not this time, Karen. Rachel's got a deadline to hit, but we'll schedule something for later."

Much later, like once he got a handle on his teams. Besides, he knew how badly Ryan's initial design meeting had gone. Ryan hadn't sugar-coated it and Mark didn't need Rachel being in the line of fire, especially when it was his fault the fire was so hot to begin with.

"A deadline, really?" Karen pushed past Ryan and shook Rachel's hand.

Any hint of Rachel's anger, or even her annoyance at Mark, was gone. Instead there was nothing but the 'happy to meet a fan' face of the famous writer. But when he looked closer, the signs she was still mad were clear.

A slight tightening of her forehead. A smile that didn't reach her eyes.

He knew what *that* kind of smile looked like. She'd nearly knocked him over with it a handful of times.

So when Ryan finally got Karen out of the room and Rachel turned that not-true smile on him, he was ready for it.

"My, that was nice of you, speaking for me like that."

"Hey, you're the one who hasn't been sleeping well," he said. "When is your deadline anyway?"

Rachel's smile slipped. "Tonight."

"Tonight? Shit. And you drove all the way over here to yell at me?"

"No, absolutely not. But this is an investment and I couldn't possibly ignore a call like that..." her voice trailed off.

Mark smirked. "And?"

"And yes, I drove here to yell at you. Okay? But now that I've done yelling, I should get back to work."

Rachel stood, slipping her purse on her shoulder. "You do plan on handling this, right? I mean, with the everyone?"

"I'll talk to them today."

He held open the door for her, but she didn't move to leave. The silence grew more uncomfortable by the second, made him more aware of the other, unspoken issue between them. An issue they'd have to deal with at some point. Not now, though, not when he had designers planning a mutiny and she had a book to finish.

Rachel seemed to think the same because she only nodded and gave another not-true smile. "Just, just call me."

She clicked past him, moving quick in those tall heels of hers. Her hair brushed his face and he caught a scent of vanilla and honey, then it was gone, just as she was gone.

Mark closed the door behind him, listening to the door's soft click to know it was fully shut. Call her? He *had* called her, brief and purely business calls, but they were calls.

Problem was she wasn't talking about *those* kind of calls.

Mark glanced at his unplugged phone. He needed to return that call she'd interrupted, needed to talk with his designers and get them to think outside their giant egos.

Screw it. He'd deal with it all later. Instead, he grabbed his gym bag to go work off this typical mood seeing Rachel brought on. Whether they were arguing or ripping each others clothes off, there was definitely a mood she cast over him.

He had no idea if this was a good sign or not.

Probably not.

They had a long way to go before Cupid was finished, if he could convince his employees to stick around for the long haul.

One thing was for sure, Karen had given him the perfect idea to bridge the gap between him and his employees.

They might not like romance, they might not Rachel Clare and everything she represented, but they did like a good party and he had the perfect excuse to throw one.

CHAPTER 30

Rachel pulled her Corvette up to the valet and leaned forward, gazing up at the Space Needle. Just looking at it made her palms sweat. That was a really, really tall building. If she could even call that thing a building.

What had Mark been thinking having the announcement party *here* of all places?

"You sure you're going to be okay?" Nick tugged at the collar (of the tucked-in shirt she'd insisted he wear). "Just looking at that point gives me the creeps."

"You know, how about we not talk about it?"

After all, if she didn't discuss or acknowledge just how high up the banquet rooms were, then she wouldn't notice, right?

She smoothed her hands over her navy blue cocktail dress, the silky fabric clinging to her waist and hips. The valet, decked out all in black, opened her door and his polite smile slipped as she stepped out. He recovered himself and asked if she was a guest at FastPlay Games' party.

A silly question since she didn't dress up like this for just any old occasion. "Yes, unless they moved the banquet rooms to a place not quite so high up?"

She could hope, right?

"Sorry, miss, but there's a gentleman who's been waiting for your arrival." The valet nodded over her shoulder and Rachel turned.

Her breath caught in her throat.

Mark waited by the curb, hands tucked in the pockets of his dark, perfectly tailored suit. The only color was the deep red shirt he wore, but it only made his blue eyes stand out more. She stepped forward, the silk dress wrapping around her, showing off her curves, her legs.

He watched her and she could see the blue of his eyes changing to midnight. A look that left absolutely nothing to her imagination. Even though the kiss had happened months ago, she remembered that look.

Remembered the promise in that look.

"Rachel." He held out his arm.

Her hands shook as she accepted his arm and she hoped he hadn't noticed. "Do all your investors get the VIP treatment? Escorted by the famous and powerful Mark Ashe?"

"The only famous and powerful one here is the girl on my arm." His voice purred, swirling around her, deep and promising.

Nick cleared his throat. "Good to see you, Mark."

Mark tore his gaze from Rachel and she sucked in a breath of wonderful air. How did he do this to her? Every time she saw him she got caught up in his gaze, in the way her stomach decided to take dance lessons.

Mark released her long enough to shake Nick's hand, and then he claimed her arm again, as if to prove something to Nick. What that was, Rachel hadn't a clue.

Besides, at the moment, she had a bigger issue to worry about: the elevator ride.

At least the short walk was comfortable, not like several of the other employee wives and girlfriends who were already doing their best to smile and hide their wincing as their feet protested their dressy footwear. Though beautiful, their shoes clearly weren't meant for walking.

Unlike hers.

The silver strap heels fit her in a way only money could buy; they weren't just gorgeous, they were comfortable, too. Just in case she had to run away screaming or something.

Or stomp away from Mark before she killed him.

Or yank him into the nearest dark corner.

Either way, she and her comfortable shoes were prepared.

Mark was also apparently prepared for the elevator ride, keeping up a quiet hum of conversation with Nick, his free hand carefully resting on her arm. A solid presence, a reminder she would survive this.

What she wasn't prepared for was the elevator doors sliding open to the dozens of faces turning their way. FastPlay's employees. Yes, she'd been prepared for their interest, but not their complete and absolute attention.

On her.

Already she heard the whispers, the confirmation that yes, she was the angel investor who funded Cupid, the game that would finally be revealed to the whole company.

Rachel smiled, but her grip on Mark's arm tightened as he led her into the crowd, a crowd that turned as they passed, gazes following them. Nick, her darling, wonderful brother, stayed by her side. When Mark broke off to shake hands with Ethan, Nick tapped her shoulder.

"You okay?"

"You mean am I going to pass out? I'm not sure yet."

Nick frowned as he scanned the nearby crowd, the people pressing in, clearly wanting to meet her. "You're normally fine with being in the limelight."

"Yes, but this is... different. These people don't want to meet me."

They hadn't come to hear her speak, to ask for autographs. She was in their *world*, a video game world where romance and everything Rachel represented wasn't welcome.

Nick kissed her forehead. "It'll be fine. I'll do the talking thing, maybe drop in a few hints about your career and how rich you are. Rich always makes people happier."

"You're such a *doll*, Nicky."

"You know I love you. Make sure this guy looks after you." He nodded at Mark, then disappeared into the growing crowd.

She would have liked to have made some snappy, empowering comment like her not needing someone to look after her, but she'd already caught enough dark, unhappy looks to know that wasn't true.

Not here, anyway.

Mark had kept his promise about being more open, sharing what was happening with the company and those employees who had started on the pre-production steps of Cupid.

Rachel could easily pick out those individuals, both the happy and the unhappy ones.

"Rachel!" A familiar female voice burst behind her.

She let go of the safety of Mark's arm, and turned.

She didn't need safety when it came to Karen, her one true fan in the whole company. Karen had also done her duty in keeping Rachel informed of the team's morale, just in case Mark slipped up in that department again.

Karen rushed forward, sporting a sexy, black evening gown as she embraced Rachel. Ryan followed at a more sedate pace behind her, and shook Rachel's hand when Karen finally let go.

"Ms. Clare."

She smiled at him, pleased to see both of them here, and pleased to see her influence of all-things-romance had influenced their own bubbling relationship.

Here, she thought, was at least one man who understood what her novels were about. And that was exactly what she needed in a lead designer, someone who believed in her work.

The thought made her smile falter. She glanced at Mark, who was finally turning his attention back to her, and then instead greeted Ryan and Karen. The polite greetings continued and Rachel was quickly lost in a sea of new faces and names.

It helped when Mark also mentioned a person's title, which helped her put faces to the names both Mark and Karen had talked about.

There was one person whose name Rachel didn't need to ask. He came forward, practically shoving his way through the crowd, using his larger weight to do most of the work for him.

To say he was unhappy was a vast understatement. If there was one person who'd been pissed to be on Cupid, it was Brad. Brad, who was also unfortunately, a very loud, constant complainer. A person who Karen admitted she was worried about bringing the rest of the team down.

Brad stopped only a few feet from her, clearly meaning to push into her personal space. Rachel lifted her chin. She wouldn't back away; she wasn't about to give him the satisfaction.

Still, she flicked her eyes to the side, but Mark was gone. Gone to talk to another employee?

Either way, he wasn't here and he wasn't about to save her.

She didn't need saving.

"Brad. I'm Rachel."

She held out her hand, keeping her charming smile in place when the only thing she wanted to do was slap him. This man, and everything about him, reminded her of Daniel. The kind of person who looked down on her work, who sneered at her for what she did.

"I'm surprised you had the nerve to show up." Brad glared at her, pupils slightly dilated. He'd clearly already started on the booze, and had had quite a bit from the smell of it.

"Well, I am financing the game after all. And your position. I think I *should* be here."

Those beady eyes of his narrowed even further. "You think you can come in here, throw all your money around like you own us? You haven't a clue about what your trash will do to us, do to this industry."

Brad spit at the last word, a few drops splattering onto Rachel's face. She dropped the charming smile for the really pissed off woman that she was. He'd said the one thing, the one thing she couldn't handle.

Trash.

That was the word had Daniel used. The word, for many years, she believed in.

"The only trash out there is those games that claim they have interactive, complex stories. And before you bash anything I've written, I suggest you sit down and learn to read first."

Brad growled, stepped forward and reached for her, but a hand landed on his shoulder, stopping him. Rachel breathed, relief coursing through her, but when she looked up, smiling her thanks, it wasn't Mark who'd saved her.

It wasn't even Nick.

It was Scott.

CHAPTER 31

*B*rad, I think you're quite finished here. Why don't you sit down and eat some of those olives you left in your glass? Get some food in you before you embarrass yourself and this company."

Brad towered over the skinny accountant, but apparently the realization that Scott was an owner was enough. Not enough to shut him up, but enough to get him to back down before Rachel had to put her new, comfortable shoes to some use.

Like kicking out and nailing the bastard in the crotch.

"The only person embarrassing the company is her," Brad muttered. But he went when Scott directed him towards the tables.

"I'm sorry about that, Rachel. As you know some people aren't happy with the project."

She'd gotten *that* message loud and clear. "Thank you. I didn't realize some people were this unhappy. Mark's mentioned some, but nothing like this."

She scanned the room, but the people had nearly doubled since she first walked in. She couldn't spot Mark's tall frame anywhere.

"Mark," Scott sneered.

The way Scott said his name made Rachel snap her attention back to him. Disgruntled, maybe? Unhappy?

Wary, she watched him, not sure what was going on. Scott had always been one of her biggest advocates. As soon as he saw the potential for this game, and the success (including the money it could make), he'd been on board.

So, why the sudden change?

Rachel was observant, an important quality in a writer. She might not know what made Scott look at her like this, but she knew something was going on.

"Yes, Mark," she said. "We talk. He's keeping me informed of Cupid's progress."

And the employees.

"I see. I didn't realize you two were still working so closely."

Rachel tucked a strand of hair behind her ear to buy time, to figure out what was going on.

"Yes, well, he's the CEO after all. You know, I'd love to put my coat down. Do you know where I'm sitting? Mark didn't have a chance to show me before he was pulled away."

Scott's face went blank.

She went on, "Mark's told me about the presentation, though he didn't go into details."

"Ah, yes, of course." Scott recovered, straightened his shirt, and smiled at her like nothing was wrong. She didn't believe it for a second. "Well, I can't give away any details myself, but I can show you to your seat."

Her answer about Mark and the 'time' they spent together was apparently enough to satisfy whatever was on Scott's mind, but when he offered his arm, she hesitated. She wasn't sure why, just she didn't want him touching her.

Again, there was that look from Scott, as if he noticed her hesitation.

Rachel felt someone step up behind her, their presence invading her space. Great. First Brad, then Scott and now... she glanced behind her and sighed.

Thank God, Mark had finally decided to show his face.

A face that didn't look too happy as he glanced from Rachel to Scott's offered arm. "Thanks, Scott, for looking out for Rachel. I got tied up back there. Any problems?"

This last he directed to her. She shook her head. It was easier then explaining just how many problems she was having right now. And easier to pretend she was just fine and would survive the evening.

Scott backed off as Mark claimed her arm. The thought 'claim' made her instantly look down at their arms. Sure enough, his right hand settled over her arm, practically trapping her to his side.

Her stomach swirled. Her fingers slightly tightened around his muscular arm, an arm without an ounce of excess fat. And my, Mark did look good in a suit.

Rachel blushed and looked away, only to see Scott still staring after her, his forehead creased. There was that look again.

"Have you been having any problems with Scott?"

She thought about the way he phrased it. "Not more than usual, why?"

"No reason, just wondering."

Rachel didn't buy it for a second. So there *had* been problems. Another part of his life he wasn't sharing with her? Probably. That seemed to be the foundation of their relationship.

Except, of course, they weren't in an actual relationship. So if he had secrets, he could keep them. It obviously wasn't any business of hers. The only thing of was her business was the game itself.

She could tell he wanted to ask more, ask what Scott wanted with her, but they were stopped by more employees and by the time Mark got himself free, they'd arrived at their table. A table that happened to have a perfect view of the Seattle skyline.

And the long, long drop down.

Rachel swallowed, gripped the chair as hard as she could and did her best not to look down. She settled for the next best thing, glaring at Mark.

"You did this on purpose."

He shrugged, but he smiled at her, playful. "I asked for the best seat in this house. How was I to know this was the spot?"

"I don't know, maybe something about the view," she growled.

Mark's smile grew. He touched her chin with his hands, a touch as playful as his smile. "I guess that means I don't need to worry about you running off in a rage. You'll be stuck with me. All night."

The idea of all night, the deepening of his voice, set her stomach into tap-dancing mode again. It was all she could do to sit in her chair, body and hands shaking at the thought of him touching her again.

At least this time her shaking wasn't from the height, but from Mark... and the promise she heard in his voice. She was supposed to be mad at him, supposed to still be holding a grudge for lying to her about the employees.

Apparently her brain and racing heart weren't on the same wavelength.

Mark settled in beside her, and because the table wasn't spacious meant they had to sit rather close. Quite close, actually, as in his legs brushing against hers the whole time.

The other two owners, Scott and Ethan, joined them. Neither had an actual date, like her or Nick, but they'd invited friends. Friends who she quickly dismissed as boring women who didn't know the first thing about games.

Nick was his usual, charming and engaging self with Mark right along with him. That was fine, it meant Rachel could lose her focus in the conversation and since she couldn't quite tear her mind away from Mark and how close he was, the way every brush of him sent a whole new wave of electricity racing from her feet to her head.

It was probably a good thing all she had to do was smile and nod.

When dinner ended, Rachel found herself again at Mark's side, but not in the same way she'd been earlier. Dessert had been served and everyone was finishing off the last of their cheesecake and crème Brule, when Mark stood. A waiter handed Mark the microphone. He twirled his fingers with hers and helped her stand.

"Mark, what's going on?"

Thankfully, he hadn't turned on the microphone yet.

"The announcement."

"I don't think you need me for this."

"Need you? Rachel, you're the star of the show."

"What?"

Her mouth fell open. She would have protested, would have ducked back to her seat, except Mark took that moment to welcome everyone.

And she realized where he'd stopped. Right in front of the glass windows framing the long, long drop. She clutched at his arm, mentally cursing and planning his painful death.

Already she could see the stares, the curious faces turning their way. Yes, this was what everyone had been waiting for.

Everyone except her.

She scanned the room until she found Brad, seated near the back, arms crossed over his chest. No, she wasn't looking forward to this in the slightest. Mark might think this was a good idea, but she had no idea how she could make it through this alive and in one piece.

Everyone wanted to know who she was, what involvement she had with the project, and she was sure quite a few were wondering what her relationship with Mark was.

Mark, finally, told them. Just not the last bit, the part she would have liked an answer to as well.

And how did he break the news?

By telling them the truth.

"Let me introduce, Rachel Clare, our investor and the creator of Project Cupid." He swept his arm towards her. "A project that has been heavily influenced by her work and if we play our cards right, a project that will not only send quite a few shock waves in the industry, but might make us all quite rich."

There was that 'rich' comment again.

Rachel stared at her brother, pleading for him to come and save her. But Nick remained sitting, not happy, but sitting.

He shook his head once. He wasn't going to bail her out. This was for her to deal with; this was the other half of their bet.

If she wanted to make this game, she had to prepare for the opposition she was going to face. Opposition like Brad.

Mark motioned to Karen, who turned on a short video for Project Cupid. Rachel blinked, not sure what to expect, then froze as the preliminary sketches and drawings flashed before her, and in the background, the commentary Mark had asked her to write... and to narrate.

She listened as her own voice explained the project, introduced the designers to their audience, and described the vast number of women simply waiting for someone to step up and give them a game worthy of them.

A game that took women seriously.

Her eyes filled with tears as the sweeping audio mirrored the character sketches, the artwork. This, this was her game. Her romance video game.

She was really doing it and just like Mark promised, it was everything she'd envisioned. He'd found a way to make her game, and a way to respect both her and all women out there.

Rachel tore her attention from the screen. Mark was watching her, lips tugging into a smile when he saw her tearing eyes.

"You did it," she whispered. "Why didn't you tell me?"

"I wanted it to be a surprise."

This, this was more than a surprise. It was more than she could have ever wanted. It was him, believing in her. Believing in her romance.

The video faded and Mark took Rachel's hand, holding her at arms' length.

"Rachel Clare is a number one New York Times bestselling writer, a writer whose decided it was time to make a game for women, a real game, and fund it herself if she had to—which she is." Mark added, his tone light.

This got a few chuckles from the crowd, but Rachel could barely hear over her thundering heart.

"You might ask what a 'real game for women' is." Mark nodded at the screen. "Well, that's it. A romance video game. A game being written by one of the top romance writers in the industry."

The chuckles and quiet laughter died.

Dead, awful silence filled the room.

Unless Rachel counted that hammering of her own heart. She was pretty sure the entire room could hear it as well.

She knew Mark expected this. After a bomb like that not even she expected sunshine and flowers. But this? This shocked silence?

At Mark's nod, Karen stepped away from her laptop. It was Karen who broke the silence, Karen who spoke to the crowd. Karen as a woman, as a reader of romance and she addressed all the women there.

"How many of you recognized Rachel when you saw her tonight?"

A few hands went up. All of them were women.

"How many of you recognized her name?"

More hands.

Karen put her own hands on her hips. "Come on, men. I know you've gone grocery shopping before. How many of you walked by the book aisle and saw her name? Or better yet, how many of your mothers read her books at the family barbecue or at Christmas dinner?"

This time, several men reluctantly raised their hands.

Rachel let out a breath she hadn't realized she was holding.

Mark squeezed her hand, reassurance she knew, but she didn't feel it. She felt like she was in that awful dream standing naked in front of her classmates.

And wasn't she?

Wasn't she standing here naked, baring the truth of who she was to these people? People who were already judging her, people who'd never heard of her, who'd never read a romance?

"Now," Mark said, "let me you show you *why* FastPlay is taking a chance on this kind of game. Remember that 'getting rich' part I mentioned earlier?"

Mark didn't let her escape to her seat like she wanted. He kept her at his side as he flipped through the slides, explaining to his company, his employees, what he was doing, why he was making this game.

She saw the numbers sinking in, saw their jaws slowly loosening, dropping. But the part that made her smile, that sent a thrill through her was the women.

The pure excitement in their faces. This game, *her* game, was for them. Everything she did, even standing up here bare-butt naked, was for them.

Rachel scrounged for the last of her confidence and managed a true smile since Mark had yanked her up here. This was her game and they were actually doing it. Mark was convincing his company *this* game could only be made by them.

Even as she smiled, he tugged at her hand and she couldn't help but wonder, did he finally believe? Did he believe in what he was saying?

Did he believe in her game?

Did he believe in her?

She squeezed his hand back, wanting to share her joy—share their joy and their success as people stood up, asking questions.

Questions that were going quite well, including the comment about everyone attending who had needed to sign a non-disclosure statement before being admitted inside.

"Secrets reign supreme in this industry and this game most of all," Mark said, all easy smile and charm. "I'm sure you can understand why."

From the corner of her eye, Rachel saw movement. Someone standing.

Brad.

She turned to warn Mark, to direct him towards the danger, but he didn't catch her look. He gestured for Brad to speak and Rachel's stomach plummeted.

Brad's voice boomed across the room. "What you mean to say, is do we all understand what this trash will do to our name? To this company?"

CHAPTER 32

$\mathcal{M}$ ark kept his smile on even though he wanted to reach out and wring Brad's neck. Already he felt the mood in the room shift, nurturing the discontent, the worries and fear he knew everyone had felt when they'd heard the words 'romance video game.'

Karen had warned him, had told him the kind of trouble Brad was stirring up. Why hadn't he listened? Why hadn't he gotten rid of Brad?

Everyone turned towards Brad, who stomped his way to the front. Yes, he definitely wanted everyone to see him, to hear him.

"Romance," Brad spat, "doesn't belong in our industry. It'll never sell and we'll be run out. Laughed at the second someone hears about our game, when they see this trash listed on our resume." He pointed a finger at Mark. "You and that woman will destroy all of our careers."

Mark knew why he hadn't fired Brad. Knew why he'd kept Brad on the team. Deep down, Mark agreed with him. On some level, Mark still fought with those very words Brad now spoke. Brad didn't believe in this game, didn't believe in what Rachel was trying to accomplish.

Mark didn't know if Cupid would mean the beginning of the end for his company. He didn't know if they released Cupid if they'd be black-listed in the industry.

Brad's finger swerved towards Rachel, the sudden motion making him sway. "That's why you don't want us leaking the information because you know damn well what it'll do to us."

Beside him, Rachel stiffened. She slowly untangled her fingers from Mark's hand, as if she could sense his doubts. Her head lifted, staring at each person in the room, challenging them to speak up.

"You're not the first person to feel this way about romance novels, about the genre I write in," she said coolly. She didn't look at Mark, or even at Brad "And you won't be the last."

How many times, Mark wondered, had she heard this argument, heard that romance novels were trash, were insignificant and weren't worth the paper they were printed on? Not even worth the non-paper of electronic books?

Rachel moved away from Mark, her dress catching the dim lighting making her seem taller, seem otherworldly. Everyone's gaze drew towards her, to her flaming red hair and her temper... a temper that had drawn him towards her since their first meeting.

Rachel's gaze swung towards the women in the room. "Ladies. Quite a few of you have read my books and if not mine, another author's *romance* novel. 'Trash' as so many people call them. Not a novel at all."

She set her hands on her hips, and even though Mark couldn't see Rachel's expression, from the sudden blank look on Brad's face, Mark was sure he'd just been given Rachel's death-glare.

A glare Mark knew all too well.

"Congratulations, Brad. You've just insulted every woman in this room. I hope you didn't bring a date because she might not be too happy with you either."

But Rachel wasn't finished, even when Brad's face paled. This time, she swung her glare at the rest of the room.

"None of you men have to respect my books. None of you have to respect *me*, but you damn well better respect the women in your lives because I highly doubt they'll stand for your arrogant attitudes much longer."

Mark eased down from his spot by the projector screen. Even

from here he could hear the spark in Rachel's voice, the temper she really was going to let loose unless he got her out of there.

Rachel turned, as if sensing him and he froze. Now the death glare was aimed directly at him.

"And they *shouldn't* stand for it," Rachel snapped. "Not any longer. This isn't about you, or your so-called 'respectable' game titles. This game is about *them.* So buck up, boys, grow some balls, and make a game that was meant for them."

Rachel didn't wait for the crowd's reaction as she headed toward the elevators, didn't wait to see the shocked faces slowly melting into surprise mixed with admiration.

Nor did she see every woman in the room stand up and clap.

She didn't see, but Mark knew she heard. Her steps faltered as the first claps started, then louder as more joined in. As the men stood up, clapped as well, joining with their wives and girlfriends.

That was when he realized she didn't need him to fight this battle. He wanted to be at her side, to defend her against Brad's accusations—even when his own thoughts were so conflicted. He still wanted to be with her, to support her.

But she didn't need a hero, not like the ones she wrote about. She was her own hero, had been for a long time.

The realization bothered him, but not enough to quit. Not enough to pack up and toss the towel in because damn it, he had some balls and he was going to show that proud, courageous woman what she'd done to him.

Which was turn everything he believed in on its head.

No, he didn't know what this game would do to his company, or what the inevitable outcome would be, but he still wanted—no *needed* her by his side.

Mark stormed after her.

Nick caught up to him and had just enough time to pass over Rachel's purse. "Take care of her. I'll make sure her car gets home and the dog's fed."

At least, that's what Mark thought Nick said.

For all he knew, he could very well have warned Mark that if he touched his sister he would die.

Mark didn't give a shit.

He caught up to Rachel right as she was getting on the elevator—by herself. She looked up, glared at him, and punched the 'down' button. The doors closed shut. Mark gave himself enough time to curse, then rounded on a waiter popping out of a nearby door.

"Stairs?"

The waiter jerked around at Mark's bark and pointed behind him. Mark took the stairs two at a time. He tripped on the cement steps, his dress shoes not meant for running, especially running after a pissed off Rachel. He reached the ground floor just as she did.

Rachel stepped out of the elevator, face slightly pale from the ride down, and he shoved her back inside.

"What are you—"

"You think you can run out on me like that?" he roared.

"I'm not *running*, I'm *leaving* your terrible party. I've heard enough of that shit to last me a lifetime and I'm—"

The elevator doors slid closed behind them. She scowled and tried to shove him aside. "Will you move? I need to go."

"Damn it, Rachel. You're not going anywhere unless it's with me."

He grabbed her and yanked her to him. She fell against him, losing her balance. He wrapped his arms around her, holding her close so she would understand he meant it. She couldn't leave. Not without him.

Mark held her with everything he had, and then when she lifted her head to yell at him with everything she had, he kissed her. He kissed her with all the words he couldn't yet say.

Words he didn't know he wanted to say.

But the kiss? Yes, he said everything with the kiss. A kiss that ignited every inch of his body, a body he pressed against hers, showing her his need.

He needed her. Needed her in his life and needed her to yell at him until he believed in this game.

He couldn't do it alone; couldn't do any of it without her.

His kiss was relentless and he didn't let up until she softened against him, until her arms circled around his neck. Accepting his need. Wanting his need in return.

She moaned against his lips. Rubbed her body against his. Shit, he could practically feel her heat through the silk dress. A wanting heat, a heat begging him to finish this.

Mark broke away. Rachel stared up at him, eyes glazed, but still just as sharp as always. He was pleased to see her ragged breathing matched his. Very pleased indeed.

"Rachel," he whispered against her lips. "Come home with me."

Come home with him. Stay there. Never leave.

"I..." her voice trailed off.

The elevator doors dinged open. An elderly couple stood there, tickets in hand. They were clearly going up to the top, to the Space Needle, and the last thing they expected was Rachel pressed against the elevator wall, one leg wrapped around Mark's leg.

Mark glanced down even as Rachel scrambled away. When did she put that there?

"Umm, sorry," she muttered, straightening her dress he'd somehow hiked higher up her hips. "Please excuse us."

The older man blinked, then gave Mark a big grin. One of his front teeth was missing. "Don't mind at all, if I dare say."

"You dare not." The older lady slapped his arm.

Mark gave them both a grin, told them to enjoy their own ride up since it was such a romantic evening. He also kept a firm hold on Rachel so she didn't bolt.

Knowing her, and knowing that seemed to happen every time they had a mind-blowing kiss, she would try to. She didn't disappoint.

She also hadn't thought about her 'escape' very well because the second the cold air hit her she froze, wrapping her arms around her bare, smooth arms. "My purse, my jacket. I forgot them. I have to go back up and—"

"Purse is here."

She snatched it from Mark and rifled through the contents. "Where's my ticket?"

"Nick's taking your car home. He's also gonna feed the dog."

Her teeth chattered and her entire body, from her arms to the curve of her breasts just visible above the top of her dress were covered in goose bumps. "Nick. And what, what about me?"

"I thought I told you." He shrugged out of his jacket, plopping it on her shoulders. "You're coming home with me. No more running, Rachel. No more stopping this."

He wouldn't let her run. Not this time.

He just hoped when she decided to run it would be into his arms and not away from him. There was only one way to find out.

The valet pulled up his comfortable, reliable Civic, and Mark opened the door for her. "You coming?"

CHAPTER 33

To say this was bad on so many levels was an understatement, a giant understatement. Of course, that did nothing to answer the question of why she was still here.

Mark came out of the kitchen, two glasses of red wine in his hands, but it was his shirt, with the first two buttons undone that might be part of the reason why she'd hadn't already left. Two undone buttons revealing the tiniest glimpse of skin, of the hard muscles she'd briefly touched.

Muscles she wanted to taste, to run her tongue down. Rachel dropped her head, deciding her fingers looked very interesting at the moment.

This was why her being here was such a bad idea.

Yes, she wanted to sleep with him, badly, but plain old physical attraction wasn't causing her to blush or her sudden uncertainty. No, whatever was causing this reaction was something more, something she wasn't ready to accept.

"Here."

He offered her a glass, his fingers brushing hers.

She shivered at the touch, at the promise he was passing on to her.

She glanced up. His eyes had darkened again. They only did that when he was either mad at her or when he wanted her.

Mark was doing nothing to hide his attraction, as if he wanted her to know, wanted her to see.

"Mark." Rachel's breath came out in a short, jagged gasp. "This, this isn't a good idea."

She said the words she'd been thinking the second she'd stepped outside the Space Needle, the cold slicing through her silky dress and through her raging hormones. It parted the haze surrounding her, a haze which appeared whenever this man came near her.

"Why not?"

He slid onto the couch beside her, a couch that suddenly felt much smaller than it was. He filled the room, filled her senses until there was nothing left but him.

She laughed, or tried to. It sounded more like a dying croak. "Pick a reason. We're business partners. I'm funding this game."

She couldn't believe she'd known him for this long already, that he'd been in her life, and she'd managed to keep him at arms' length. Or herself at arms' length.

They seemed to trade off in that department, depending on their moods.

But now there was nothing arms' length about Mark. Instead, he set his glass on the coffee table, pulling her closer to him.

She wanted to resist, because resistance would be the sensible thing to do. But the way he looked at her, the way she hummed in anticipation, waiting for the kiss she knew was coming.

Waiting for what came after the kiss.

"You still haven't given me a good reason." Mark's hands brushed her cheek and she moaned at the touch, arching her head closer. "Rachel. You have no idea what you do to me."

She opened her eyes, not sure when she'd even closed them. She felt the haze surrounding her, but they needed to talk about this. She needed to know where he stood before this went any further.

"I can feel very well what I do to you, but we still need to talk about this. Mark. There's a reason we haven't..."

"You mean, why we haven't slept together yet?"

She nodded, feeling relief he'd said it for her. It was one thing for her to believe they had this attraction from the beginning, it was another to actually say it aloud. She could have been wrong.

Or worse, she could be the only one feeling... whatever this was between them. But it was more than just attraction. She knew it with a certainty that terrified her.

Mark slid her closer and she sucked in a breath when she felt his hardness pressing against her thigh. Okay. She was definitely not wrong; he was very, very attracted to her.

"We haven't slept together because we've somehow managed to keep our heads on whenever things got too heated." He nuzzled her neck. "But I think I'm done keeping my head on straight when it comes to you."

"And the business? The relationship, I mean?"

Relationship.

Rachel's eyes closed at the word. For a moment, fear rolled through her so sudden and so strong she couldn't move. She hadn't just meant the business relationship, but the personal one.

The one she hadn't allowed herself to have since Daniel; the one she *couldn't* have.

"We keep them separate." He trailed kisses down her neck, each one reaching lower and lower. He plucked the glass from her hands.

She'd forgotten she'd even been holding it.

"Mark." She gasped as he tugged the strap of her dress lower with his teeth. "There has never been anything separate about this relationship, business or otherwise."

It wasn't what she'd wanted to say, but she couldn't make herself say the other part. The need to trust him tugged at her, scared her more than what might happen with their business relationship if their personal one didn't work out.

Business was one thing. Her heart was another.

She was scared shitless.

He grinned at her. "Guess it's a lost cause, keeping the two separate, huh? And maybe we shouldn't bother. Seriously, though.

Watching you tonight, standing down a roomful of men who hated everything you stand for, everything you are. I've got no worries about your ability to stand up to me, Rachel. If this doesn't work out, if things go south, you'll grab me by my balls and make me listen to reason."

His hand caressed her cheek again, sending another hundred tingles rushing through her. "Just like you've been doing since I met you."

She felt the truth of his words, but she felt more. Felt what he wasn't saying. That was the part making her chest tighten, making her blink back tears. Scared her.

Mark respected her writing and what she did for a living.

He respected her.

"How do you know this won't end badly?"

She was stalling, she knew that, but with her head in such a whirl she couldn't think straight, couldn't see past the haze he clouded her with.

Mark brushed aside a tear with his thumb. "I don't. I also don't know if this is a good idea, but I must have gotten all these empowering thoughts from your books. I'm not going to walk away because it's safer, because it's the smart thing to do, just because something might go wrong."

"Those books are about make-believe people falling in love, not real life people dealing with a business partnership."

His eyes darkened even further, if that was possible. "And who says we aren't?"

Rachel's breath caught. Her whole body froze, both in fear and excitement as her stomach rolled at the thought, at the possibility. Mark's lips brushed hers and paused. Waiting for her, waiting for her decision.

His words changed everything.

The promise, the possibility in his words. Somehow, she'd known this had never just been about sex or attraction, not with them.

That was what made her hand shake as she gently touched his cheek. Shaking both from excitement and fear.

Mark waited, giving her the chance to say no. But was that what she wanted? Did she want to trust him with herself, now and every day? Did she want to see where their story ended, even if there was no guarantee of a happily-ever-after?

Rachel lifted an arm around his neck, pulling him closer. She wouldn't let fear control her life. Not anymore. Not when she had so much to gain from standing up and following her heart, regardless of where it might lead her.

"Maybe it's time I took my own advice."

Mark smiled against her lips. "Is that right? Which advice is that? You gave out quite a bit tonight."

"The part about growing some balls."

Mark chuckled, his breath tickling her lips, her throat. "You may not have a physical pair of your own, which is a good thing, but trust me, you've definitely got a set."

Rachel couldn't help her fingers sliding down his chest, sliding lower . Yes, he did have quite a pair himself. The second her fingers brushed him through the fabric of his pants, Mark groaned, low and throaty.

"Enough, Rachel. Please."

She stroked him again, putting a little more pressure. Mark's groan turned into a growl. He swept her into his arms in one movement, cradled her close as his mouth descended on hers, as he kissed her, devoured her.

Rachel tugged at his shirt, fumbling with buttons. Too many clothes. Too much separating them. No more waiting.

She needed this man, needed him inside her.

Needed him in her life.

Mark practically carried her as they stumbled to the bedroom. He somehow managed to open the door without letting her go until he finally slid her onto his bed. He followed right behind, pressed his body against hers.

Rachel arched up, the heat within her growing at his touch. A touch that still wasn't enough. She needed more.

She grabbed at his shirt. She didn't bother with the buttons. The ones left unbuttoned scattering to the floor, followed quickly by the shirt, as Mark tossed it shirt over his shoulder.

Rachel leaned back, taking in the sight of him, the defined abs she'd known were there. But knowing and seeing were two completely different sensations.

She ran her fingers up and down his chest. Touching him, feeling every inch of him. Then she did the same with her lips and tongue, following the same path. Meanwhile Mark knelt there, waiting for her to finish, eyes closed.

"Enough. It's my turn."

He kissed her, pulling her back to the bed. Then it was his turn to trail kisses down her neck, down her arms. He unzipped her dress, sliding the straps down and then the rest over her hips, over her legs.

His hands, caressing her through the silk, made it even more electrifying. A touch which had her humming in anticipation, wanting more. It had been so long, so incredibly long since she'd felt this way.

Since she'd let anyone this close.

"You're beautiful," he murmured. "And your legs..."

He kissed her from her knees all the way up her thighs, slowly trailing closer to the one place she wanted him to touch, the one place that would relieve this sudden aching need.

"Your legs, a mile long. They're exactly what I'd imagined they'd look like." He unclasped her bra, making her wait as he paid the same attention to her breasts. First one, and then the other.

It was glorious, every second, every moment with him burning itself into her heart. She felt herself building, higher and higher. She wanted him close, wanted him in her arms.

Wanted *him.*

Rachel yanked his head to her and kissed him, showed him just how much she needed him. Mark answered her kiss in return, pressing his bulging pants against her bare legs.

"No more waiting, Mark."

She needed this, needed him.

Mark broke away, breathing hard. Their gazes met. There was no going back. Rachel didn't want to go back. She wanted to go forward, running forward, running to see where this led.

She wanted to trust herself with him and she did.

She slid his pants down his long, lean legs, then dragged his boxers down to his ankles, where he kicked them off. He returned the favor, peeling off her lacy black underwear until they finally rested against each other, skin to skin. Nothing separating them, nothing but each other and this choice. Their choice.

Mark held her gaze. Fear held her for a moment, and then she shoved it aside. She would do this, she would trust him.

How could she not? Especially when the more she was with him, the more she realized it was already too late.

She was already falling in love with him.

Just like in her books.

Rachel lifted her lips and slowly kissed him, then she guided him to her, into her. She forgot all about fear.

Instead, she remembered what it was like to love, and to be loved in return.

CHAPTER 34

Sunlight spilled over the bed and Rachel blinked. She rolled over, burying her head under the pillow. Definitely wasn't time to wake up yet.

Except the pillow wasn't as fluffy as usual. Nor, she realized, did she have navy blue pillow covers.

Realization dawned slowly. This wasn't her usual pillow. This was *Mark's* pillow. His pillow because she'd spent the night.

Rachel smiled even though it was too early and she really should go back to sleep. Every inch of her felt wonderful, relaxed and... alive.

Yes, 'alive' was the right word. For the first time in a long time she felt alive, happy.

She also really needed to pee.

Mark's side of the bed was empty, but she heard him shuffling around in the kitchen. No matter, she'd rather empty her bladder in privacy. She also saw he'd left her a towel in the bathroom, a towel that matched his bedspread.

Rachel fingered the towel, not caring she was standing on the cold tile completely naked with goose bumps covering every inch of her. His thoughtfulness touched her in almost the same way he'd touched her last night. It was the little things that made her smile, made her heart twist in excitement.

She didn't take a long shower. She simply washed her hair with his shampoo and conditioner, then dug around in the cabinet until she found a spare toothbrush. By the time she came out, red hair still damp, Mark had fresh coffee brewed, right alongside a generous helping of bacon and eggs.

When she slid into the bar stool chair, he paused, mid-turning of the bacon, and stared at her. Probably because the only thing she had on was one of his shirts. A shirt that did nothing to hide her bare, mile-long legs as he called them.

"You know, I was going to suggest something along the lines of, 'Rachel, you should bring some clothes and leave them over if you like.' But now, I'm thinking *hell no*. You can't have any of my drawers."

"Is that right?" She smiled, slow and luxurious at the very thought. He already wanted to offer her space.

Rachel yawned, her body reminding her that while this was cute and fun, she needed coffee. She wiggled her toes to get Mark's attention. "So what does a girl have to do to get some coffee around here?"

"Other than head back to the bedroom with me?"

"But the bacon would burn."

"Honey, I can always make more bacon." He grinned as he pulled out a cup.

Mark didn't burn the bacon. In fact both the bacon and eggs were fantastic. It surprised her, though she wasn't sure why. "I didn't realize you could cook."

"I haven't exactly had you over lately."

"No, I guess not." They had both been too busy hiding from each other, hiding from this attraction. "And I guess that'll be changing?"

She hated the slight tilt to her voice, the slight quiver of uncertainty.

Mark leaned across the kitchen table, gently touching her cheek. "I truly hope so. And to be fair," he pulled away, "I don't normally have a lot of time for cooking. There are still plenty of times where I don't even come home to sleep, let alone cook or eat."

She ate another slice of bacon. "So, you can now? Time, I mean. Shouldn't you be at the office?"

Mark snorted, grabbing another helping of bacon for himself. "I'll get in when I get in. You think I'm going to rush out on a half-naked, wet-haired woman who's only wearing my shirt? Hell, no. Especially when I'm the guy in charge."

That, she thought, was a very good thing because she didn't want to rush out. She wanted to sit here, to enjoy the morning with him.

Even better was the relaxed air between them, even though they'd put a damper on their attraction after last night (yes, more than once), it was still there, still humming between them. But now she could focus on him and realized there was so much she didn't know.

Like Mark knowing how to make bacon without actually burning it or under cooking it. She smiled at the thought, realizing how much she enjoyed learning something new about him.

Mark slid the newspaper towards her. "Oh, I wanted to tell you, you made the *Times* list again."

She blinked at the newspaper, not quite sure what he was talking about. "The *Times?*"

"You know, the list. The big all important 'New York Times Best-seller' list? I thought that was something you writers cared about."

Sure enough, there was Rachel's latest book, *High Mountain*. It was rated number one. "Oh. I'd forgotten that one was out already."

Mark blinked at her. "Forgotten? Isn't this important to you? I mean if not this," he gestured at the newspaper, "then at least knowing when your book is actually being released?"

It took her a moment to realize they were looking at this from two, very different perspectives. "Let me put it this way," she said. "How many games do you release in a year?"

"In a year? We sometimes go two to three years between releases. It takes a long time to make a game."

She nodded. "Well, I release quite a bit more. Per year. Anywhere from five books to ten. That's how quickly I write. When you have that many books coming out, all the time, you just sort of forget about one you wrote a year or two ago because that's how long it takes from me turning in a finished novel to seeing it on the shelf."

Mark glanced at the newspaper, then back at her, shaking his head. "So that book you just finished… it won't be released for two years?"

Rachel nodded. "Something like that."

Mark raised his eyebrows. "We really are in two different industries. Doesn't your agent or whatever call and remind you of these things?"

"I don't have an agent. I have an attorney." Rachel took a long, glorious sip of her coffee, then added a tad bit more creamer. Mark liked his a little blacker than her.

"No agent." There was that dumbfounded look on his face again.

"I guess there's a lot we're still learning about each other."

"I guess so."

But Mark didn't seem bothered by this, merely circled his arms around her waist, pulling her closer so he could have his first, long morning kiss.

"And I can't wait to see what I learn next."

Neither could she.

And she was all for learning more about Mark, but not in the evening gown she'd worn the night before, especially when he mentioned she should come into work with him.

Today.

"What?" she said again, not sure he'd heard her right.

Mark was buttoning up a shirt and she was momentarily distracted from the vision of his chest—a vision she'd had another chance to get up close with after breakfast.

He stood barefoot in the bedroom, jeans fitting snugly on him while Rachel stood in his shirt—and no pants.

"The office. I think it's important if you came in today. A ton of people are going to want to meet you, ask questions. It'll help smooth things over."

Yes, this was a rational, smart business move but this still didn't fix her problem.

"And what about my clothes?"

He grinned, getting another nice eyeful of her legs. "I guess we have to run to your place real quick."

"Unless you want your whole company getting a nice, long look at my legs, I'd say that's a very good idea."

And it had been a good idea, especially since Allie nearly ran her over in excitement as they walked through the door. Nick might have fed her, but Allie clearly needed more 'me' time than just a bowl full of food.

Mark offered to take her outside while Rachel changed. He and the dog raced out the front door and Mark barely remembered to grab Allie's leash.

Rachel shook her head, a smile on her face. She'd not only gotten lucky with the perfect dog, but seemed to find the perfect man to go with the dog. That was a rare find indeed.

She slipped out of her evening dress, hanging it so she could take it to the cleaners. She changed with a quick efficiency, not knowing how long Mark would be gone and not wanting to keep him waiting.

Her voicemail blinked red, and since Mark and Allie still weren't back, she pulled out a notepad and hit 'play.'

"Hi, Rache."

The pen slipped from her fingers.

Daniel.

Daniel was calling her.

"Surprise, I know. Didn't think to hear from me, did you? Look, I was just reading the paper this morning and right there was your name. I just wanted to call and wish you congratulations. Knowing you, you probably don't even know what I'm congratulating you for. You made the *Times* bestseller list again."

Rachel deleted the message before Daniel finished. "I don't need your congratulations. I haven't needed it for years."

Her stomach rolled, tightened. She did not need his congratulations, especially when the only thing he ever called her about was her success—and the money he knew came with it.

Well, she was done—absolutely done—with him.

The front door opened and Allie bounded back inside, rushing over to show Rachel the fun she'd had on the short walk. Mark stood framed in the doorway, his smile slipping as he noticed her tense posture.

"Rachel? Everything okay?"

"Yes." She put the notepad away. "Everything's fine. Just a call I hadn't expected."

Or wanted.

"A publisher? Book deal gone bad?"

"Nope, nothing that serious. Just my ex-wanting to cash in on another successful novel." She kept her tone light, but....

Mark's eyebrows lifted. She'd known he'd be curious, known that mentioning Daniel would open a whole new gate of questions. Questions Mark deserved answers to.

But they were also questions that would rip a big, giant hole in her happiness and so far, this had been the best morning she'd had in years. She wasn't about to let Daniel take that away from her, too.

She held out her hand, which Mark took. "We're late. I promise I'll tell you all about Daniel and how he nearly destroyed my writing, but not now."

Mark searched her face. "Is this going to be a problem?"

She shook her head. "He's been out of my life for years. I don't even want the memories of him to ruin this."

Mark nodded, but she could tell he was only letting the matter drop for now. He'd bring it up again, and that was fine. There was nothing about Daniel she wanted to hide, but there were parts of her still healing, still mending.

Especially like the part about her falling in love again. That was definitely a conversation she wanted to take slowly.

CHAPTER 35

Mark watched as Rachel heard the message. Saw her stiffen. Even from where he stood at the door, he could see she was upset. Allie thumped over, as if sensing Rachel's distress as well, and nudged Rachel's hand with her giant head.

Mark took all this in at a glance. He wanted to fold his arms around her, to hold her close. To tell her what he thought of her writing, of the successes she'd made of her life.

He didn't.

Her words, clipped and tight when she mentioned Daniel, told him she didn't want to be held, didn't want to be protected. So, he stepped back and forced himself to stand there and let the dog comfort Rachel.

The ex, Daniel, might be out of the picture, but he wasn't entirely. Even now, he still dug his claws into Rachel, emotional claws as well as the controlling ones.

It didn't take a huge leap to realize a huge part of Rachel's stubbornness, as well as her insecurity about her writing, came from that asshole.

Mark would give her space, though, give her distance. But at some point she'd have to let him in. Have to let him comfort her.

He couldn't do that unless she wanted his comfort. He'd hoped after last night, after trusting him to take her home, she would want that. But sex was still only sex. Great sex sure, but it wasn't what had made the night amazing for him.

It was the look in her eyes, a look he knew mirrored his own. He hoped it had been more than sex for her, because he had a feeling it had been more for him.

Also, he couldn't help the good feeling when they walked into Rachel's large, spacious and damn-clean garage, and saw that Rachel's car was missing.

Well, not missing, exactly. Just that Nick hadn't returned it yet.

Which meant Mark got to keep Rachel close.

"Where is my car?" Rachel glared at her garage, hands on her hips as she tapped those pink heels he admired so much. "You said Nick was bringing it home."

"I did. He just didn't say *when*," Mark said with a grin. "Give him a break, Rachel. I mean, you drive a Corvette. If you let me drive your car I'd take that thing for a nice, long ride."

"Well, you can't drive my car. Ever. And I didn't say Nick could, either."

Before she realized Mark was the reason she didn't have her car, he had ushered her into his unshowy Civic. By the time they reached the office, she'd stopped complaining. Instead, she sat there quietly, fingering her purse, a worried expression on her face.

Was she thinking about Daniel? Mark wanted to ask, but kept his mouth shut. They'd have that conversation in due time, when she was ready. They had enough to deal with right now anyway, mostly convincing his gamer employees management wasn't totally cracked about this romance game idea.

Mark pulled into his reserved spot in the garage, turned off the engine, and gave her a long look. She'd composed herself on the drive. Whatever demons Daniel had awakened were safely tucked away— tucked away so deep not even Mark could see them.

He didn't like that. He wanted her to trust him, to even trust him with her demons.

"You ready for this?" he asked.

"After last night, I think I'm ready for anything."

So was he. A good thing, really, because when they entered the office, they got the whole gambit of reactions—all the way from excitement to near-mutiny. Actually, Mark was surprised Brad had even shown up for work and hadn't slid his resume under the door.

Then again, it could still be there.

He held Rachel's hand, nodding to his employees, waited while a few introduced themselves to Rachel. Quite a few women, actually, and more than a handful of men.

Men who also glanced down at his and Rachel's intertwined hands, took the hint, and backed off.

That's right boys, Rachel is taken.

This was how Scott found them: Rachel meeting many of the employees she'd met last night while Mark lingered at her side, hand resting casually on her hip. Scott's glasses slipped down his nose as he dropped his gaze to Mark's hand, then back up at Mark.

If the dark circles under his eyes were any hint, Scott had had a late night. Not an enjoyable one for sure, unlike the festivities he and Rachel had enjoyed.

"Scott. Anything I can do for you?"

Scott straightened, his tie suddenly making him more bookish, more accountant-like and not an equal owner in a video game company. "A meeting, right now, with Ethan and I. Rachel should come, too."

Scott spun on his banker shoes so fast, they squeaked on the hardwood floors. Mark didn't have a chance to ask what this surprise meeting was about. Rachel gave him a confused look, but he merely shook his head.

"I don't know, but we're about to find out."

"It's been my experience surprise meetings are never a good thing."

Too bad for both of them Rachel was right.

Ethan and Scott waited in the conference room. Ethan hunched over the table, blinking sleepily when he saw Mark. Meanwhile Scott paced up and down the room.

"Long night, Ethan?" Mark asked as he pulled out a chair for Rachel.

"A good night." Ethan gave an undisguised look at Rachel. "How 'bout you?"

"An excellent night."

Instead of lighting the mood as Mark had intended, it instead sent Scott sputtering as he stopped his pacing and slammed the door shut.

"Something wrong?" Mark sank into the chair beside Rachel. He fought the urge to drape his arm around her because he had a feeling *this* was the reason Scott was so furious.

"What do you think you're doing? You and her!"

Scott thrust his bony finger at Mark, then at Rachel. "You're together aren't you? That's where you went last night, leaving Ethan and I to deal with Brad and the problems he caused."

"I didn't really think where I went or with whom was any of your business."

"Well it is!" Scott slapped his hands on the table, jerking Ethan upright. "It is because she's our investor."

Rachel crossed her long legs. And as much as Mark hated to admit it, his gaze did stray to marvel and appreciate those legs. Damn. She really knew how to draw the eye. Perhaps that was the point, since Mark noticed that was where Scott's attention was suddenly transfixed as well.

"So," Rachel said, "it's *your* business if I sleep with someone in your company?"

Scott blinked, still not all there yet. "Yes, of course it is. Anything that would threaten the contract—"

"The contract," she went on, "has several termination clauses which must be met. Me having a disagreement with someone I sleep with is not listed in those clauses and therefore is not a viable reason for me to withdraw from my end of the agreement."

"This is still highly unethical," Scott stammered. "This whole project is at stake now because Mark can't keep his hands to himself."

Ethan yawned, still sleepy but definitely coming to. Scott's shrieks tended to have that effect on people. "Oh, *please*. Even I knew this was going to happen."

For a moment, there was quite the silence in the room.

"You knew, huh?" Mark draped his arm over the back of Rachel's chair, but instead of leaning in to rest her head against his shoulder like she'd done last night, she gently turned her chair away from him. Turned it so she could face Ethan.

"Please," Ethan said. "The sparks flying between you two have been obvious since our first meeting." He looked at Scott. "It would have been obvious to you too if you'd been paying attention."

"That's not the point!" Scott blustered.

"As far as I'm concerned it is." Ethan stood, dragging his coffee mug with him. "I voted for this deal knowing there was a relationship possibility and I expect both of you to handle yourselves profession-ally. Especially if the personal side doesn't work out."

Mark knew he would. As much as he didn't want to make this game, or still didn't fully believe in it, he'd signed the contract. That means he'd see this through to the end, regardless of what happened— with the company or with this relationship.

Rachel nodded. "I want to make Cupid. I wouldn't be funding it and fighting this ridiculous battle if I wasn't serious."

She gave both Ethan, then Scott, and finally Mark a long stare. "I plan on seeing this through to the end."

Mark thought this would make him happy. After all, she was putting the game first above all else. It was no different than his own thoughts—in fact, nearly the exact same thing, word for word.

They'd see this game to the end, no matter what.

But it didn't explain why he suddenly wanted to look away from her, to not see that intense, focused gaze, or the chair no longer resting beside his.

Maybe because their relationship was in second place, while the first prize—the main prize—was still on the horizon.

Cupid.

Rachel's game.

Which was silly. They hadn't known each other very long and this was what he wanted—what was best for the company. They'd make this game and whenever they were together in a professional capacity, they'd act as if nothing had changed between them.

And he was fine with that. Right?

Mark didn't have much time to think more about his and Rachel's relationship, not when the second they stepped out of the conference room they were put to work.

As Rachel had stated, the game came first, and right now he had a whole heck of a lot to take care of. Even if the revealing of Project 'Cupid' to the team had been a success, there was still a ton of work to do, especially now that the game was in full production.

And, first things first, he dealt quickly and efficiently with Brad's mutiny, firing him for cause, especially after Brad again verbally attacked Rachel and the 'trash' she wrote for a living. Rachel kept her distance after that confrontation. She distanced herself from everyone, including him. He didn't know exactly why, but he understood the reaction and let her be.

At least Scott kept his distance from both Mark and Rachel.

Not to mention, the calls from Forged Legends had finally died down. All in all, the game was slowly moving from 'headache' to only a mild annoyance.

It still wasn't Mark's game, still wasn't the game he or most of the employees wanted to work on, but it was the game deal they'd been handed.

For better or for worse, FastPlay Games was making a romance video game. The only questions now were if whether or not they could do it, and if Mark would survive the project.

When Rachel kissed him on the cheek, telling him she had to get back to her book, he knew his chances of surviving had improved radically. Especially when he saw her excitement as her project came alive before her eyes.

This game might not be for him, but they really were making the right kind of game for a whole, brand new audience. And that, he knew was worth it.

CHAPTER 36

To say Cupid wasn't running smoothly would be the giant understatement of the year. Even after a full year of pre and full-on production.

Granted, Mark had expected this. What he hadn't expected was the continued disgruntlement of his staff.

Or his co-owners. Specifically, Scott.

Mark leaned back in his chair, keeping in his groan when Scott stomped into his office and shut the door. 'Shut' was a nice word. Slammed would be more accurate.

At least Mark wasn't on the phone.

"You've got to talk with her," Scott snapped.

"And you need to be more specific than that. I do *talk* with her. On a regular basis, actually."

Mark's causal reference to his and Rachel's relationship—whatever kind of relationship that was (Mark was still working that out—even after a full six months of them having a fantastic relationship, in bed and in the office)—got Scott in a huffy temper. He spent another whole five seconds straightening his tie, glaring at Mark, then at the floor.

"Yes, I know you speak with her. That's part of this whole problem.

I just got off the phone with Rachel and she's still questioning our decision to keep Cupid a secret."

Ahh, Mark thought, this was why Scott wasn't pleased. "I'll talk with her."

"You need too. Right away. She doesn't understand and I wouldn't be surprised if she went and did something foolish."

"Rachel isn't going to do anything. I'll talk with her, okay?"

This appeased Scott enough that he actually left Mark's office without bringing up yet another sore spot on this project. You know, like Cupid itself. Or saying anything specifically about his dating Rachel.

For once.

Mark rubbed his shoulders and worked at the knot there. He didn't have the magic touch Rachel had when it came to working loose his knots. He had a sudden thought of maybe showing up at her place and asking for a back rub.

The thought made him smile, but then he remembered the three meetings he had this afternoon and all the emails and questions he had to follow up on.

Man, he'd had no idea what a nightmare Cupid would become. Not because of Rachel, as much as Scott wanted to think so. But just simply the new kinds of problems a ground-breaking game created. The main problem was neither Mark nor most of the team truly understood the 'rules' of this genre, of romance.

Thank the video game gods for women like Karen and the few men who'd jumped into this thing with both feet. As much as he enjoyed the challenge, Mark himself still couldn't get his other foot in the water.

Not that he was holding back, but he knew that to make this game work, to give it his all, he had to fully believe in the game, in what they were doing. There was some part of him, hidden and buried deep, that didn't want to let go.

Even with this year of production, of creeping closer and closer to their deadline, of seeing Cupid coming together, he still had reservations.

Mark hadn't kept those secret from her. If he had then he knew she'd be suspicious. After all, these were the same reservations he'd had from the beginning and they didn't just up and disappear because he wanted them to.

No. Cupid itself had to convince him, and yes, the game had done a good job but there was still something missing, something he couldn't quite put his finger on.

Mark glanced at the phone. Should he call Rachel now? At least that way he'd be sure not to forget to talk with her about it.

Generally when they saw each other in the evenings, with her coming to his place or him going to hers, they barely talked about work. Oh, he talked with her throughout the day and she was fantastic about making herself available to him and his staff when they had questions, but when it came to the evenings, they tended to get lost in each other.

Their evenings were free from work and he found himself enjoying that. When he left his office for the day, for the first time in his life, his office didn't follow him home.

Screw it. He needed a break and it was time for lunch. He'd pick up some Chinese and surprise her.

With that, Mark popped into Ryan's office, told his lead designer he'd be out for a few hours and if there was any questions he needed from Rachel. Sure enough, Ryan had a bunch which Mark dutifully noted.

Rachel, like always, was busy writing. When she answered the door, the smile she gave him made the whole thing worth it. Everything from taking a chance on a relationship with her to this game, was worth it.

"A surprise lunch?" She held open the door for him, while Allie bounded out to give Mark a nosy head butting and smelling of the Chinese bags.

"I thought we both could use a break. Move over, dog."

Mark nudged Allie out of the way, swept Rachel close and kissed her. It was a long kiss, the perfect kind of kiss for a lunch break, and the kind of kiss that woke up more than just his hunger.

It was a good thing he told Ryan he'd be gone for a few hours.

Rachel deepened the kiss. Already he felt her fingers working loose his shirt buttons. "Should we eat before the food gets cold, or should just heat it up later?"

"I'm up for later if you are."

Which, by the third button, she clearly was.

Later was exactly what they did. For the food, not for their time together in the bedroom. Mark ran his hand down her bare back. Her soft, perfect skin sent more of that desire through him. "You know, I could get used to this. Coming over for lunch, spending a few hours lounging in bed."

"If you did then we'd never get any work done."

Rachel turned, the sheet falling enough to show her breast. A breast he happened to know was also soft and perfectly smooth. He leaned forward and kissed her, light and tender. He never wanted to stop kissing her.

She laughed at his attention, kissing him back with just as much joy, before finally pulling away. "And we *do* have to get work done. And I'm still hungry you know."

"Well, some people like Chinese better after it's been microwaved."

Rachel snorted. "Including the dog."

She threw on a robe while Mark changed into his work clothes—only slightly rumpled from where he'd tossed them on the floor. Not too rumpled, but Scott would surely notice. Best to avoid that confrontation when he got back to the office.

They sat at the kitchen counter, eating from the bar stools while Allie sat as pretty as possible, waiting to lick their plates and any leftovers they hadn't eaten.

As much as Mark didn't want to talk about work, he was still on company time (technically), so he pulled out the list of questions from Ryan. They discussed them together, Rachel giving Mark general feedback.

"I'll call Ryan and talk to him myself," Rachel said, "but I really think he's got the feel for the game. It helps, you know, him being with Karen."

"Oh?" Mark raised his eyebrows. "I didn't realize being in a relationship was the key to understanding this game."

He hoped it wasn't the key because he was in a relationship, a causal, comfortable relationship with Rachel, and he still didn't 'get' this game. At least, not in the same way Ryan did.

Rachel shrugged, turning her attention to the food as she forked another helping onto her plate. "It's not that so much. It's him being in love."

Love?

Mark lowered his own fork. He hadn't quite expected that being the key she was referring to. The topic of love came up quite a bit in the office, mostly because they were making a game about falling in love.

However, the topic of love didn't come up very often between him and Rachel. At least not after a wonderful lunch break in her bed, and not when they were eating the re-heated lunch because they'd been in her bed.

"You think Ryan's in love with Karen?"

"Definitely."

She didn't look at him.

He wasn't sure why she didn't, or why it hurt.

"So, you're saying that's the key? If you're in love then you've got a deeper insight into this game?"

Again. Not something he wanted to think about.

"No, I just mean it helps him see what women want from this game. He's a smart guy. He knows how to make Karen smile, what makes her heart race, what makes her look at him in that special way."

This time Rachel did look at Mark. Her smile was soft and whimsical, as if she was hiding something from him.

He had no idea what, but this conversation had moved into new territory, ones he wasn't ready to deal with yet. Everything about Cupid was hard; everything about it made him see the world differently. First, it was making games differently and now, they were discussing love. From the very day he decided to found FastPlay Games, Mark hadn't had time for love. This company was his dream and that dream needed his undivided attention to see it through the coming problems.

And there were always problems.

As much as Rachel talked about love, or as much as Ryan enjoyed being in love with Karen, didn't change the fact they had some big battles ahead of them. Battles such as the press and what was going to happen if they learned too soon the kind of game FastPlay was making.

Bad publicity could destroy all their work before they'd even had a chance.

"Rachel, there's something else we need to talk about."

Rachel's smile vanished. She tried to recover, but her smile didn't reach her eyes. "Okay. What is it?"

Mark might have picked up a few things from reading all those romances, enough to know what Rachel said and what she meant were two different things. But he didn't know enough to understand why she was suddenly nervous or what had caused it.

He wasn't Ryan, who suddenly seemed so intuitive when it came to women. Mark wasn't. He was just a guy trying to make the kind of game that felt impossible to make, and the only reason he was making it because if anyone could do it, it was this woman. So long as she didn't destroy everything by talking to the press.

"Rachel. Scott said you want to announce the game. We've talked about this. Talked about why. You can't do that. Not yet. I know it's different in the book publishing industry, where you want your fans to know about the newest book, but with Cupid..."

He shook his head. How could he make her understand?

"If news got out about Cupid," he said, "we'd need to release clips and demos for the game ahead of schedule. And generally, 'ahead of schedule' means buggy and unpolished. Or, a ton more work for our team. We can't risk that not now, at least. And especially not with a game that's as groundbreaking as Cupid."

"Oh." She dropped her fork. "That's what you wanted to talk about."

He blinked. Hadn't she just heard him?

"Well, yeah. What did you think I wanted to talk about?"

"Nothing."

There went his red warning flags. She said 'nothing' but she really meant to say something else and didn't.

Women. How the hell was he supposed to understand women when he couldn't even understand the woman he was sleeping with? And how the hell was he supposed to make a game for women if he couldn't understand one?

This was why he'd hired women specifically to help on Cupid. It was also why he consulted with Rachel so much.

But neither helped him understand why she suddenly seemed more distanced from him, as if there was something else she wanted to talk about. The hell if he knew what that was. It wasn't like he could read her mind.

And sometimes, he was glad he couldn't, especially when she gave him that kind of cold shoulder.

<h1 style="text-align:center">CHAPTER 37</h1>

The second Mark left, Rachel stared at her closed front door. "*Love*, you idiot. I thought we were talking about love."

They were talking about love, but not about *Mark* being in love with her. Nooo, they were talking about *Ryan* being in love.

"Which is why I'm staring at my front door, talking to myself," she muttered. "Because I'm such a romantic idiot."

She ran her hands through her hair, pulling at the strands. "Just a big idiot getting caught up in one of your own stories and now you're starting to make one up about yourself."

A story that was clearly not true. At least, not the love part.

There was plenty of romance, plenty of sexual tension, and well, plenty of sex, but love?

Love was definitely missing at least from one side of the equation.

Rachel glared down at the robe she wore, at their half-finished Chinese food and Allie still waiting patiently for her scraps. Rachel sighed, not really feeling like fighting herself or the truth staring her in the face, and cleaned up.

She tried not to think about Mark as she showered, but that was impossible.

So was writing.

227

And so was focusing on her characters falling in love.

Rachel glared at her computer screen. This was an important scene to write. It was the scene where the hero realized he'd fallen in love with the heroine.

She got to her feet. She needed a walk. A nice, long cool walk, with the last traces of winter hanging on—after all, winter lasted for quite a long time in the Seattle area, sometimes (and often) well into spring. Still, the crisp, biting air would help clear her thoughts because the last thing she felt right now was love coming from her heroes. Not the fictional hero she was writing about or the real-life hero she thought —hoped—she'd met.

Rachel bundled herself up, grabbed Allie's leash, and together they headed out the door, only to bump into Nick coming up the walk.

"Hey," he smiled. "Heading out?"

Rachel held onto Allie, barely managing to keep the dog from jumping Nick. "We were going out for a walk. Want to join us?"

"Yeah, I would actually."

Rachel hadn't a clue why Nick was there, or why he was so withdrawn. But she knew her brother, and knew he'd come around when he was good and ready to. Still, the cool air was enough to distract her from thoughts of Mark.

And love.

They headed for the park, one of Rachel's favorite places, mostly because of all the ducks and birds that visited the man-made fountain-lake. And with it being a clear day, they weren't the only ones out.

Nick kept his silence, hands tucked in his pockets. Finally, after they'd circled the park once he'd thought about the problem enough where he could finally talk to her about it.

"So, uh, how's Cupid going?"

Cupid? Rachel glanced up from petting Allie. Cupid was the reason Nick looked so forlorn and sad?

"It's good. Why?"

He shrugged. "Just wondering, is all."

Which was the biggest cop-out she'd ever heard. "Come off it, Nick. Will you just tell me what's on your mind?"

"Really. It's nothing."

"You know, I get enough of this from Mark. I don't need it from you too."

Rachel turned, fully intending on stomping out of the park, leaving Nick running after her, when his hand shot out and grabbed her arm.

"What about Mark?"

"Of course that's the part you'd pick up on. Look. I don't need my brother to protect me."

"Yeah, you do. When it comes to men, you do."

She pursed her lips. "Come on, Allie. I don't need to hear this."

Rachel shoved Nick out of her way.

"Oh, come on, Rachel. Just tell me. What about Mark?"

"The fact is, it's none of your business."

Nick jumped in front of her. He looked, desperate almost. Worried. She'd never seen him like this before and it surprised her. "Just tell me, okay?"

The way Nick said it, how he didn't even hide his worry for her, was the reason she said anything. At least, that's what she told herself anyway.

"Nothing. I mean, I'm falling in love with Mark and I just don't know if he feels the same about me."

Nick closed his eyes, briefly. "You're in love with him?"

"Yeah. I'm just not, well I'm not sure what to do about it."

Or what to do about her fear, a fear that hadn't left her even after six months of being with him.

He nodded. "It's okay. I knew that."

Now it was Rachel's turn to blink. "Knew that? How? I didn't even know it!"

He shrugged. "You're my sister and Mark's the first guy you've, well you've actually let into your life. Since Daniel, anyway."

Right. Daniel.

Rachel looked away, turning her attention to the two dozen ducks being fed by children at the park, with their smiling parents watching nearby.

"Does Mark know?"

"Know about Daniel or me being in love?"

There was a pause.

"Christ, Rachel. You haven't told him either?"

"I couldn't. I've been, too afraid, I guess."

Even after all this time. Maybe because so much of their time and energy focused on Cupid and not on each other. Big conversations of them looking into the future?

For some reason, they shied away from them.

"I think we're just trying to get through this project. It hasn't been easy and a lot of people are still worried about something happening to our relationship that will hurt the business partnership."

"It is a valid concern."

"Sure, but even after six months?" She turned, raising her eyebrows. "Mark doesn't want to talk about it. Every time I bring up the subject, he changes the topic."

Or started kissing her, but she wasn't about to admit that to Nick.

Nick wrapped his arm around her shoulders and squeezed. "He cares about you, Rache. Any idiot can see that."

"Caring about and loving are two different things."

"You want him to love you?"

Nick's question caught her off guard. Rachel fumbled for an answer and realized, suddenly, she didn't have one. If Mark did love her back, then... what? It'd mean they were moving into old territories for Rachel.

Territories like moving in, proposing, and... marriage.

Fear gripped her so strong she would have stood there for another few minutes if Allie hadn't decided it was time to get walking again— practically tugging Rachel behind her.

Nick stayed by Rachel's side as if he understood exactly what she was feeling. He probably did. After all, Nick had been the one to help Rachel put the pieces of her life back together after Daniel nearly destroyed her.

They headed back to Rachel's house. The walk helped ease away her fears, enough so she could focus on Nick. "So. Are you going to tell me the truth? You gonna tell me why you're here?"

Nick frowned, then sighed. "Knowing you, you'll never give up until I tell you. I just wanted to see how the game was going. I caught a buzz in the rumor mill, something about FastPlay and their new 'innovative' title not working out the way they'd hoped."

Rachel shook her head. "I haven't heard anything like that. Sure Cupid's a bit rocky, but Mark doesn't seem worried. Working hard, yes, but not worried."

They'd arrived at Rachel's house. She unlocked the door and took Allie's leash off. The dog headed towards her water bowl, leaving Rachel and Nick in the doorway.

"Do you think there's something going on?" she asked.

"I'm not sure, but generally, rumors have to come from somewhere. And generally, there's a core of truth in them."

"Did you hear anything more than that? Like Cupid being a romance game?"

Nick shook his head. "I gave Mark a call on my way over, told him what I knew. But right now, it's just vague, dire predictions. But if that much got out…"

His voice trailed off, which was fine because Rachel picked up his thought for him. "Then it's possible Cupid itself, and what it is, could get out."

Nick nodded. "It's something to be worried about. How have, how have things been with the other owners?"

"Ethan and Scott?"

"Yeah."

She shrugged. "Okay, I guess. Scott's been keeping to himself, which makes me happy, and Ethan is wonderful as always."

"Oh."

She knew that tone. "What is it, Nick?"

"It's probably nothing, but I saw Scott the other day at lunch. He was with those guys from Forged Legends."

Rachel frowned. That was… strange, but not completely unheard of. After all, she knew Mark still kept in touch with Forged Legends and several other publishers. "Isn't Forged Legends the publisher funded their previous title? *Last Man?*"

"Yeah." Nick's expression cleared, not quite so worried but it was still there. "I'm just worried about you, is all."

Rachel kissed him on the cheek. "And that is exactly what big brothers are for. Do you want to come in? Have some coffee?"

"Better not. This is my lunch break and I should get back."

Lunch break. Just the thought of her earlier lunch with Mark made her blush. It was a good thing Nick liked to take a later lunch than most normal people.

Nick half-turned, then stopped. "How is Mark handling the game? I know he wasn't happy about making Cupid."

She thought about their conversation regarding love. The way he seemed to disregard it. She shrugged. "The same. He still isn't convinced Cupid will sell, but he's trying. I can't force him to believe."

"Well, at least he believes in *you* so I guess he isn't a total jerk." Nick hugged her. "Take care of yourself. And tell him the truth."

She hugged him back. "Which truth?"

"Both. About your past with Daniel, and that you love him. He might be dating my sister, but Mark still is a good guy."

"I guess we'll see about that."

Rachel closed the door, still uneasy about Nick's sudden appearance. And maybe Nick was right. As long as Mark believed in her, wouldn't that be enough?

And just because she was in love with Mark didn't mean he needed to know. So long as she was happy with what they had, that would be enough.

Wouldn't it?

Love, at least, was easy enough for her to write about even if it didn't come so easily in her life.

Rachel lost herself in her day to day life. Working on her books, writing short stories when the need hit her, and of course, working on the game. Part of her had wanted to distance herself from Mark and the growing feelings she felt towards him, but he was a fixture now, whether she wanted him to be or not.

They spent most of their evenings together unless they had deadlines either of them were working on.

Busy and happy, that was her life. Just like this nice, steaming cup of coffee was the start of her morning—even if Mark had taken off before she'd gotten up (and used up all the hot water).

The phone rang.

Allie wrapped herself around Rachel's legs as she reached for it, balancing her coffee in the other hand. "Hello?"

"I'm sorry to disturb you, but are you Rachel Clare?"

Rachel glanced down at the caller ID. A local number. "I'm sorry, who is this?"

"I'm with the Valley Reporter and I have heard from a reliable source you're funding a romance video game, code-named 'Cupid.' Would you care to comment?"

The coffee slipped from her fingers and spilled all over her counter. She thought that was plenty of comment.

CHAPTER 38

When Mark got into the office, threw off his coat, and saw the two dozen phone messages he knew something was wrong. Also, the nearly thirty new email messages filling his inbox was another big tip off.

He didn't bother with the messages or the emails. Instead, he opened up his favorite gaming news website, Your Game Insider, put his coffee carefully out of reach, and swore when the headlines popped up.

FASTPLAY GAMES MAKES A 'PLAY' AT ROMANCE

Times are tough in this economy, but are they so tough a highly respected, sought-after developer switches from making well-received, innovative titles to making... a romance game?

"Son of a bitch." He scanned the article, his jaw clenching the more he read.

Their game had been leaked.

Here was everything, absolutely everything. In-depth references of all the publishers who'd turned Mark down in the months before he'd met Rachel. The deal he'd thrown back in Forged Legends' face to make this 'bodice-ripper' instead.

If he hadn't been sitting down, he would have fallen down. Someone had told the news everything.

He gripped his armrests, fingers digging in the more he read.

He'd tried to keep this a secret. He'd hoped to save his company's reputation by keeping the lid on Cupid for as long as possible, at least until what they had to show was enough to surprise the socks off anyone who saw it.

But someone else had other ideas. They'd even gotten a hold of a some of the concept art, and which one did the leak pick?

A kiss.

A god damn kiss.

"Rachel."

It had to be her.

Brad was gone, long gone by the time that art was made. Not to mention he wouldn't have had easy access to it—even if he were still buddies with employees here. And Scott—Scott had just as much to lose as Mark. They needed this game, and their reputation.

Rachel was the only one who wanted to get the truth out there about her game.

The only one, who made sense.

Mark snatched up his phone, punched in the number for speed dial. Nothing. Her phone went straight to voicemail.

He didn't know how she did it. How she got the art or how she'd even figured out which site to contact. Had she gotten it from his laptop when he'd spent the night?

It was possible. Every bit of it was possible.

He'd told her to leave the press alone.

Why would she do this?

"Calm down," he said to himself. "You don't know it was her."

He didn't.

Brad. Scott. Both were possibilities. And there was everyone else being forced to work on this game—except they, just like Scott had a damn good reason to keep Cupid a secret.

All of their jobs, their reputations, were on the line just as much as Mark's.

Someone like Rachel, though, someone who wasn't really part of the game industry, had a lot less to lose. As much as he hated the assumption, the sickening lump in his gut told him he was onto something.

Rachel didn't have a stake in this company. Or its reputation.

But would she do this? After all, this was her game too, her money. And he dare hoped, her relationship with him.

He remembered her this morning, naked except for sheets and heavy blankets. He'd kissed her on the forehead and she'd murmured a question about coffee.

Coffee which he always remembered to make before he went into the office.

She couldn't have done it.

His tight gut said differently.

Mark didn't have a chance to call Rachel again because Scott stumbled into his office, glasses barely staying on his face. "I told you to talk with her. It's everywhere, *everywhere*."

"I did talk with her." Still no answer from Rachel. He slammed his phone into the receiver. "Are you sure it was Rachel? It could have been Brad."

Brad. That was an obvious possibility, but why would Brad wait so long to blow their secret?

Mark shook his head. He'd done the exit interview with Brad. Brad had been embarrassed by the game. He wouldn't willingly tell his own mother about it.

Still...there were so many possibilities. But why would anyone do this? This article, everything, even the slur about Rachel, was an attack. An attack meant to bring FastPlay down.

Which meant whoever had been the leak meant to hurt FastPlay, meant to destroy it.

Mark thought through different the scenarios, tuning out Scott who kept at it. Mark's phone rang, but caller ID said it wasn't Rachel.

The only person he wanted to talk with right now was Rachel.

And as if his thoughts had conjured her, there she was, standing in his doorway. Coffee stained her white blouse and she had her purse in a tight grip.

Scott rounded on her. "Who did you speak to? Someone high up? Only someone with your connections could make this thing spread like a virus across the entire internet."

"*Me?* You think *I* did this?"

"Who else would it be? You're the only one not part of this company. We told you to keep away from the press!"

Mark knew that look, knew the way her eyes narrowed. She was about to bust Scott in the chops. "Scott. Get out."

"You have no right to—"

"I said *out.*"

Scott huffed once more, but he didn't argue. Instead, Mark heard him going down the hall, telling everyone how it was over, how their cover had been blown and there was no way Cupid would survive the bad reputation. But they'd hold it together. Keep moving forward.

Even with all the bad press.

The worst part was, Mark didn't know if Scott was wrong or right. He didn't know if Cupid could survive the sudden wave of negativity, of bad publicity. He'd need to act quick and fast. Needed to get the right information out there and hope it was enough to mitigate this mess.

Right now, however, he couldn't think about that idiot. Not when Rachel stood before him in her own righteous fury.

For a moment, they stared at each other. Mark wasn't sure if she was going to punch him, cry, or walk out. Probably all three.

He at least wanted to do the third.

"Did you tell the press?" he asked, voice quiet.

"No. Did you?"

Mark closed his eyes, feeling a slight relief at that. He'd hoped it wasn't her, hoped she hadn't gone behind his back. Of course, he shouldn't have doubted her in the first place. This was her game, even more than his.

It was her damn money.

"Did you?" She threw her purse onto his table. "Did you tell the press so you could get out of making Cupid?"

"Out of making Cupid?" Mark's head shot up. "What are you talking about?"

Rachel jerked her thumb towards the closed door—and even through the closed door he heard Scott spouting more doom. Shit. Had he really been that desperate when he signed on Scott as a partner?

"I know you're not happy with this game." Rachel took a deep breath, lifted her head and met his gaze. "Did you leak the news so you could back out of our deal?"

"Of course I didn't. How could you even think that? This company means everything to me."

The phone rang. Another publisher or another news reporter looking for a comment. Mark didn't answer.

He couldn't right now even if he wanted to, because right now he couldn't think straight. Couldn't see past his anger, not when everything he'd built was crashing down around him and all because of this woman—a woman with a vision to make a romance video game.

A woman who'd gotten his name because of fate's lucky draw of the cards.

"I *knew* this would happen." Mark moved around his desk, slow and deliberate. "I knew when news got out it'd ruin us."

"And what, you're saying this is my fault?"

"It's your game."

"And you signed a contract with me." Rachel crossed her arms and glared. "You could have said no. If this is how you really feel then why did you sign the damn contract?"

"I never wanted to!"

The words rushed out of him and it felt good, so good to finally get them out there. To tell her the truth.

"I didn't want to sign the contract but I didn't have a choice because you'd already convinced the other two to go along with your little romance idea. And not one of you took a minute to think about what this might mean to my company, about what would happen when news got out."

Mark knocked several folders off his desk. Papers fluttered in the air, landing around a stunned Rachel. Good. He wanted her to be surprised, wanted her to know exactly how much her dream of a romance game was costing this company, was costing him.

Frustrated beyond belief, he just needed to take it out on someone, on anyone.

On Rachel.

The one who was responsible.

"I walked away from a damn fine publishing deal because of you. And now you have the audacity to point the finger at me, suggest that I set up *my own company* to take the fall?"

She opened her mouth, but he didn't let her speak. Not when he had to get this off his chest. All of it.

"Why can't you just admit you made a mistake? That you're wrong about this game? Why can't you just let us get back to making the kinds of games people respect?"

The door swung open. Ethan stood there, hand raised in a knock, and he stared at both Mark and then at Rachel. "Umm, is this a bad time or should I come back later?"

Rachel's bottom lip trembled, but she lifted her head high. She ignored her eyes, now watering with tears—tears that made Mark freeze as he suddenly realized what he'd just said.

Suddenly realized that yes, he had meant every word he'd said.

Rachel grabbed her purse, then faced Mark. She didn't look away.

"I'm sorry you feel this way. Sorry you felt you were trapped into a making a game you clearly didn't respect. You, of course, can go back to making all the shoot 'em up games you damn well want to. And while you do, I'll continue writing books that sell better than all your games, books that mothers talk to their daughters about because they can't help it."

Rachel stepped closer, now a mere inches from him. A closeness they'd shared just this morning. Already he missed that closeness, that comfort, and knew he'd never have it again. Not after what he'd said.

Truth or not, he'd crossed a line with her. He'd known it the second the words were out. But there was no going back and he wouldn't deny them.

"They talk about my books..." Rachel's voice caught. Tears slipped down her cheeks and she wiped them away with her coffee-stained sleeve.

"They talk about my books because they can't help falling in love. They don't care if the plot is the same as something else they've read or how the story ends, so long as it's happily ever after. You might not respect my books, or this game, but there are millions of women out there who do."

She stepped back, giving both Ethan and Mark her full attention now. "You're right. This is my fault. I've clearly made a mistake in hiring your company and," this part she said to Mark, "and the company I keep."

The phone continued to ring, went to voicemail again just as another call came through.

The press. Wanting a statement.

The ringing phone was the only thing Mark could hear as Rachel walked out of his office and out of his life, her head held high.

She didn't look back.

He didn't go after her.

Couldn't, because she was right. This was a way out for him and for the company. If they got enough bad publicity from the leak, a bad enough reputation, it could kill Cupid before they even finished it.

And a game like Cupid, a game whose very concept would equal bad publicity, was a death sentence.

Just like the one they'd just been handed.

"I think," Ethan scratched the back of his head, "she just dumped you *and* the company."

Mark's head spun. She had, hadn't she?

The question he needed to deal with was simple: was that what he wanted?

The problem was, he had no idea what the answer was.

But just thinking about her walking away and never coming back, was enough that he nearly ran after her.

He didn't, though. Couldn't.

Because he had a company to think about, a company to run—and this decision, for good or bad, was his to make.

Did he go after Rachel? Did he keep making a game he didn't believe in?

Mark took a long, deep breath. "She might have just dumped me, but she didn't dump the company."

Ethan cocked his head to the side. "You gonna go tell that to her? If so, I'm gonna heat up some popcorn and watch her kick your ass."

"I don't need to talk to her. We have a contract and she's not pulling out. I'm not letting her."

She could pull out *after* he delivered Cupid to her. Not before. Not until he fulfilled the terms of the contract.

He wasn't going to let her give up, walk out on him or this game.

How could he, especially when he was in love with her?

CHAPTER 39

Rachel stumbled out of Mark's office, not quite seeing right because tears blurred her vision. She had to get away. Had to find some place where she could breathe, compose herself—long enough for her to get home, long enough for her to grieve in peace.

How could she have been so completely wrong about him? How hadn't she seen it?

Rachel got to her car and rubbed at her eyes until the tears stopped. But they didn't stop, not for a good long while. Frustrated, she yelled and slapped at the steering wheel.

Why did this always happen? Why, when she got close to someone, when she was ready to open her heart the truth came out?

Mark didn't respect her. He didn't respect her or the stories she wrote. Just like Daniel hadn't.

This was absolutely nothing like her novels. There would never be a happy ending to her life.

She slammed on her steering wheel again.

Rachel flipped open the phone and hit Nick's number. He answered on the first ring.

"Rachel—"

"Shut up." She snapped. "You knew about this, didn't you? That's why you came over to talk to me. You *knew something* was going on and you didn't fucking tell me!"

There was pause at the other end of the line.

The pause was enough for the tears to come back, to clog her throat again.

"Christ, Rache. Don't cry. I didn't know anything specific. I told you everything I knew and I tried to warn Mark, but without details or knowing who the leak was—"

"Oh, screw you, Nick. What you didn't tell me was how damaging information about Cupid could be. You didn't tell me it could *destroy my game!*"

She hung up and threw the phone on the passenger seat. She was so absolutely finished with men. Completely done.

Men in her love life, men in her family life.

If having no men in her life meant she could have an honest, lie-free life, then that was exactly what she'd do. Besides, that's why she had the dog.

She didn't need Nick.

She didn't need Mark.

She also, definitely didn't need the man standing on her front porch, shielding his hands as he looked in through her window. She pulled into the driveway.

She didn't need to see his face to know who it was.

This, apparently, was her day to deal with the awful men in her life. Well, the hell with them. She was done, absolutely done bending to their will and judging both her and her work.

Rachel jumped out of her car, slamming the door behind her.

Daniel came towards her, arms extended in a hug. As if she'd hug that asshole.

The second he saw the look on her face, the arms fell. "Uh, hi, Rachel. I wanted to surprise you."

His deep gaze took in her tear-stained face and red eyes, as well as her previously white, now mocha colored blouse. She didn't give a shit. She was done giving a shit.

And to make matters worse, Daniel stood there just as well

groomed in his tailored suit as always. Yeah, she'd love to see him throw the 'I need money' line at her, not when she *knew* how much that suit cost.

Rachel crossed her arms and glared at him. "What the hell do you want?"

"I told you. It's a surprise visit."

"No. It's not. You want something from me, probably money, and the answer is 'no.' It will always be 'no,' so please stop wasting my time and don't come by anymore."

She stormed past him. When he didn't move fast enough, she gave him a good shove with her shoulder. Asshole. She meant it. She wanted him gone and out of her life.

"Fine. You want to know why I came?"

"Not really." She dug for her keys in her purse. She heard Allie by the door, thumping loudly against it with her body. Rachel really wanted to see Daniel's expression when he realized she didn't live alone anymore.

"I read the paper."

"Good for you." Where were her damn keys?

"Look. I came over here to be nice, to give you some good advice, and this is how you treat me?"

Ah-ha, found them! Rachel yanked out her keys and glared at Daniel from over her shoulder.

"Daniel. I happen to remember every single derogatory comment you ever made about my career and my writing. I'd say I've *earned* the right to tell you to get the hell off my property and leave me the hell alone."

Daniel's face clouded over. She knew that anger, knew she'd hit him exactly where she wanted to.

Daniel couldn't handle being talked back to; he couldn't handle not being in control. Just like he'd never been in control of Rachel or her writing.

Which was exactly why he'd been so harsh, both with all the time she spent on her writing and how she'd failed again and again, struggling to find the story, to improve her craft.

"Your career?" He spat on the porch. "As if anyone could call romance writing a career."

"I'd say those giant checks I get from my publishers is all the proof I need."

"You want to make another mistake with your life, then go ahead. You want to go forward with this project, with a romance video game and ruin any last bit of credibility you have, then go ahead."

Daniel stepped closer, towering over her.

Well, like hell she was going to let him do that.

Rachel shoved the key into the lock and turned it. The door clicked open. On the other side, Allie jumped up, thunking against the closed door once again. Daniel's attention flicked once to the door, but he was too mad to pay attention. Too worked up.

He had something to say to her, something else to try and make her feel worthless.

But it wouldn't work. Not this time.

"You think I'm making a mistake?" she asked. "I'm surprised you still care."

"Sometimes I don't know why I bother. Here you are, wasting your talent. I always knew romance was sub-standard and anyone with a lick of taste wouldn't be caught dead reading it. What was I supposed to do when my *wife* was the one writing that shit?"

"Shit." She tilted her head. "I suppose you're right. My writing is shit. Now that we've got that out of the way, how about you leave? For good."

"We can still fix this you know. We can drop this whole game thing, we can pick up where we left off in our relationship. Work this out."

"*Our relationship?* Ha! Didn't you really mean to say *my money?* Well, Daniel. I'm already in a relationship. Would you like to meet her?"

"*Her?*" Daniel nearly backed right off the porch.

"Yes. Her."

Rachel opened the door and Allie burst out, furry tail wagging in excitement at the new 'guest.'

She'd never seen Daniel that pale—or run so fast in her life. He was at least one asshole she knew was now completely out of her life. And as far as Mark was concerned?

She was done with him, too.

The only person she had a relationship with was her dog, and that was exactly how it was going to stay.

No more men.

CHAPTER 40

Mark rubbed at his tired eyes. Two weeks. Two weeks of non-stop damage control. He needed sleep, needed a break, needed... hell, he needed a two-month vacation in Hawaii.

In fact, as soon as Cupid was finished he planned on whisking Rachel away, putting her on the earliest flight, and not coming back to Seattle until he caught up on sleep.

Of course, that depended if Rachel still wanted anything to do with him.

He was pretty sure she didn't. Especially when she hadn't returned any of his calls.

At least all his business calls had been dealt with. All the emails replied to. All the interviews completed.

It hadn't been easy. No one had wanted to listen, had wanted to even give him or this game a chance.

And the only reason it had worked as well as it had was because of Rachel—and her yelling at him before she'd strode out of the office. Her speech to him had been perfect, and he'd happily stolen every word of it.

It had bought him time with the other development companies, publishers, and of course, the press. When he'd gone out and defended a woman's right to have a game made specifically for her, there was only so much nay-saying the press could do.

Not unless they wanted to step over the line.

A line, which surprisingly, had quite a few angry women in the gaming industry. They had sided with him and the press had backed off.

Not much, but enough. Enough to buy him some time.

The video clips, screenshots, and art he'd released hadn't been as polished as he'd wanted, but they'd done the job. Sure there was still lots of speculation on the game, of even making a game with this kind of scope—if telling a romance story where the player had choices would even work. But like Mark told them, they wouldn't know until they played Cupid now would they?

So, one crisis was taken care of, but he still didn't know what to do about the other one, the larger one.

He had no idea what to do about Rachel.

Nick knocked, popping his head in Mark's open door. "Hey. Ryan was on his way out. He let me inside."

Nick. Another person Mark hadn't talked to in two weeks, even though he'd tried calling. He hadn't been sure if Nick had hung him out to dry or simply sided with Rachel.

"Mind if I come in?"

Mark glanced at his swamped desk, at the paperwork piling up and overflowing over the side. "Yeah. Sure. If you can find some place to sit."

"I'll manage."

Nick did manage, even though it included lifting a paper pile nearly half his size and depositing it on the floor.

"I hope that wasn't important."

Mark shrugged. "The word 'important' is a bit relative these days anyway. Now. You mind telling me what you're doing here? Or are you just going to hit me for hurting Rachel?"

Nick paused, half-way into sitting down, then shook his head. "No. I'm not going to hit you. You sure as hell deserve it, but then I'd have to let you hit me in return."

That was not the response Mark had expected. "Why would I hit you?"

Nick ran a hand through his short brown hair. It looked like he hadn't shaved in at least a day as he had a nice stubble growing on his chin.

"Because. I heard the rumors about Cupid being leaked, yeah I told you, but shit, man, what was I supposed to think when I saw Scott with the Forged Legends executives?"

"Forged Legends?" Mark leaned forward over his desk. He didn't care about the papers he pushed off to the floor. "What are you talking about?"

"A couple weeks ago I saw Scott at lunch with those guys from Forged Legends. I told Rachel about it, but we both thought it was the normal stuff, just the normal networking you owner-types do."

"Scott," Mark growled, "doesn't do the networking. I do."

Nick slouched further in his chair. "The thing is, shit, I didn't give it much thought and then when I heard about the press, about Cupid getting out... I thought you knew. I thought you were the leak."

"Me?"

Mark felt another flash of anger. The same anger he'd felt at Rachel when she'd accused him of the same thing.

"This is my company," he said, forcing himself to keep himself from either yelling or growling. "The last thing in the world I'd do was leak this kind of information, the very kind that could drag my company down."

"I know. I mean, it didn't make much sense to me either, but what else was I supposed to think? You weren't thrilled about this game to begin with and even now you're not thrilled."

Mark figured Nick had a few more seconds before he let loose his pent up anger and punched his now ex-friend. "I think I've heard enough, Nick."

"No. No you haven't because I saw Scott again. Today. This time, not with executives but with a couple of reporters. The only reason I knew they were reporters was because they were wearing press badges."

Press badges. Reporters.

"How do you know what they said?" Mark was surprised he could speak so calmly, so in control. On the inside, he was seething. He was so furious, ready to explode, to throw Scott out of the office by his glasses.

Because he finally understood what Nick was trying to tell him, what Nick had first missed when he saw Scott with the Forged Legends executives.

Instead, Mark forced himself to take another breath. Nick still hadn't answered.

"Nick?"

"I eavesdropped, okay? It was some follow up interview. It was Scott who told them all about Cupid, all about my sister. He told them about the projects you'd pitched and none of the other publishers would support."

Nick ran a hand through his hair. "Look, you're my friend, and you're my sister's… hell, I don't know what you two are now, but you're making her game. This is your company—"

"You're right. It is my company."

Mark stood. He walked around his desk and held out his hand. "And it looks like I still have some work to do. Some house cleaning."

Nick glanced down at the offered hand and shook it. He smiled. "I'm really glad to hear you're not the asshole I thought you were."

"I'm not so sure about that. I still hurt your sister."

Nick's smile faded. "Yeah, you did. I did too but you definitely hurt her worse. You gonna make it up to her?"

"I'm going to finish her game."

Nick frowned for a moment, measuring Mark, still not letting go of the handshake. Finally, he nodded. "It better be one hell of a game."

"It will be."

Because he'd promised it to her. And he'd show her he never backed out on his promises. Ever.

First, though, he needed to deal with Scott.

The next day, Mark called a team meeting. Ethan and Scott were there, as well as Ryan and his design team, programmers, artists. Everyone except for Rachel.

He tried not to think about her missing presence, how he wanted her there to share in this moment.

Mark shook his head. He needed to focus. This was a company matter, an internal one. He'd deal with the company first, then he'd deal with Rachel and hope his begging and apologies would be enough to let him explain.

Not like explaining would do any good. He'd spoken the truth, told her how he felt about the game, and he'd hurt her. Deeply. An apology wasn't going to be enough.

He didn't know if anything he did would be enough. He'd try, though, and that was all he could do.

Mark gazed around the room, taking in each individual, meeting their eyes. So many had been brought on, like Karen, to help make Cupid a success. Others had found they not only didn't mind reading romance novels—because even Mark had to admit it—they were good stories.

Not his kind of stories, but they were good books.

More than a few people here, he realized, had found love.

Rachel's game, project Cupid, had somehow helped many of his employees find their way, helped them understand, and find love. And now they were in danger of losing Cupid.

The battles he'd anticipated were finally here. He hadn't known the scope of those battles, or expected the betrayal, so he hadn't been fully prepared. Now, he was ready to fight. To take on the gaming world if he had to.

"I'm going to make this simple," Mark said. "I've received four resignations in the past two weeks. If anyone else would like to resign, say so now."

Eyebrows rose, whispers darted out, and were then silenced. No one spoke up. He hadn't really expected any of them to. He'd hoped this was his core group, a group that would see this through to the end.

Mark watched Scott in the back, watched the way he fiddled with his tie. His eyes glanced at the group, then back to the closed door. Always moving, never staying on one person too long and always avoiding Mark.

Good. Scott should be nervous.

"If you want to go, you'll be given a severance package and a good recommendation. Whatever your feelings are on this project, I won't hold it against you. In fact, I *can't* hold it against you."

There were a few murmuring at this. Ethan raised his eyebrows, a clear question, but he said nothing.

Mark got to his feet. "I can't hold it against you because I feel it, too. I feel the doubt, the questions. Should we be making this game? Will this destroy every shred of our reputation?"

Mark tucked his hands in his pockets. "Yeah, I've questioned Cupid from the beginning. I wasn't sure, wasn't sold on the idea. Not like Ethan or Scott. I won't hold those feelings against you either, but I will say this. I'm not giving up. I don't care what they write about us or if they review our game with the lowest scores possible. I don't care. If I give up, if you give up, then they've won."

For the first time since Mark signed onto this project, since Rachel first blurted out her desire to make a romance video game, it felt right. This felt right. That it should be this company, *his* company to make this game.

"Like I said at Cupid's announcement party, FastPlay makes innovative games, games on the edge. I'd say Cupid qualifies. I'd also say, screw the reviewers and the game industry. We're not making a game for them. We're making a game for women."

For Rachel's audience.

Heads nodded, approval lighting the faces of his team. He should have done this earlier, should have talked them through this first battle. But he hadn't been prepared. Something had been missing.

It had taken Mark's talk with Nick to figure out what that was. Now, he knew.

Mark crossed his arms, took two steps towards Scott whose jaw slowly dropped to the ground. Scott's cheeks reddened.

That's right, you little prick, Mark thought. *It's your turn.*

"Isn't that right, Scott? We're not making a game for the rest of the industry now, are we?"

"Of, of course not."

"Good. Didn't think. So. Mind telling the team why you told *Your Game Insider* a different story?"

Scott paled. He shot up from his chair and ran for the door. He didn't get far. Not when Ethan slid in front of him with Ryan right behind.

Mark may not have expected this betrayal, but one thing was for sure. He was finally getting rid of a partner he should have tossed a long, long time ago.

CHAPTER 41

$\mathcal{N}$ick banged on Rachel's door for the fourth time that day. "Damn it, Rachel! You changed the locks!"

Yes, yes she had, and she was damn proud of herself for remembering to.

Rachel sat at her table, trying to focus on the newest contract from her publisher—a contract that had quite a few 'little' changes to it. Changes she hadn't agreed on but they'd snuck in there, expecting her to sign without noticing.

A very, very bad move on their part. She was in an angry kind of mood, the kind where she was going to tell them exactly what she thought about that.

A mood she'd been in almost constantly since she last talked with Mark a month ago.

"Rachel! I left you alone long enough. Now open the door."

Allie sat by the door, tail wagging, giant smile on her face as she stared at Rachel as if to say, "Well, aren't you going to open the door?"

"No. I'm not."

She had, absolutely, nothing to say to her brother.

Too bad Nick wasn't going to leave it at that.

257

He kicked—actually kicked—her door! "I will break a window if you don't open up."

Rachel got up from her chair. Her idiot brother would do it too. "Do that and I'll call the cops."

"Fine! So long as you talk with me."

Rachel growled, told Allie to get back, and then unlocked the chain she'd had installed with the new lock. She yanked the door open and glared at her brother.

"What?"

"Finally!" He barged in, knocking her aside.

There went her plan of shutting the door in his face. She slammed the door and turned, hands on her hips. Her scowl lowered a little when she saw how haggard Nick looked.

Her brother didn't look like he'd slept in weeks. Although, to be fair, she also looked like hell.

"Can we talk now?" he asked. "Or do you need to do some more yelling? Maybe hit me."

"I don't know. That depends whether or not you're going to be honest with me."

"Good." Nick headed to her fridge and pulled out two beers, opening both of them.

"You know I don't drink beer." Except for those book-completion celebration pizzas she *used* to bring over to Nick's. She didn't mention that.

He held it out to her. "Why do you have it, then?"

"It's not mine."

Nick's eyebrows rose. "Ah. Mark's then."

She snatched the beer from him. "Fine. I'll drink it and you can tell me what you want, and then you can get out."

He shrugged and settled onto her couch, tapping it for Allie to join him, which she happily did. Rachel had a feeling Nick wasn't going anywhere any time soon.

Great. He was one of the last people she wanted to deal with.

"I came to apologize, Rachel. And to tell you that you can't keep shutting me out."

Rachel sat on the loveseat across from him. She tipped back the beer and had a small sip. Stella. It wasn't bad. She could see why Mark would like it.

Mark.

Rachel immediately put the beer down. "Why? Why can't I keep shutting you out?"

"Because you haven't got anyone else. I know you haven't talked with Mark in weeks."

She flinched when Nick said Mark's name. Nick noticed, his eyes sharpening on her, but he didn't say anything.

"You need me around. I'm your brother and hell, you shouldn't be going through this alone."

Rachel shrugged, hoping to make light of it. "Going through what?"

"That the guy you're in love with said some pretty awful things to you, things you happen to be a little vulnerable to, thanks to a previous asshole guy you were in love with."

Every time Nick said 'love' Rachel flinched. Why did he have to be so damn perceptive?

"Okay, okay fine. I am in love with Mark, but that doesn't matter. I made a mistake with him and—"

"Have you been following the news?" Nick asked.

Rachel shook her head.

"Your boy's holding his own. I think, I think you'd find his reasons for making this game pretty spot on." Nick set the beer down and leaned over the coffee table. "Rache, I'm pretty sure you bitched him out with those words."

She shrugged. So what? It didn't meant anything.

"Well, since you're not talking to Mark, I thought you'd like to know what's been going on with Cupid. And an apology."

There went all of Rachel's warning flags again. She sat closer to the edge of her seat. "You better tell me the truth this time Nick or I swear—"

He lifted his hands. "Look, when I saw Scott with those guys from Forged Legends I didn't think anything of it—just like you, remember. But then, when word about Cupid got out, I thought Mark was involved. Turns out, I was wrong, but only partially. It was Scott, Rache. Scott's the one who leaked the news to the press. Not Mark."

Scott?

The realization swept through Rachel. She sank back into her leather couch and listened to Nick. He told her about seeing Scott with the reporters, what he overheard.

She'd been wrong. It hadn't been Mark.

But Mark had still said those things. Mark was the one who didn't respect her.

Rachel took a deep breath and grabbed her beer. Her hand shook, but she ignored it. She'd nearly canceled the game contract a half-dozen times since that day. She'd had the phone in her hand, ready to call her lawyer to cancel the contract.

She still could, if she wanted to.

For these past couple of weeks she'd been floating aimlessly, lost. She didn't know what to do, what direction to take. All the people she'd trusted, who she would normally ask for advice had hurt her.

"I don't understand," she finally said. "You still haven't explained why you're here. Or why you're telling me this."

Nick a ran hand through his hair, something he only did when he was really nervous. "Mark sent me. Now, don't get mad. He asked me to talk with you and I wanted to come. He and Ethan are still waiting on your decision. They need to know, Rache, if they should keep moving forward with this game or if they should look for another deal."

Rachel's legs felt stiff and wooden. She clutched her stomach with one hand, still held the beer in the other. Leave it to Nick to ask the one question she didn't have an answer to.

But like it or not, she needed to give FastPlay an answer.

"I know you," Nick said, "you're the type of person who never gives up."

Rachel wiped at her cheeks and was surprised to see they were wet. She was crying? Why was she crying?

"Why?" Nick set his beer down and got up. "Why are you giving up now?"

"Because I'm tired of being a failure. I'm tired of people like Daniel and Mark judging me, judging my writing, what I do..." She couldn't stop the tears, couldn't stop the hurt.

She'd tried so hard to ignore the pain, the way her heart ached and bled slowly until there was nothing left. Every inch of her hurt, day in and day out. The hurt never went away.

Nick pulled her to him and kissed her forehead. "Rache, you know you're not a failure. You've never been a failure. Not once in your life have you failed."

How could he say that when she had a failed marriage and a string of failed romances to her credit? She called herself a romance writer, but she couldn't even get the love in her own life straightened out.

"You're not a failure," Nick said again.

He pulled her away and made her look at him. "And I'm not going to let you fail. You're going to make this game and you're gonna show my arrogant industry exactly what you're made of. If there's anyone who can rock my industry to its core, Rache, it's you."

She closed her eyes as another wave of hurt hit her. But to move forward with Cupid would mean seeing Mark, working with him again.

Hadn't she agreed she wouldn't let her personal relationship get in the way of the business one? But hadn't he already told her how much he hated Cupid?

"Look at me. It's your choice, Rachel. Your choice to either walk away or take the fight to them, to all those guys like Daniel. No one else can do this but you."

It was her choice. Her choice to be a failure or to pick herself up and be something more.

To be something greater.

CHAPTER 42

*M*ark was waiting for Nick's call.

He and Ethan sat in the conference room, an unopened bottle of Vodka on the table. Either way, they'd be celebrating or they'd be grieving.

Ryan, followed by Karen, crept into the conference room. They weren't the only ones. Soon enough, the whole team was packed into the small room.

It was also starting to get a bit warm.

Ethan came back with another half dozen paper cups. "Probably should have picked the bigger conference room to wait in."

"Yeah."

Ethan opened the vodka and began pouring out shots. On just this one night they'd silently agreed drinking on company property was allowed. They hadn't meant to extend that invitation to the whole team, but it was a little late to back out now.

Mark glanced at his phone, still silent on the table.

He should be the one over there, the one talking to Rachel. The one apologizing to her.

It had been Ethan who said no. Ethan who talked some reason into

263

Mark. If anyone could talk to Rachel right now, and convince her to move forward with Cupid, it was Nick.

Not Mark, not the guy who'd flat out told her he didn't want to make her game, who'd blamed all the company's own problems on her.

Mark was definitely *not* the right person to talk with Rachel.

He clenched his fists, ignoring when Ethan handed Mark his own vodka shot in a plastic cup. He still should be the one over there, asking her to forgive him because staying away was literally eating him alive.

Karen came over and lightly touched Mark's shoulder. It took a moment for him to notice.

She smiled at him, which he thought was supposed to be encouraging. It wasn't.

"Cheer up, Boss. It'll work out. She knows how you feel about her."

"I doubt that." Mark carefully took Karen's hand off him. "I doubt that because one, I sure as hell don't deserve it, and two, I just figured it out myself."

Karen gave him another smile and pat on the shoulder. "You'd be surprised at how intuitive women are. She knows."

Then she left him alone with his silent phone and the silent conference room which everyone had now overheard their exchange that Mark Ashe, Creative Director and CEO of FastPlay Games, was in love with Rachel Clare, their investor and famous romance writer.

Karen didn't say 'love' but she hadn't needed to. The meaning was pretty damn clear. No one said anything. Most looked away from him.

After all, Rachel didn't want anything at all to do with him. Which he again, deserved.

His phone rang. It was in Mark's hand before he realized it.

Ethan and the others sat forward on their seats, inching closer as Mark answered it.

The call came from Nick. Not Rachel.

"Nick."

"That was fast, man. What were you doing? Waiting by the phone?"

Mark's fingers tightened on the phone. "You know, Nick, now's probably not the best time."

There was a pause on the other end. "Right. Can't say I blame you. Look, go ahead and tell Ethan and whoever else is there the deal's still on. She still wants to make the game."

Mark sank back in his chair, the tension leaving his face, his neck and shoulders finally relaxing. "Seriously?"

"Seriously."

Ethan didn't even wait for a nod. He knew Mark well enough to know they'd been given the green light. Cups were lifted into the air, cheers all around, even a few people slapped Mark on the back.

He didn't care. All he cared about was the woman who wasn't here.

"Something else?" Mark asked. He knew there was something else, could feel it in his gut.

"Yeah, I'm…shit I'm sorry about this man. But she said the only way she'll go forward is if she doesn't see you."

To say Nick's words cut him right to the bone would be putting it lightly. Try cutting right to the heart. He deserved it, deserved every bit of it. But it didn't make it hurt any less.

She didn't want to see him. Ever.

"I understand." Mark got up, pushing away his cup. There'd be no celebrating for him. Not until he had Rachel back in his life.

Mark left the room, shutting the conference room door behind him, but he could still hear the cheering inside, the excitement. Completely at odds with the silent hallway.

"You know I'm not going to give up, right Nick?"

"If you gave up I think I'd really have to hit you. She cares about you, a lot, but she's really hurting right now."

Hurting. Because of him.

Mark leaned his head against the wall. It looked like the only thing he could do now was eat his own words. Prove to Rachel, once and for all, just how much this game meant to him.

Romance game or not, he'd never made a game that had so completely turned around and changed his life. It was also the very same reaction Cupid was going to have on the whole gaming industry.

Of course, it had taken Rachel walking out of his life to realize just how much making Cupid meant to him, and not only that, but how much *she* meant to him.

There was no way he was letting her go, not without a fight. And there was no way he was letting Cupid go down without a fight either. Even if he had to take the whole industry on.

That, of course, was exactly what he planned on doing.

CHAPTER 43

Ethan stormed into Mark's office—err, Mark's temporary home since he hadn't been home in a couple of days. Check. Make that, a couple of months.

Or. Fine.

More than a couple of months. Closing on a year.

Ever since Rachel had walked out of his life, he'd thrown everything, *everything* into finishing this game. Making the game it should be.

"Have you seen our critic score? We're getting creamed out there."

Mark rubbed at his chin, surprised to feel just how much his stubble had grown. He needed to get home if just to shave. "I saw. It's not looking good."

Ethan kicked a small trashcan. There was nothing in it. Mark had put it there just for kicking purposes. It helped.

Most of the time.

Right now, though, Ethan looked about as good as Mark. They were both stretched to the breaking point and now... now they were dealing with the most arrogant, game critic jerks out there. The same ones who'd been slandering the game since Scott leaked Cupid.

And their review scores weren't looking good.

"This is bullshit. They're not reviewing the game as if it was a romance, as if it was a game for women they're, they're..." Ethan threw up his hands and kicked the trashcan again.

"They're reviewing it like any regular game." Except this wasn't a regular game. Just like movie critics couldn't fairly compare a drama to an action movie. They were two completely different beasts.

Unfortunately, Cupid was by far the first of its kind and not only did the reviewers not have any what to do with it, they also didn't care to be 'fair' either. They wanted to bury FastPlay and ensure they never made another title again.

"The hell with this." Mark stood up and grabbed his coat from the hanger. "We're not marketing the game for these jerks anyway."

"So? What else are we supposed to do?"

"We're gonna do what we should have done from the beginning. We're going to market this thing to the people who are going to play it."

They were going to get the news out to the women, the people who didn't care about review scores, the people who only cared about a good story and falling in love.

Mark pulled out his phone and hit Rachel's number. She hadn't talked with him in months. Nearly a year. Any go between was first handled by Nick, and then eventually by Ethan.

But Mark?

She'd been serious when she said she didn't want to talk with him.

"Come on, Rachel," he murmured into the phone. Ethan's eyebrows shot up at that. "Pick up."

Of course, she didn't.

He'd even thought about getting a new number, but decided that would be too deceitful. Not the way to win her heart.

Except if he couldn't see her, then he couldn't win her heart now could he?

Mark left a message, but doubted she'd call him back. "I need to talk to her, to talk to someone who knows romance."

Ethan shrugged. "I'd let you talk to my girlfriend except I don't have one since I'm putting in 60 hour weeks."

"You're not the only one." But something Ethan said pulled at him.

He frowned, then dug into his desk, searching for that small slip of paper.

"What are you doing?"

Mark dumped out the entire drawer and rifled through it.

"Have you finally lost it?"

"I lost it the second I agreed to make a romance game. I'm only now just finding my way back to reality."

There! Mark spotted a small, pink business card.

A card with a woman's number on it.

A woman who could hopefully save his ass.

After all, wasn't that one thing women did so well?

Mark got lucky. Stacy picked up on the first call and he reminded her who he was, the guy she'd met at the Bellevue Barnes and Noble and who asked her questions about romance and video games.

"Oh?" There was a slight tilt to her voice. Your *game*. Does that mean you've made it?"

Mark winced. Right. They'd sure done a fabulous job getting the news out there, hadn't they?

This was something he'd needed Rachel for, to work out with her directly, but she'd shut him out.

It was okay. They still had time.

"Yeah, Stacy. The game's pretty much ready to launch and this is part of my problem—no one knows about it. I need to market this to women and I haven't a clue how."

"I see." She said that last as if she was pretty unsure, and pretty uncomfortable by the call.

"Look. Any advice I'd appreciate."

Ethan leaned on Mark's desk, nodding towards the phone and asking 'who's that?' Mark ignored him.

"Game reviewers are eating us alive. I don't care about them. They're not the people we made this game for, but I have no idea how to get it into the right hands. Do you know of any book clubs or large groups of romance readers? We want you to play the game, to tell us what you think—and good or bad—to tell all their friends about the game."

"Is this, is this something you'd be able to set up?" Stacy asked.

At least now she'd gone from wary to curious.

"It's a play test," he said. "We bring a whole bunch of you in, feed you lunch, and you just play. We've had a few small groups but we need more. Lots more."

Ethan nodded at this point, but that probably had to do with the 'more women' aspect. Ethan really hadn't been getting out much either and any kind of distraction would work—especially the long-legged variety.

Like Rachel's.

Shit. Mark closed his eyes. Focus. Think about one woman at a time.

"Will Rachel be there?"

Mark groaned. This must be an internal woman sensor thing. "No. She wont."

Stacy paused. "You pissed her off again?"

"Of course, I did." No point lying about it. "I'm trying to make it up to her. I need this game to sell for her."

He could almost see Stacy tapping her nails on her chin, thinking. "I'll tell you what. You get a whole bunch of signed copies of Rachel's latest book and I'll make sure the women never stop coming into your office."

Mark sighed. "You have no idea how much you've just saved me."

"This, Mark, has absolutely nothing to do with you. It's for Rachel. She's talking up a storm about this game. You might be inept at getting the word out, but she's been nonstop about it for weeks now."

This surprised the hell out of Mark. He thanked Stacy and then caught Ethan up to speed. Ethan was just as shocked as Mark.

"Seriously?"

"That's what she said."

And sure enough, Stacy was right. Rachel had been having one press conference after another. Talking to readers face-to-face, scheduling book readings, having question and answer sessions with her readers.

"Shit," Mark muttered. "She even has a demo."

"Oh. Yeah."

Mark snapped his attention to Ethan. "*Oh, yeah*? What does '*oh, yeah*' mean?"

Ethan scratched the back of his head. "Just that, umm, I happened to remember Rachel asking for that."

"And you didn't tell me?"

Shrug. "I forget. Things have been a little crazy."

That was the understatement of the lifetime. But he had to hand it to her, Rachel was brilliant at business. She was doing all the right things, using her brand to get the word out about the game.

If only she'd let him help.

Well, he was now and he'd do everything he could to make sure news of Rachel's game—of *their* game spread like wildfire.

CHAPTER 44

$\mathcal{N}$ick handed Rachel a bottle of water while she fiddled with her dinner napkin. This was it. Her last speaking event.

The room was filled with women, mostly writers, and many of them were also her fans. This was the largest gathering of women writing romance, an annual conference which she attended every year.

No one treated romance better than Romance Writers of America, and if there was anyone she needed to talk to about this game, it was them. They were her support, her anchor. She'd never have gotten where she was today if it hadn't been for their help, their knowledge, and their support.

Now she was here, asking for their help to realize her dream, her dream that women in games be given the same respect, a fair shake and a nod that they were a market.

"You nervous?" Nick, wearing his own tux and tie, a tie he was again fiddling with.

"You're nervous enough for both of us. Stop that." She reached over, straightening his tie. "You look great."

"It's hard to think so when you've got all these women are staring at you."

"In most cases, guys would be happy about that whereas you? You're *nervous*."

"Hey, this isn't my usual event. Remember, I'm the guy who stays up late playing games and hardly sees the sun. I let you drag me all the way across the country, so cut me some slack." He straightened his jacket. "You sure I look okay?"

Rachel leaned over and kissed his cheek. "You look great, Nicky."

She wouldn't have gotten this far without him. He'd practically picked her up and forced her back on her feet. And when she started this crazy marketing scheme, going directly to her audience and telling them about Cupid, he was right there beside her.

The place where Mark should have been.

Rachel's smile fell and she leaned back. She hadn't spoken with him, directly, anyway, since that day. He tried calling every so often, but she never answered. Still... she glanced again at her phone, silent on the table.

Of course he wouldn't call now. There was no way he could know tonight was the big night for them, her chance to make the biggest push ever to their audience.

And even if he had called and wished her good luck, it wasn't like she'd have answered it. Still... seeing his number, seeing his name come up would have given her that extra push to go up there and do her best.

Rachel slipped the phone back into her purse. She'd gotten this far without Mark. She didn't need him now.

Their table had slowly filled up, a couple members of the RWA Board, other writers and their guests joining them. The seat next to her remained empty. She didn't see a name tag, and no one else seemed to know who was supposed to be there.

"Maybe someone who canceled, last-minute?" Nick shrugged. "Haven't you got enough stuff to worry about? You've still got to be your nosy self?"

Rachel slapped his arm. "Be nice."

"Why?"

"Because *I'm* nervous."

And because she missed Mark. Missed his companionship, his smile, the way he made her laugh.

Sandra, one of the conference coordinators, came over to Rachel. "Are you ready? They're about ready to begin."

"Yes, of course." She'd managed a smile, but it quickly dissolved into a tremble when Sandra turned away.

Why was she so nervous?

Nick didn't seem to notice, as if he had something else all together on his mind. Maybe that's what was distracting her?

She wasn't distracted because of Mark.

He was back in Seattle, not here in Atlanta. And after tonight, she'd be finished with this game, finished with him—no matter what happened. Whether Cupid tanked or if it sold half as well as she hoped, it didn't matter.

She was done with the game industry, done with anything that reminded her of Mark.

Sandra was at the podium, welcoming everyone and Rachel tuned her out, scanning the crowd. Over a thousand people were here, mostly for the chance to network, but many of them had come to listen to her keynote speech.

Rachel stood, feeling her cue coming just as Sandra turned, arms extended towards Rachel. The light fell on Rachel and clapping so loud it was like a dull roar filled her senses.

Rachel smiled as she made her way to the front. A true smile. All these people were clapping, were cheering her on. It was humbling, to say the least, and this was exactly what she told everyone there.

"Humbling because at one point, I started my career right where you are. Writing like crazy, trying to convince some poor editor to take me on, to take a chance on me."

Everyone watched her, listened with rapt attention.

"And some of you had loving, supportive spouses back home. They wanted you to succeed, offered to clean the dishes so you could get fifteen minutes—or if you were lucky, another hour —of writing before it was time to put the kids to bed."

She hadn't had that support and she told them that, told them how she had to fight through the rejections, both for her manuscripts and at home.

She'd fought alone.

"I struggled and I pulled myself out of it."

She choked up at the memories. Memories of Daniel always did this because she couldn't help but relive them, even if this briefly. "I was determined to succeed, no matter what. And I did. I fought tooth and nail, like many of you. Now I'm standing here before you again and I want to tell you about another struggle I've recently faced, the struggle of finding respect in an industry who sees women mostly in scantly-clad outfits and slinging giant swords or a pair of handguns."

From the corner of her eye, Rachel saw Nick who nodded at her. It helped, having him there, to share this story.

"It started with a bet." Rachel took the microphone from the podium, and adjusted the skirt of her dress so it didn't tangle in her legs. "A bet with my brother actually—he's sitting right there ladies, and yes he's single."

That set off another whoop of cheers and cat calls, making Nick blush as bright red as her hair.

But it gave Rachel the smile she needed, the smile to go on as she told them about Cupid, what she went through, the negativity she and the game even now were faced with.

"Will there be a happy ending? I don't know. But I've succeeded with what I set out to do. That was earn respect."

Respect.

Just the word made her think of Mark.

Her smile wavered.

"Respect is something you earn, and sometimes, no matter how hard you work or how much we try as romance writers, we'll never earn it. It'll never be given to us. Because we write romance."

She swallowed, pushing back her tears. "Because romance isn't worthy. It's not real fiction. It's trash. Yes, I see your heads nodding. You know exactly what I'm talking about."

Rachel turned and noticed movement coming from the back of the room. People were moving forward. She blocked them out, or tried to.

But there were too many people—not the usual got-up-to-use-the-bathroom in the middle of a speech.

A lot of people.

People following one tuxedoed man. A man with the brown, unruly hair she instantly recognized.

Mark.

Mark and the entire FastPlay team. And they were making their way to the podium.

Towards her.

CHAPTER 45

Stunned, Rachel couldn't say a word. Not when her eyes met Mark's, when she saw the familiar deep blue. Every inch of her cried out for him, hope and fear mingling until she had no idea what she was feeling.

Except shock. Shock was definitely at the forefront.

Seeing Rachel distracted, her audience turned to see where she was looking—and more specifically—who she was looking at. Murmurings rumbled through the ballroom.

Some people stood up to get a better view.

Mark kept right on coming forward. He only had eyes for her. He didn't even stop when Nick joined him.

Mark joined her on the stage, taking the steps two at a time.

And the whole time Rachel couldn't move. She just stood there with her mouth hanging open, heart pounding.

His smile. It was everything she remembered, everything she longed for.

"Mark," she whispered.

He stopped beside her and she felt every inch of him, as if waves of heat were streaming off him. Tears pricked her eyes. He'd come here. He'd come here for her.

"What? What are you doing here?"

"What I should have done a long time ago. May I?" He nodded to the microphone.

She handed it over, felt the sizzle when his hand brushed hers. She nearly dropped it, but he was there, easily taking it from her.

And then, he turned to the audience. Rachel forced herself to swallow, to switch into 'Rachel Clare' mode for her fans and colleagues. But no matter what she did, she couldn't smile. Couldn't pretend she was happy to the crowd.

Not now. Not with Mark here, standing beside her.

"First off, I'd like to apologize and introduce myself. I'm Mark Ashe, boss of this crazy team over here."

He pointed toward Cupid's team and the spotlight dutifully swung over. "They insisted on following me down here. You see, I'm not the only one who wanted to make an apology. And not just to Rachel, but to all of you. Women who love this genre, women we didn't really believe in until we started Cupid."

Mark reached into his jacket and pulled out a copy of her game. Rachel's game.

"The first romance video game ever made. A game made for smart, intelligent women like yourselves. A game Rachel had the vision to see and to force asses like me to pay attention to. Even when we didn't want to."

Rachel barely heard him. She couldn't take her eyes off Mark. He stood there, easily at her side, not at all nervous by the hundreds of women waiting to hear what he had to say.

Rachel had already said her piece, had told them about the trials making Cupid. About how no matter how she worked, she couldn't convince this one man, the one man she needed to convince.

The man she loved.

She wiped at a tear before it fell. Her gesture caught Mark's attention and he paused, taking the time to stare at her. She felt it then, in his gaze, his intensity, she felt his sorrow.

He was sorry for what he'd said, for what he'd done.

"I'm sorry for not believing in you," he said. "The truth is, I didn't understand what romance was, not until I experienced it for myself."

Rachel's breath caught in her throat. Romance?

"The reason," he told the audience, "you buy Rachel's books, why you buy the books written by all the other authors here, is because you want to fall in love. That's the draw. Not the happy ending, but the falling in love. I didn't get that, didn't understand until I'd fallen headfirst myself. Right about then is when I realized how big of an ass I'd been, and of course, like any of your good books, my realization came too late."

He turned to Rachel, his attention only for her. "But now that I have, I'm hoping there's still a chance for that happy-ending, because I really want the happily-ever-after. I need it, Rachel. I need you in my life."

Rachel's head spun, spun so much she was surprised she didn't fall right off the stage when she closed the distance between them. Tears blurred her vision.

She wrapped her arms around Mark's neck. He pulled her close and lifted her off her feet. She didn't hear the cheers or the claps, didn't hear anything but Mark as he bent his head toward her.

"I love you," he whispered. "And I think I've loved you since you pulled out of that red Corvette with those mile-long legs of yours. Forgive me for being an ass. Please."

"There's nothing to forgive. You made my game. You believed in my game enough to see it through. You believed in me."

"I've always believed in you, Rachel. Always."

And it was true. Every word of it. She felt his truth, felt the rightness in his words, his touch, his lips as he kissed her.

Cupid might be finished, might be on the shelves and in the hands of women all across the world, and they would determine whether or not Rachel's dream would become a reality.

But their lives, hers and Mark's, and their happily-ever-after, was only just beginning.

HOME RUN: A NOVEL

Author of *Second Chance*

CHRISSY WISSLER

To find true love, first step up to the plate.

Home Run: A Home Run Novel, on sale now from your favorite retailer. Turn the page for a sample chapter from that book.

In the world of girls softball, fun no longer matters. Colleges. Scholarships. Laurie Stevens fought this her whole life. A former college star who walked away from it all. Now, a coach for twelve-year-old girls, she faces the same challenge.

A challenge that hits home when former Major League Baseball player, Jack Evans, and his lonely daughter, walks onto her team and into her life.

"Home Run," a novel about dreams, romance, and, hope for the future.

"Wonderful book, chockfull of unexpected surprises. If you like sports novels, you'll like this—even if you don't like romance. If you like romance, you'll like this—even if you don't like sports novels."
—Kristine Kathryn Rusch, *USA Today* Bestselling Author.

CHAPTER 1

The softball cracked off the bat.

Laurie slid to the edge of her overturned bucket. Nearly tipped herself over as she leaned, closer and closer to the chain-link fence. Her metal cleats scraped on the dugout's cement floor and she pushed as if she was the one turning and running, running to catch the high, flying ball.

Just like she'd done, hundreds, no *thousands* of times before.

Laurie gripped the chain-link separating her and the field she'd practically grown up on. Gripped it hard until her own memories, of pushing off the buzzed short grass and racing to make the catch, faded. Until it was just her and her team again.

Until it was just little Suzie Turner out in right field.

Suzie, with her bouncing pigtails and smile as wide as the field, turned and ran. Her deep pink uniform, with the white lettering of her last name and the number one, reflected the heating, sweltering sun. But despite the sun and its beating-down glare, Suzie hadn't been dozing or drifting off. Not this time. This time she'd gotten a good jump. Had seen the hit. Had seen the softball flinging in her direction; the very second it'd happened.

It would be close.

Very close.

Laurie watched as Suzie glanced over her shoulder. Took in the distance. And, like Laurie had taught her, kept on running.

"Come on. Come on," Laurie chanted.

The ball arched, high, then higher. On the field, the other team's runners sprinted for the next base. Flinging dust and dry dirt into the air until it formed a cloud so thick Laurie could barely track of that white speck in the sky.

It was either the winning hit. Or the losing hit.

Meanwhile her team, her wonderful amazing team, shouted. Called out to each other. Asked for who had it.

Suzie answered.

Behind Laurie, the roar and cheer of parents froze. A collective, indrawn breath like Laurie's. Like Hugh and the handful of girls beside her in the dugout. They all waited. Watched.

Suzie, still running, still pumping as hard as she could, stretched out her arm. Opened her worn, brown leather glove—and that flying, spinning softball landed smack in the middle.

Just like they'd worked on.

Just like they'd practiced.

Laurie leapt up from her bucket. Pumped a fist into the air and let loose a walloping cheer with Hugh and her girls.

And unlike anything they could practice, it was when Suzie turned, with a face filled with so much shock Laurie could see it clear from the dugout.

Along with that big, gigantic smile.

They'd won.

Won the game, yes, but for Laurie, and what really mattered, she'd won that smile.

Except Laurie heard the unmistakable *thump, thump* behind her. So loud, so clear, it dwarfed the cheering parents.

Laurie's own smile slipped.

She glanced over her shoulder, and sure enough, there was Dan Richards, jumping down from the bleachers—yes, from the lowest step—and waddling towards the dugout. His rolling belly, and the

Slugging Angels T-shirt barely tucked into his jeans, hanging on by the slightest fold. But it was the red, scrunched face, the glinting eyes that held her.

She swallowed a curse (always mindful of her words around her girls—regardless of the currently cheering, very loud bodies).

The dust from the softball's impact hadn't yet cleared, let alone the umpire's usual shout of, "Game over!" before Richards was ready to let her have it.

Again.

Along with spewing angry spit all over her.

Just great.

She knew exactly what this was about. And how it would turn out.

Laurie fingered the sunflower seeds in her khaki shorts pocket. Just looking at Richards gave her a sour taste. And his temper. She might as well add in a mouthful of salt... except, no. She needed to deal with this. And without a mouthful of sunflower of seeds.

Yeah, she'd deal with it.

And do it the only way she knew how.

The only way she could.

She smashed her pink, *Slugging Angels* ball-cap on her head, squashing her ponytail flat, and prepared for some good ol' coach-to-parent battle.

Hugh, her co-coach and team owner, leaned against the fence. His wrinkled, leathery face was already tanned from the unrelenting southern California sun, a tan that was always better than hers.

He noticed her attention. And who it was on.

"You got this one?" Hugh asked. "He's a bit high-strung today."

"Just today? Hell, I'm surprised he hasn't blown out his knees from all the bleacher-jumping he's been doing."

Hugh lifted his eyebrows, which disappeared into his white mop of hair. "Careful there, Coach. Never know who's listening."

Referring to the five girls streaming out of the dugout, screaming and cheering at the top of their lungs. Laurie smiled and shook her head. "I think I'm safe."

Safe from being overheard (for now), but not safe from a determined and angry dad like Richards. A dad who, at times like this, hit a little too close to home.

Laurie shoved aside the memories, but they latched on. Held her. Gripped her so hard that, for a moment, it wasn't Richards stomping towards her, sneakers brushing the reddish-brown dust into the air. Wasn't Richards wearing that complete, disapproving look.

A look that said no matter how hard she worked, no matter how hard she trained, it wasn't enough.

She'd never be good enough.

Except this *was* Richards.

Not her dad.

And he was yelling at her. A coach. His daughter's coach.

Laurie dug her cleats into the cement, scraping and squashing the memory away. She wasn't a player anymore. She was a coach; a *good* coach, and she just flat out didn't have time to deal with the past—not if she expected to handle Richards.

And be nice about it, too.

Dealing with irate, know-it-all parents required a delicate touch. It was an art, one Laurie had picked up over the years. She'd seen all kinds of softball parents, from the most understanding and loving to the kind who pushed their girls until the game of softball changed from a fun sport to a job.

Those were the kinds of parents Laurie wanted to slug. And with good reason.

It didn't matter how many of these parents she'd met over the years or how many 'talks' she'd had with them. It never got easier. The memories were always there, lurking, waking up at just the right—and the wrong—moments.

"Enough, Stevens," Laurie growled to herself. "Focus."

She'd have to use her best tactic. Quick and to the point.

And it was the only way she'd get through this with her shredded self intact.

Laurie grabbed her old, reliable, 25-ounce Louisville Slugger bat and went to head Richards off.

A good bat, one she'd used in her high school days and all the way through college. Still of use to her, even now, even after that career had long ended.

Her girls ran from the field and into the dugout, all nine mingling with the other five racing out. Leaving Laurie trapped in the middle.

"We did it, Laurie!" Suzie leaped in the air, hugging Laurie around the middle. "Did you see my catch?"

"I sure did. You were great!" Laurie leaned her bat against the fence, temporarily relinquishing its comfort, and held up both hands for the team's high-five jumps.

Parents were one part of her job, this was the other. The better one.

Suzie jumped, stretching her short fingers towards Laurie's hand, and completely missed the double high-five.

Not that Suzie cared, or any of the other girls for that matter. One by one, they jumped, missed, and then tried again. Hugh gave his usual deep, barrel laugh, the one their girls loved, before shooing them into the dugout to clean and pack up.

Richards reached the field, face red, steam practically spewing from his ears. That last fold from his T-shirt finally untucked and now flapped around his middle.

Time for business.

Laurie finished the last couple of air high-fives and hefted her bat.

Lacey, the only girl who hadn't lined up for the high-fives, was standing off to the side, cleats still on, glove still clutched in her fist. Refused to enter the dugout. She towered over the other girls, both in height and size. Already pitchers on the other team were sending Lacey wary glances whenever she stepped up to the plate because any bat of Lacey's that touched the ball practically ensured it would go far.

To the *fence* far.

And she hadn't even hit her growth spurt, which meant there was a good chance she'd be a hell of a hitter once that kicked in. Not much of a runner, though, and if that attitude kept up, she'd not be much of a softball player, either.

But it was the attitude that was the problem.

A big problem.

One that, if Laurie didn't get a handle on—and on *Richards*—meant Lacey would go down a path darker than the one she'd gone down.

At least Laurie's teammates (when she'd played) had always liked her. At least they'd never been *afraid* of her.

Lacey gave Laurie a smug smile, the one kids got when they knew their parents were gonna knock some serious sense into you.

Hugh noticed Laurie's gaze and leaned closer, keeping his voice low and jolly so the girls wouldn't suspect trouble. "You sure? You know he wants Lacey to start more."

Laurie lifted her eyebrows. "You mean, this would go easier if you talked with him and not me?"

Which was true. Mostly because Hugh was male and to Richards's mindset, that meant he was much more willing to understand his position as Lacey's father.

But she understood his position just fine.

After all, she'd had a father just like him.

This was her team as much as Hugh's and whether she liked it or not, parents came with the territory. Even the ones that brought up bad memories.

"Thanks, but I'll handle this."

She needed to. Because, maybe, one day, she could move on.

Hugh glanced pointedly at the bat resting on her shoulder. "That's part of what I'm worried about, girl. You play nice, remember?"

"I always play nice." *When they do.*

Thankfully, she was saved from Hugh's response as the girls, Suzie in particular, had quite a few highlights of the game they were sure Hugh had missed seeing, and therefore had to enlighten him.

Lacey still glared at Laurie, still refusing to come into the dugout. Clearly she wanted to be near the action of her dad ripping Laurie a new one.

"Go get packed up." Laurie pointed into the dugout.

Lacey merely lifted her chin. Triumph.

Not today, kid.

With girls like Lacey, girls who thought they knew everything, there was really only one way to deal with them.

Be bigger. Stronger. Then maybe, somewhere down the line, they'd be willing to listen to something softer.

Kinder.

"Get packed or sit the next two games."

"That's not fair! I'm one of the best players. You need me out there if you want to win."

Laurie straightened. Took a deep breath to calm herself. Lacey was getting to be too much like Richards. The same arrogance. The same driving desire she'd seen countless times back on her old teams.

No matter how much she wanted to, she couldn't yell at Lacey. Couldn't even tell her how dangerous this road was and where it would lead if she wasn't careful. Because Lacey wouldn't listen.

Not yet. Maybe not ever.

For some girls, they never did.

"We're not here to win. We're here to have fun."

Lacey knew that. All her girls, and their parents, knew that. This was a team that had fun. The day it became a job for them was the day Laurie quit.

"Pack up or sit out. Your choice." Laurie spun, her cleats digging nicely into the hard-packed dirt, and headed Richards off before he reached the dugout.

This wasn't a conversation she wanted her girls to overhear.

But to appease Hugh, she gave Richards her best smile, though she did swing her bat nicely onto her shoulder. Might as well appeal to his male sensibility and appear strong. It might work in her favor.

"What can I do for you, Mr. Richards?"

"Coach," Richards growled. "This is the second game you've sat my daughter."

"Actually, I was pretty sure she was playing first base just now."

"You know what I meant." Sweat streamed from his face and his giant nostrils flared. "She should be starting. No one else on this team can pitch or hit like Lacey, and you sat her!"

Laurie's smile wobbled as her temper flared. "You know very well why I sat her."

"Do you think I'm just going to sit around and let you ruin my kid's chances? Ruin her shot at a great future?"

"Dan. Your daughter's twelve. She isn't even close to the age where—"

"Every game is important! Every game she has a chance to catch someone's eye. A coach on an 18-and-Under Team even."

"Eighteen? Christ, Richards, she's only twelve!"

But he didn't hear her. Couldn't. Already too lost in big dreams and an even bigger future.

"Maybe even scouts. High school. Hell, college. *And* if you can't teach her, if you can't be the great coach we thought you were, then you're wasting our time."

Her head swam.

Richards was honest to God thinking of Lacey for an 18-and-Under Team?

When it came to travel softball teams, age didn't exactly matter. Travel teams were the intense version of this game. More than any school or high school or league team. These were the teams that traveled to different cities, different states even, all with the end goal in mind: playing for college.

Just not Laurie's team.

Which was why she was coaching girls so young. Young enough that those big, lofty dreams didn't matter. Having fun was what mattered.

But if you were good enough to play with the big girls, and on those teams where seniors dominated, then you'd play with the big girls.

If you were good enough.

If your parents agreed it was the right move.

Laurie couldn't think of one instance where it was the right move. Not for a girl barely twelve. Not for Lacey.

It certainly hadn't been for Laurie.

The field tilted slightly. Red-brown dirt and the green, trimmed outfield temporarily trading places. How many times, for how many of her own years playing softball, had she heard Richards's exact words? Those exact same dreams?

Sometimes, they'd even come from her own, misguided lips.

Richards stepped forward, breaking the hold her past had on her. She needed to focus. Needed to be right here, right now if she was going to do Lacey any good.

She had to talk him down.

Laurie didn't back up. Not even when he pressed close enough she could practically taste his own sweat on her tongue. She squeezed the comforting rubber on the bat's handle. Dirt slid under her nails.

Focus. Stay calm.

"You still think you're some great hot shot?" Richards continued. "Well, I got news for you. You ain't in this sport anymore. You're a has-been, and the fact that anyone even remembers you playin' is a miracle."

This time, he leaned so close their noses nearly touched.

It took all of Laurie's control not to slug him. This man, no matter what she said, no matter what she did, would never understand.

Would never listen.

And *that* hit too close to home.

Enough to re-stir her anger. To push through the air that was trying to hard to catch in her throat. To clog there and keep her captive.

Not this time.

Not ever again.

"So you tell me," Richards growled, so close the sweat from his brow heated the already sun-hot air between them, "who the hell do you think you are sitting my daughter?"

"Her coach."

Laurie tapped her bat gently on her shoulder.

A reminder.

Richards's eyes zeroed in on it, but he made no move to back down or back up. Not like she'd expected him to.

"I'm the coach," she said again. "Lacey's coach, just like every other girl on this team. I'm also not going to stand here and let you yell in front of these girls. You have a problem with the way I run this team? You don't like the way I coach? That I don't measure up to your inflated expectations of me? Fine."

Another tap of the bat.

Richards's eyes jerked back to her face. They widened. Just slightly. As if *finally* realizing the danger.

That, just maybe, he'd gone too far.

"When Lacey joined this team, I made myself clear. We're not here to train your daughter for college ball. My girls are here to enjoy the game, to have fun." Laurie's breath hissed out, low and dangerous. "And if you ever yell like that in front of my girls, you and Lacey can get the hell off my team."

They glared at each other.

Richards looked away first.

Laurie risked a glance at the dugout. Hugh had done his part, keeping the young-ins away, focused on the small candy bars he was handing out on account of their second win of the season.

Even Lacey had been distracted by the promised treats. Good. Meant that they could finish this before it got any worse. Of course, quite a few of the parents had crept closer, hoping to overhear.

That was at least one thing that never changed from team to team, or parent to parent.

The gossip.

Laurie leaned back. "Do you have any problems with that?"

It was a trap question, and the way Richards's eyes narrowed, he knew it too. He and Lacey could quit the team; that was their choice.

She didn't resent them for it, but this was also her team.

She had choices too.

"Now," she gestured towards center field. "Why don't we have that talk, take a short walk, and work this out?"

She brushed past him. Her hand tightening on the bat. *Patience. Just another parent, one who if all the signs pointed correctly, wouldn't last long.*

Parents like Richards never did. They always had their own ideas, their own big dreams for their kids. The kind of dreams that usually ended up with two words: *college* and *scholarship*.

Why was she even doing this? Why was she fighting so hard when no one wanted to listen? What was the point?

They reached center field and Laurie thrust aside all her doubts. Richards would sense them, like a shark smelling blood.

Their talk went about as well as expected. Richards was furious Laurie hadn't started Lacey (again), and of course, was adamant that when Lacey had shoved their catcher Mandy, it was not in fact, a shove.

"Shove or not a shove," Laurie said. "I don't give a shit."

Richards's mouth clicked shut. He blinked. A softball coach for twelve-year-olds didn't do much swearing. It came with the job. There were times, however, when such words were needed.

Necessary, even.

Like now.

"A gentle, friendly shove is still a shove and I won't have fighting on my team. I warned Lacey and she decided to back talk to me. So, I benched her for the first half of the game. Hugh agrees with my decision."

That last comment effectively cut Richards off at the knees. He couldn't go plead his case to Hugh, not if Hugh was already on Laurie's side.

"If you want her playing," Laurie said, "then I suggest you talk to her."

Lacey's fighting habits had started almost immediately after her parents separated. That, however, wasn't Laurie's business. There were certain topics where it wasn't her place to say anything. At least not until kids like Lacey made it Laurie's business.

Richards might not be pleased, but he couldn't argue her points. He didn't say he agreed with her; no, that wouldn't be up his alley, but he nodded anyway and went to collect his daughter.

Lacey had that gleam in her eyes, the triumph for having her dad stand up for her, which immediately died when Richards shook his head.

Not this time, kid, Laurie thought to herself.

Of course, Lacey had no idea, and would never know, that the real person who'd stood up for her had been Laurie.

She watched them leave and the muscles in her right shoulder pulsed. She rubbed at the knots and hissed. A leftover reminder from her softball days, the muscles still hurt, still got tense whenever something like this happened. As if her body, along with her mind, refused to let her forget.

She lowered her arm. Right now, the last thing she needed to remember was playing softball and dealing with her dad, the coach.

"You gonna help me out here?" Hugh came up beside her and dumped a handful of softballs into the bucket.

"You bet." It was exactly the kind of distraction she needed. She and Hugh loaded up the ball buckets and equipment bags into the back of Laurie's somehow still running pick-up.

The weekend hadn't been a hard one, not for their team, anyway. Only two games on both days, though the spring season was only just getting started. They'd be soon seeing their girls once during the week for practice, then on the weekends. Switching between three and four games a day, every week until the summer season closed.

Still, the park—with its four, well-used softball fields—was already deserted. Teams, parents, and their kids seemed to vanish the second the last pitch was thrown. It made the park more relaxing, more inviting as if it needed the quiet to settle in for the night after a long day of roasting hot dogs, French fries, and mounds of ketchup.

But right now, with her shoulder pulsing and Richards's accusations rolling around her mind, not to mention her own damn memories, the last thing Laurie felt was peace.

She packed her bat and slammed the tailgate door. Her truck shook slightly.

Hugh lifted his eyebrows at her. "It went that well, huh? Got a bit of extra steam to work off?"

"Steam is too generous. Try really pissed off."

"I can see that. You want to talk about it?"

"No."

Hugh merely looked at her.

"There isn't much to say. I told him to back off. Lacey pushed Mandy, regardless of how he wants to dice it."

"I noticed he stopped yelling."

Laurie shrugged. "Not hard to do when you carry a bat."

And if you have no problem using it, if push comes to shove.

Hugh let the bat comment slide. But he looked at her, like he always did. Just like he always knew why she needed it for these talks.

The bat, as much as the softballs and the very fields her team played on, were part of her past. A direct link, and a reminder, of the kind of coach she refused to be.

"You okay?"

She knew what he was asking. And why.

"Yes. No." Laurie leaned against her truck and rubbed her shoulder, the muscles still tight, still pinching. "It'll come up again. It won't be the last talk."

"Unless he decides to take her to another team." Hugh sighed. "I'm getting too old for this. It didn't always used to be this way, you know? Parents thinkin' they know what's best, even if they don't know anything about the game."

"It's not you. And it's not me. The game's changing."

It had started to change when she was Lacey's age, when it was Laurie out there being yelled at by her father as he pushed her to do better, to excel.

She rubbed her forehead. What was wrong with her today? Why all these memories and why now? Was it just because of Richards?

Sure dealing with him usually brought on the bad times, ones that no matter how many times she buried them, just kept digging themselves free.

"I thought I could change things, make a difference in their lives."

Hugh reached over and gripped her shoulder. "You are. Why do you think parents keep lining up to join?"

They joined because regardless of what Richards thought, Laurie and Hugh were excellent coaches. They had a knack for bringing up the best talent, for nurturing girls. The problem was she and Hugh were merely the dinosaurs who refused to go extinct. That was the real problem. The one neither wanted to bring up.

Teams nowadays didn't care about having fun. They wanted results. They wanted the best chance for the kids to get that college scholarship.

It didn't matter if the kids were only twelve-freakin'-years old.

Laurie bit her tongue and kept her thoughts to herself. So did Hugh.

One day, they'd have to accept it, but until then well it didn't matter so much did it?

"Still," Hugh reached his arms up above his head, his old bones cracking and creaking as he stretched. "Sittin' all day on that damn bucket—I'm definitely too old for that."

"Whatever you say, old man."

Hugh laughed. "Old? Damn straight I'm old. Girl I remember when you were no taller than our Suzie-pie. About just as freckled too."

"I was always taller than Suzie. And I only had two freckles." She knew because she'd counted nearly every day.

Hugh scanned the empty parking lot, a lot that had been recently filled with the more expensive cars and BMW's. That was southern California living for you. Laurie's beat-up truck was the only one of its kind on game days.

"But you're right," he said. "Times are changing. It's not the same game as when you came through. A different world." He shook his head. "More kids will be like Lacey, more dads like Richards who think they know everything."

Laurie dusted off her pants a final time, not like it did much difference. She seemed to be covered in as much dirt as her girls. "It's still enough the same."

She hoped it was, that there was enough reason for her to stay, to keep playing the game she used to enjoy so much. "As long as there are kids who want to play good ball, who want to have fun, then I'll still be here."

She'd still coach. She'd make sure at least one girl had the experience she never did. As long as she never crossed that line, the line that so many coaches had no problems stepping over, she'd keep coaching.

Yes, she still spent most of her days helping out kids—or trying to. Most kids, especially the lovely high school age ones Laurie taught, didn't appreciate the help. But out here, on the field, this was still her life.

Even as hard as that life had been at times.

But she'd learned, the hard way, that she couldn't stay away.

This, *this*, was where her heart was.

On the field.

"I know you will, kid." Hugh slapped her shoulder. "I've no doubts about that."

Laurie nodded, but kept her mouth shut. She had her doubts, and Richards in all his anger, had reminded her of them.

To continue reading "Home Run," visit ChrissyWissler.com or your favorite bookseller.

Any Normal person thinks magic a myth. Anyone worth knowing, knows differently. Magic wanted and it took. Free pizza delivery, free Wi-Fi, freewill.

All of it, fair game.

Blessa of the Blessings Bridge made sure all her landing platforms, from the golden arches to the inter-dimensional voids, remained clear of seaweed and seagull shit. An important job, really. Essential, even.

Too bad she hated it.

The Blessings Bridge will transport you to living, breathing world where magic resides alongside freeways, fishing piers, and funnel cakes. A world you never knew about, but always knew existed... right outside your backdoor.

By joining my list you'll receive wonderful benefits such as being notified of upcoming book releases as well as the free story, *The Blessings Bridge.*

To enjoy your free copy of *The Blessings Bridge* and keep up with the latest news and releases, go to chrissywissler.com/free-book/ and chrissywissler.com.

ABOUT THE AUTHOR

Chrissy Wissler's writing has garnered praise both from readers and professional writers. Readers love her characters and the emotional grip she engenders.

About her novel *Home Run*, *New York Times* bestselling author Kristine Kathryn Rusch said: "Wonderful book, chockfull of unexpected surprises. If you like sports novels, you'll like this—even if you don't like romance. If you like romance, you'll like this—even if you don't like sports novels."

Chrissy's short fiction has appeared in the anthologies: *Fiction River: Risk-Takers, Fiction River Presents: Legacies, Fiction River Presents: Readers' Choice, Deep Magic,* and *When Dreams Come True*. She writes fantasy and science fiction, as well as a softball, contemporary series for both romance and young adult.

Before turning to fiction, Chrissy also wrote nonfiction for publications such as *Montana Outdoors, Women in the Outdoors,* and *Jakes Magazine*. In 2009, *Inside Kung Fu* magazine awarded her with their 'Writer of the Year' award.

Follow her online at ChrissyWissler.com. To enjoy another story by Chrissy Wissler and to keep up with the latest news, releases and more, go to: chrissywissler.com/free-book/

For more information:
www.chrissywissler.com
chrissy@chrissywissler.com

ALSO BY CHRISSY WISSLER

Home Run Series

Home Run

Romance Video Game Series

Second Chance: Novel

Anything Possible

Changing Perspective

Enchantment Avenue

Searching for Sanctuary: Novel

Dragons in Preschool: Short Novel

The Blessings Bridge

Pixie Dust Cupcakes

Christmas Weather Witch

Unfreeze a Heart

More than Nurture

Elven Heritage Series

Hidden in Mist

Hidden in Truth

Hidden in Shadow

Hidden in Fire

Hidden in Flight

Hidden in Spirit

Hidden in Desire

Hidden in Memory

Hidden in Time: Novel

Hidden in Lore: Collection #1
Hidden in Myth: Collection #2
Hidden in Legend: Collection #3

Little League Series
Swing Away: A Little League Novel
Prom Dates & Softball Bats
Throw Like a Girl, Catch a Date
Fly Away
No Crying in Softball
More to Life than Softball
A Pitcher's Unexpected Date
A Catcher's Christmas Wish
Stolen Bases, Stolen Kisses
Softball Baby
Off-Balance
Batter-Up Pucker-Up: Collection
Everlasting: Collection
All or Nothing: Collection

www.ingramcontent.com/pod-product-compliance
Lightning Source LLC
Chambersburg PA
CBHW030606170726
48283CB00002B/489